DEC 13

121\

THE RANGER

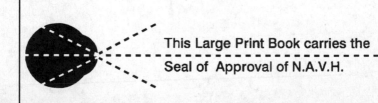

This Large Print Book carries the Seal of Approval of N.A.V.H.

THE RANGER

ACE ATKINS

THORNDIKE PRESS
A part of Gale, Cengage Learning

Detroit • New York • San Francisco • New Haven, Conn • Waterville, Maine • London

GALE
CENGAGE Learning·

LIBRARY OF CONGRESS CATALOGING-IN-PUBLICATION DATA

Atkins, Ace.
   The ranger / by Ace Atkins. — Large print edition.
     pages ; cm. — (A Quinn Colson novel series) (Thorndike Press large print basic)
   ISBN 978-1-4104-6449-1 (hardcover) — ISBN 1-4104-6449-0 (hardcover) 1. United States. Army—Commando troops—Fiction. 2. Murder—Investigation—Fiction. 3. Mississippi—Fiction. 4. Domestic fiction. 5. Large type books. I. Title.
PS3551.T49R36 2013
813'.54—dc23   2013031177

Published in 2013 by arrangement with G. P. Putnam's Sons, a member of Penguin Group (USA) LLC, a Penguin Random House Company

Printed in the United States of America
1 2 3 4 5 6 7 17 16 15 14 13

In memory of Robert B. Parker

The true soldier fights not because he hates what is in front of him, but because he loves what is behind him.

— G. K. CHESTERTON

Don't ever march home the same way. Take a different route so you won't be ambushed.

— ROGERS' RANGERS STANDING ORDER No. 11

1

Quinn headed home, south on the Mississippi highway, in a truck he'd bought in Phenix City, Alabama, for fifteen hundred, a U.S. Army rucksack beside him stuffed with enough clothes for the week and a sweet Colt .44 Anaconda he'd won in a poker game. He carried good rock 'n' roll and classic country, and photos from his last deployment in Afghanistan, pics of him with his Ranger platoon, the camp monkey "Streak" on his shoulder, Black Hawks at sundown over the mountains. Things you bring back home after six years away, from 3rd Battalion Headquarters at Fort Benning to Iraq to Afghanistan and back again, when you didn't really intend to return home so fast, if at all. He drove south on Highway 7 and then down 9W, and kept heading south into the winding hill country that had been logged down to nothing decades ago, leaving the people scrub pines and junk trees and squashed beer cans and bottles. This part of the state had always seemed used up to him as a kid, and it looked just as used up in the headlight glow of the truck. He was headed back down to Jericho at midnight, not wanting to see a damn soul till the funeral tomorrow.

He figured nobody plans being away for that long, but when you join up at eighteen and earn your tab just before September 11th, a soldier can keep pretty damn busy. He tried to recall the last time he'd seen his mother (not caring if he ever saw his father again), and wondered about his sister who hadn't called him in two Christmases. At home there was an ex-girlfriend who'd dumped him not long after basic and good friends he hadn't spoken to in years.

He turned up the radio, a Johnny Cash version of a classic Western ballad. Quinn knew the song by heart but loved hearing it every time.

The old truck ran at seventy on a steady ribbon of blacktop unfolding from hill to hill, a path cut through endless forest that once had been traveled by horse and wagon, Tibbehah County being one of the most remote counties in North Mississippi.

After years of marching and maneuvers, sitting still seemed odd to him, although at

10

rest he could fall asleep at will and wake up just as fast. The Regiment had whittled him down to a wiry, muscular frame built for speed, surprise, chaos, and violence. His hair was cut in the standard high and tight, not even an inch thick on top and shaved on the sides, making his face seem even more chiseled in the rearview mirror, sharp angles thanks to a Choctaw grandmother about a hundred years back mixed with the hard Scotch-Irish who settled the South.

The truck's heater was cranked, and Quinn's hand was on the wheel, sitting comfortably in a black T-shirt, blue jeans, and cowboy boots. In the ashtray he kept a half of a dead cigar that he'd smoked about a hundred miles back with some bad coffee. The trip was only five hours, but it was a hell of a long time alone with your thoughts.

Another bend, another curve on the highway, and there was a speck in the light. He touched the brakes — finding them a lot less tight than the salesman had promised — thinking the speck was a spooked deer or a dog but then seeing it was the bare back of a woman, turning on long spindly legs and caught in his high beams.

He shanked the steering wheel to the right, the truck coming within an arm's reach of the hair rushing across her blank face. He was in a ditch and stuck, back wheels spinning into mud.

Quinn got out and tromped over to the girl, still standing there on the double yellow line, her breath audible against the quiet of the motor and hot ticking of the engine. There were cows calling from some place across a barbed-wire fence, and a train whistled far off. A lonesome midnight moon glowed, and Quinn called to the girl, just spotting a logging truck cresting the hill. He grabbed her hand and pulled her toward the shoulder, finding her face in his truck's headlight.

"You okay?"

She nodded.

"What the hell you doing in the middle of the road?"

"I didn't see you."

"You didn't hear my truck?"

She didn't say anything.

"Shit, I about killed you."

The girl wore cowboy boots, a miniskirt, and a sequined halter top busting at the stomach. The girl, maybe eighteen or nineteen or sixteen, was blond and light-eyed. She had tight curly hair, a small upturned nose, and was well on her way with child.

"You from here?" he asked.

She shook her head, breath clouding in

the cold.

"I'd give you a ride, but —"

She said it didn't matter and turned away, and kept walking south.

Quinn hopped back in the truck and cranked the ignition, the F-150 older than him kicking to life, and he knocked it in four-wheel drive just for the hell of it, thinking he'd never get out of that ravine. But the tires spun, and it lurched forward a foot and then five feet, and he was back on the road, following the girl. He let down his side window, slowly, and told her to get in.

She stopped and didn't say a word. She just stood there, back roads leading nowhere all around, with nothing on her, nothing to her, and then she climbed inside the cab. Quinn accelerated fast in case she decided to change her mind.

"Headed down to Tibbehah County," he said. "Jericho."

He didn't realize he'd left the radio on, catching a staticky local station. A talk-radio-show host offering his views at the decline of American morals and the nearing of the End Times.

"How old are you?" he asked.

"How old are you?" she asked.

"Twenty-nine."

"You look a lot older."

Quinn and the girl didn't speak for nearly fifteen miles.

"You can let me out here," she said.

"Nothing here."

"I can walk."

"Where you from?" Quinn asked, keeping the same speed.

"Alabama."

"You walked from Alabama?"

"It's a fur piece," she said, staring straight ahead.

" 'Specially in those boots."

"You from Jericho?"

"Grew up there."

"You know a man named Jody?"

"Haven't been home in some time," Quinn said. "What's his last name?"

The girl didn't say anything. She just stared out at the headlights hitting the ten feet of darkness ahead of them, not much to see along the road but trailers perched on some cleared land and homemade signs offering fresh vegetables, although the season had passed months ago. The nights had turned chilly; past cotton harvesttime.

"What you're doin' is dangerous," Quinn said.

"Thanks for your concern."

"Just tryin' to help."

"Why are you going back?"

"It's time."

"How long you been gone?" she asked.

"Six years and a few months."

"You do something bad?"

"Why would you ask that?" Quinn asked, a little edge in his voice.

"Just trying to talk."

"You have money?"

"You can let me off in town."

"You have people?"

"Jody," the girl said, not sounding too excited about the prospect.

"The boy without a last name."

She stayed silent and leaned her head against the window glass, a few stray cars passing, high beams dimming over the crests of hills, all the way till they reached the Tibbehah County line, the road sign spray-painted over with the words AIN'T NO HOPE. Quinn recognized some things, Varner's Quick Mart, the small high school stadium where he'd played football long after they'd been state champs in '78, JT's Garage — but JT's looked like it'd shut down a while back. The downtown movie theater where he'd seen *Fievel Goes West* with his kid sister had been turned into a church. He passed the town cemetery where he'd probably be buried alongside both sets of grandparents and a few kin beyond that, and then they were circling the town Square. A small gazebo stood in the center as a monument to all the boys who'd been killed in action since the Civil War.

"Is this all there is?" the girl asked.

"Pretty much," Quinn said. "Can I get you a place to stay?"

"I'll make my own way, thank you."

"Some churches and places might could help. Hey, look, there's a motel right across the railroad tracks over there. I'll pay for your room tonight and then you can make your way fresh in the morning. I have to check in, too."

"I know that song," she said, turning to look at his face.

"I'm not shy," he said. "But I draw the line at pregnant teens."

She didn't say anything. He gunned the motor and crossed over the tracks, circling down into the Traveler's Rest, an old U-shaped motel where the units faced outward to the highway. Quinn remembered it used to be thirty bucks a night back when the couples needed to be alone at prom time. Now they advertised bass fishing in their pond and free Wi-Fi. You used to could drive past this place at midnight and know which girls had finally given in to their boyfriends or who was stepping out.

Quinn grabbed his bag, paid for the rooms, and tossed the girl her key.

"Good luck," he said, heading to his room.

"I'll pay you back in the morning."

"Not necessary," he said. "I got a funeral to be at anyway."

"Who died?" she asked.

The funeral started at nine a.m. sharp, everyone noting that his uncle sure would have appreciated the punctuality. There were about twenty people there. Quinn expected more, but understood it was a cold, rainy morning, and it being Thanksgiving Day and all. Most were men, old veterans who'd been buddies with his uncle since Korea, long before he'd become sheriff back in '73. They held their baseball hats, decorated for whatever military branch they'd entered, over their tired hearts as the body of Hampton Beckett was lowered into the ground to the sounds of a twenty-one-gun salute, some of the old men looking like they sure enjoyed getting out the rifles and firing off a few rounds. Every damn snap made Quinn recoil a bit, and he hated himself for that, watching the flag being folded and handed to a frizzled waitress from the Fillin' Station diner, a woman that Hamp had been seeing since his wife had

17

died five years ago. There were nice words and handshakes, and then it started to rain harder and everyone ducked under their umbrellas and ran for their cars, snaking out of the county cemetery and starting the real bit of the ceremony at the VFW club.

As Quinn reached for the truck's door, Luke Stevens waded through a ditch to shake his hand. He hadn't spoken to Luke since they graduated from high school, but he looked pretty much the same, with shaggy brown hair, a handsome face and confident grin. His gold glasses were spotted with rain and his suit drenched. He just gave a brief smile to Quinn, shook his hand, and then wrapped him in an awkward hug. Luke still feeling bad about taking Anna Lee away, even though Quinn was the one who'd left. Luke being the one who'd gone to medical school at Tulane and come back to Jericho to live and die.

Quinn started to speak, but Luke had turned back to his car, where Quinn caught only the back of Anna Lee's black dress as she climbed inside and shut the door. Hell, he didn't know what to say anyway.

The VFW building wasn't much but cinder block and tin, murals of Europe, Vietnam, and Iraq painted on the walls. A sign outside

18

advertised BINGO SATURDAYS, and a CAT-FISH FRY from two Sundays back. Quinn removed his damp dress coat and loosed his wet tie and sat at a table with three old men. One of them looked around the empty room, more for show than from worry, and pulled out a bottle of Wild Turkey; another headed to the kitchen to fetch some coffee mugs.

"You been to see your mother yet?" asked old Mr. Jim, a Third Army man who from his barbershop pulpit told stories of meeting Patton, even keeping the prayer card he'd been issued since before they rolled into Belgium. His nose resembled a rutabaga, his eyes narrow and a washed-out blue.

"No, sir."

"She'll want to see you."

"Yes, sir."

"Don't be angry."

"He was her brother," Quinn said. "Doesn't seem too much to show up at his funeral."

"They hadn't spoken for some time," Mr. Jim said. "Bad words said."

"Those two argued over the color of the sky," Quinn said. "Hamp didn't talk to her for nearly a month after she called John Wayne a pussy."

19

Old Judge Blanton, small and white-haired in a black suit, cracked open the seal on the bourbon and uncorked the bottle. Luther Varner, a Marine in Vietnam, owner of Varner's Quick Mart, returned with four mismatched cups. Varner lit a long, cheap cigarette. Quinn wished he'd brought in cigars.

He felt odd sitting with them, the men always just a "Sir" and a polite handshake. Quinn was never part of the boys sitting around drinking coffee in the morning at Varner's. But here he was after doing what was expected of him in the Army, and the old boys seemed to say, "Sit down, and sit a spell. You're one of us now."

"You didn't wear your uniform," Judge Blanton said.

"I've worn it enough."

"You gettin' redeployed?" Mr. Jim asked.

"We just got back," Quinn said. "Third Batt did six months in Afghanistan."

"You see much action?"

"We always do."

"Y'all boys get called in when the shit hits the fan," Varner said. "In case of trouble, break the glass and call in the Rangers."

"I just don't know why he did it," Mr. Jim said, making a clicking sound with his cheek. He was staring into a blank spot in

20

the corner of the VFW, not listening much to what was going on around him.

Quinn watched. The other men exchanged glances. All looked down at the table.

There was a good twenty seconds of silence when all Quinn could hear was breathing and rain pinging on the roof. He sat and waited.

"You didn't know," Mr. Jim said.

"Know what?"

Mr. Jim looked to Varner and Varner to old Judge Blanton, Quinn noting Blanton must've been elected their spokesperson.

Judge Blanton took a big swig of whiskey. "Sorry, Quinn. Ole Hamp stuck a .44 in his mouth and pulled the trigger. Go figure."

2

Lena stood before the cracked motel mirror, hair wet and combed, body wrapped in a towel, thinking only a sixteen-year-old girl could be so damn stupid to find herself in Shithole, USA, knocked up and out of cash. But she'd made that decision to find Jody, and she would've walked to Texas to get the truth on why he'd disappeared into a plan that had been sold as the greatest opportunity of his entire life. He said he'd hook up with some true brothers in Mississippi and make enough money that he and Lena could stop thinking about having to stock shelves at the Walmart, or worry about paying bills or borrowing money from their kin. They'd ride into town in that big car, a car that made everyone sit up and take notice, riding up so damn high that you had to look down just to see people on the sidewalks. You could spit on their pinheads, is what he'd said with that gap-toothed smile, her being too stupid to have a trace of doubt in those words.

Her reflection had fogged up from the steam. She wiped it away and looked at herself, looking for maybe a little determination in those sleepy eyes that challenged her flip-flopping gut.

She reached into her tiny purse and found that sweet little .22 peashooter she'd stolen from her grandmother.

Lena watched the mirror for several minutes, practicing just what she'd say, arms outstretched and sighting down the barrel at old Jody, watching him shit his drawers.

"How 'bout some answers, baby, or I'll start shootin' right for that troublemaker."

Quinn found the girl's motel room empty, the bed a wreck, and damp towels on the floor. He went back to his own room and changed out of the stiff black suit and into blue jeans and boots, pressing a rolled blue shirt with a hot iron. He brushed his teeth and ran a comb over his head, although his hair had been shaved high and tight the day before, tucking all his civilian gear neat back into his ruck.

The rain slowed to a steady gray drizzle.

He asked the night clerk about the girl, but he hadn't seen her.

He asked a maid. The maid saying she'd seen the girl walking the road before daylight. Quinn looked at his watch.

He didn't want to go. But he knew he had to.

Son of a bitch.

His mother opened the door, holding a young child in her arms and a margarita in an outstretched hand. She looked at Quinn, put the drink down on a table, and hugged his neck, Quinn smelling the same oversweet perfume she'd always worn, her crying and wanting to know why he hadn't called. On the stereo was maybe the last song he'd heard her play, "How Great Thou Art" sung by Elvis Presley. Everything in the Colson house growing up had been either Elvis or Jesus. *Jesus and Elvis.* You get two of them in one song, and that sure was a winner.

Quinn hugged her back, but found it a little difficult with the boy between them.

Their house was a basic ranch built with his daddy's L.A. money when Quinn had been born. His mother had already strung Christmas lights under the drainpipes; a dime-store plaque with a Bible verse hung on the door. A faded movie poster for *Viva Las Vegas* hung over the television. He used to get so damn sick of her obsession, sometimes secretly glad that Elvis was dead so he wasn't as much competition. Quinn knew his daddy had felt the same way, maybe the reason he'd shagged ass from Jericho.

His mother was tipsy on margaritas and gospel as she pulled him inside, the television room, the dining room, and the kitchen unchanged from his childhood. In the kitchen, she asked if he wanted anything; a picked-over turkey wrapped in aluminum sat on top of the old gas stove beside some congealed green beans in a pot and half a skillet of corn bread. She still had his high school portrait under a magnet on the refrigerator next to a photo of him after basic.

"Sure," he said.

She shifted the child to the other hip, the boy curious and bright, watching Quinn as he walked to the refrigerator and pulled out a cold Budweiser. He smiled at the child, the kid maybe two, obviously of mixed race, with coffee-colored skin and soft blond curly hair.

Quinn's mother made him a plate, heated it up in the microwave, and nervously sat down. Her eyes were bloodshot, and hazier than he'd recalled. She was unsteady, not

25

knowing what to do with her hands.

"You know why I didn't come?" she asked.

"I didn't say anything."

"If it had been reversed, if I'd said those things to him, you couldn't have paid him to go to my service. He may be dead, but he'd understand. He'd respect my decision."

Quinn ate and took a sip of beer. He shrugged.

"How long are you home for?" she asked, lighting up a Kool, finding some comfort in the action. "I appreciated those nice blankets you sent. Did you see them on the sofa? And the letters. I appreciated the letters, but I do wish you'd respond to the ones I wrote. It's like we were both playing tennis with ourselves. Don't you read what I send? Did you get the toothpaste?"

"Yes, ma'am." Quinn leaned back and sipped his beer. "You could've warned me. You told me he had a heart attack."

"What's the use?" she said. "Knowing what he did doesn't help. I just wish he hadn't been such a selfish person not to think about his family."

"Because killing yourself is a sin."

She covered the little boy's ears. "Quinn!"

"By the way, who in the hell is this kid?"

His mother stood up and turned the child

around to face him. Quinn took a bite of turkey, some burned corn bread.

"This is your nephew," she said. "If you'd opened a few letters, maybe you would've known it."

"Hey there, kid." Quinn grabbed the child's tiny hand and shook it. "Where's Caddy?"

"We haven't seen your sister for six months now."

Quinn was dead asleep at the motel when he heard a banging on the door — must have been nearly two in the morning — and he stumbled, looking for his jeans and his watch, confirming the time. As he pulled back those cheap antique curtains, he spotted Deputy Lillie Virgil standing underneath a bright outside light. She'd been at the funeral, but there had been a lot of hand-shaking and good manners, and it was not the kind of place for a solid conversation. "You looked in a funk," Lillie said as soon as Quinn opened the door. "Figured we could talk later."

"It's kinda early," Quinn said, leaning into the frame, feeling a blast of cold air, the dry asphalt lit dull by the crime lights in the lot. "Jesus."

"You mind putting on some clothes?"

Quinn was wearing a pair of white boxers and walked into the room to look for his blue jeans and boots, which felt awkward and loose without laces.

Lillie looked over the room as he dressed, smiling at the way everything was as neat as a pin except for the unmade bed, everything he'd brought home packed away in the Army ruck. She ran a hand across the bathroom counter, seeing he'd wiped down the sink after shaving and hung his towel up to dry.

"You look like you want to make a fast exit," she said.

"Makes things easier to find."

"Been a long time, Colson."

"Lillie."

Lillie stood about as tall as Quinn in her boots, her curly hair wrapped up tight in a bun, Quinn recalling watching her play soccer and baseball, running as fast as the boys at state track meets. She'd always been the tomboy, the girl that women would marvel over when she applied a bit of lipstick or wore something other than blue jeans to their school prom. Lillie curled her hair and wore it down, with a sparkly dress, but she went with this shit-bag redneck — in Quinn's humble opinion — who'd tried to get her drunk and get himself laid. Quinn hearing about all this the next morning. Even in a dress, Lillie Virgil still broke the son of a bitch's nose, the hick telling everyone in town that Lillie was nothing but a lesbian. And as far as Quinn knew, that may have been true; he never saw her after she'd gone up to Ole Miss and then became a cop in Memphis. She came back to the heart of darkness to take a job in Jericho on account of a mother dying of cancer.

"I was sorry to hear about your mom."

"She suffered a long time," Lillie said. "I got your letter."

"You want me to follow you?"

"You ride with me," Lillie said, smiling, as Quinn pulled into a plain white T-shirt and reached for a flannel shirt, buttoning up. "I'm supposed to be on duty, and if someone sees my car out here, someone is going to complain. And if someone complains — well, you're the military guy. Shit rolls one way."

"Who's in charge now?"

"Wesley Ruth is acting sheriff."

"God help you."

"Amen."

"How 'bout some coffee?"

"Dixie Gas opens in two hours."

"Couldn't this have waited?"

"Nope." She shook her head and walked

out, leaving the door wide open, crawling into the Jeep Cherokee marked TIBBEHAH COUNTY SHERIFF'S OFFICE to wait.

The night flew past back roads and trailers and endless fields of harvested cotton, spindly and dry in the moonlight. The rain had let up, and steam rose from the fields like wispy phantoms. Lillie rolled down the windows, and Quinn could smell the damp earth and decaying crops, and all of it felt oddly comfortable in the cab. The scanner crackled while Lillie remained silent, one hand on the wheel while she took slow, gentler turns on country roads, breaking through patches of fog. She lit a cigarette and blew smoke out the window.

"Who've you seen?" she asked.

"The Three Wise Men . . . My mother."

"I saw her this week. You knew she wouldn't go to the service. She had it out with your uncle over Caddy's baby. Hamp was an old man, and that kind of thing, the child being black, didn't set too well with him. You know what your mother said?"

"I can only guess."

"She said that Elvis Presley used to go to black dances down in the Delta and that he would've been a black man if he'd had a choice."

"Yep, that's what she'd say."

"She say what happened to Caddy?"

"She didn't know."

"She's in Memphis."

"I don't want to know."

"Strung out."

"Not my concern."

"Jesus, Quinn. You sure grew hard."

"After a point, you have to give up on some people. People wear their own paths. Just where are you taking me?"

"You know, a lot of folks want to see you," she said, flicking the cigarette butt out into the night. "Boom didn't mean to miss the funeral. He wanted you to know he had to attend to some personal issues. Between me and you, he's having a mess of adjustment problems, and who can blame him after all he went through. But he's going to be okay, I believe."

"Which arm did he lose?"

"His right," Lillie said. "You know, they gave him weapons training at Walter Reed to help him adjust. He can drive but won't. For some reason he hates being behind the wheel."

They turned off 9W and onto a county road, taking a hard turn into a long valley filled with cows, grazing in the headlights, a long stretch of barbed wire on cut cedar.

She headed west at the crossroads and shined her lights up onto the dark house. His uncle's home was a two-story white farmhouse built in the 1890s by Quinn's great-grandfather, a hardened farmer who'd once shot a man dead over ownership of a creek.

"I loved your uncle."

"He knew you were too good for this place."

"He didn't kill himself, Quinn."

"Oh, hell," Quinn said. "Do you realize that every time someone sticks a gun in his mouth, someone doubts it? What's the official version, 'He was cleaning his weapon'? I knew a kid in basic who'd been in and out of juvie, obviously off his medication. He offed himself in a toilet stall. How many people clean their weapon sitting on the john? You don't need to protect my feelings. I'm not religious. I don't believe he's burning in hell."

"Would you shut up long enough for me to explain?"

Quinn shut up.

"Johnny Stagg found the body," she said. "You know he's on the board of supervisors now?"

Quinn didn't speak. Johnny Stagg was the poster child for white trash who'd crawled their way out of the backwoods. The man, now in his fifties or sixties, started out working angles at a shithole retirement home, getting the elderly to sign away their family land for his comforting friendship. People say Stagg logged out half the county that way, raping the earth down to the soil and trying to make himself respectable in the process.

Lillie said, "He called the funeral home to fetch the body."

"What else could you do?"

"I saw your uncle. Crime scene was a mess with dumb shits tramping over everything. State people should've been brought in."

"What difference does it make?"

"We won't know now," she said. "Wesley called it an accident and said any further questions would only sully Hamp's reputation."

"Maybe he's right."

"I found that .44 way out of reach, and an entry point that wouldn't make sense to a blind man."

"You're a loyal friend," Quinn said. "But my uncle wasn't Jesus Christ."

"Did I say that?"

Lillie got out of the Cherokee, still looking tall and athletic in blue jeans and a slick brown sheriff's office jacket. She moved up the steps, motioning at Quinn to come the hell on, opened a screen door, and then ripped through some crime-scene tape.

"I'll come back tomorrow," Quinn said, not really sure he wanted to face that kitchen where the old man had stumbled with the .44 and contemplated the world being so damn unlivable that he'd just as soon check out. There would be reminders, as Quinn knew a person can hold a lot of blood, and that shit isn't just a grease stain on this world.

"Suit yourself," she said, holding the key in the palm of her hand. "These are yours now."

"Come again?"

"He left everything he owned to you. Didn't your momma tell you?"

Lillie Virgil handed Quinn the key. Quinn shook his head and stepped up to the front door.

3

Lena hoped she'd found Jody when the trucker dropped her off at the pulp mill just outside the Jericho city limits. She'd met the old, gray-headed guy at the Rebel Truck Stop off Highway 45, where he'd said sure he'd be glad to take her to town, and the man had seemed all fatherly and simple till he began to massage her skinny knee between gearshifting. She began to talk of her morning sickness and diarrhea, and the knurled fingers moved, and he kept his eyes on the blacktop before letting her out. She walked the rest of the way, the walking keeping her focused and sane and of the right mind to get to Jody, to ask him why he'd left her like he did, promising to return when he made a little money and make right by her.

The company road wound for a quarter mile, the air smelling rotten as an outhouse, till she found the office, a busted trailer up on concrete blocks. Wasn't anyone there when she knocked, and she kept walking toward the corrugated-tin building and the smokestacks blowing out the rotten air. She used a red bandanna to cover her mouth, soon spotting three men on lunch break, sitting atop blocks and eating sacks of hamburgers from the Sonic Drive-In. They were skinny and wild-eyed and didn't say anything to her, averting their eyes from her long legs and bulging stomach.

"Y'all know a boy named Jody?"

She described him, placing her hands on her hips.

They shook their heads.

"Heard he may have been working here."

She described him again right down to the long blond hair, jug ears, and pimples on his cheeks. She told them he had a tattoo on his left hand of a Chinese symbol of some sort.

"There's a boy started with us couple months back, but he don't go by Jody."

"What's his name?"

"Booth. Charley Booth."

"Is he here? Can I see him?"

One of the men chewed his hamburger for a good long while before answering, the other workers looking to one another with little grins on their filthy faces.

36

"I guess," he said. "He's still in jail, selling drugs to some black folks. Does that sound like your boyfriend, miss?"

The men snickered like a bunch of kids.

Lillie dropped Quinn back at the Traveler's Rest, where he got in his old truck and drove toward the Fillin' Station diner at the edge of the Square. A group of old farmers sat at a back table, drinking coffee and smoking cigarettes and talking crops and local politics in a mixture of grunts and coughs. Many of them had mud and cow shit stuck to their rubber boots, and the texture of their skin was like parchment. They complained about cattle prices and the rain that had ruined the cotton crop. Quinn could see their battered pickups parked outside like horses tied to the post.

The waitress — the older woman who'd accepted the flag from Hampton's casket — kept refilling their coffee in thick mugs and shuffling back to the kitchen before bringing Quinn out a plate of country ham and eggs.

Quinn introduced himself. She said her name was Mary.

Mary was of medium height, medium weight, with pale blue eyes and hair dyed an unnatural brown. She looked like dozens of people he knew. About the only thing of note about her was the strong perfume she wore that cut through even the scent of bacon and cigarettes.

"Your uncle kept newspaper clippings about you in his family Bible."

Quinn nodded and sliced off some of the thick, salty ham and placed it between a split biscuit.

"You check on that dog of his?" she asked.

"Didn't know he had one."

"Dog's name is Hondo," she said. "Got one blue eye and one yellow."

"You want the dog?"

"Me and Hamp were not cohabitating."

"Sorry," he said. "Just figured you might want him."

"He's a good dog," she said. "I sure like that dog."

"I'll keep an eye out."

"You want a refill?" She walked away, looking as if she might cry.

Old photographs of Little League teams and old football champs, dead city leaders with their obits attached, and publicity photos of celebrities who'd once stumbled into Jericho hung on the old paneled wood. People his father would've known, most local country music singers or television anchormen. But he'd heard Johnny Cash had once stopped in town, back when the town diner had been on the Square, before the meeting spot became the Fillin' Station. Quinn didn't even realize he'd stood up as he searched for Cash's photo, following that long wall of the town history, some of it his own: the story from the Memphis paper about the ten-year-old boy who'd survived two weeks alone in the woods after being separated during a hunt, the headline reading COUNTRY BOY DID SURVIVE. Quinn saw a younger version of himself standing between his father and his uncle. Uncle Hamp being the one who'd searched for him in what had seemed like a thousand miles of forest where Quinn had fished and hunted and made fires and for a long while thought the whole world had caved in on itself and this was all there was left. A second yellowed newspaper from 1990 read LOST LOCAL BOY FOUND.

Mary returned and found a pack of cigarettes in her apron, quickly lighting one with a pink Bic. She waved the smoke out of the way and watched Quinn sit back down, having an almost motherly look about her as she saw him grip another ham biscuit. "You get his guns?"

"Not yet."

"What about his .44?"

"I imagine the sheriff's office has that."

"Wish you'd get it melted. Would you do that for me?"

"I will."

Mary looked over her shoulder, and the old men stared back at her, knowing she should head back to the kitchen and bring back their damn free coffee. But she finished the cigarette, seeming to not give a damn, her face seeming like it just might break but then suddenly finding composure.

"You see this comin'?" Quinn asked.

"No, sir, I did not."

"Was he drinking again?"

"I didn't know he'd stopped," she said. "That man sure liked his whiskey."

"But it hadn't gotten worse?"

She shook her head. "What he done shocked me probably about as much it shocked y'all. Did you know he promised to take me on a cruise to Mexico? We used to go down to Biloxi and Tunica all the time."

"He hadn't mentioned any troubles?"

"We didn't talk about private matters," she said, shaking her head. "We just had sex."

"Not while cohabitating?"

"We helped each other along."

"Is there anything of his you wanted?"

She shook her head and gave a weak

40

smile, stubbing out the cigarette. "That house is gonna be more trouble than it's worth. You do know about the note he owed?"

"Come again?"

"Your uncle borrowed some money against the land."

"He was broke?"

She shrugged.

An elderly couple shuffled in through the glass door, the bell jingling above them, and found a place by a propane space heater where they could warm their old bones. The old man helped his wife take off her wool jacket and waited until she'd sat down. Mary punched out the cigarette in a tin tray and glanced back to the kitchen. Order up.

"Which bank?"

"Wasn't no bank," she said. "He borrowed from Johnny Stagg. You know ole Johnny?"

"You know, that's the second time I've heard that son of a bitch's name since I got to town."

"Quinn Colson."

"Wesley Ruth."

"Don't I still have a warrant 'round here for you?"

"Statute of limitations."

"You did steal that fire truck, didn't you?"

41

Wesley said, grinning. "Just between us?"

"I think I had some help," Quinn said and gripped his friend's hand.

Wesley kept on pressure-washing mud off the tires of the sheriff's truck, the truck that still bore Quinn's uncle's name on the front doors. He then lifted each boot, hitting the mud off the soles, telling Quinn he'd spent the last four hours looking for some teenagers who'd broke into Mr. Varner's store overnight and stole ten pounds of hamburger meat, some buns, ketchup, and four gallons of sweet tea. "I just drove around till I smelled the burgers and walked back into the woods, where they were having a cookout. Even invited me to join 'em."

"You charge them?"

"I got 'em in a cell to scare the shit out them," Wesley said. "It's up to Mr. Varner what to do. They didn't do much damage to the door. I think one of them boys is half retarded or high on dope. Maybe both."

"I hear you're acting sheriff."

"Can you believe that shit?"

"You'll do fine."

"You like being in charge?" Wesley asked. " 'Cause I sure as shit don't."

"I'm a platoon sergeant. I got forty teenagers who think I'm an old man. I'm the one they call when they get hauled in for drunk driving or beating someone up."

"Never thought either one of us would make thirty," Wesley said, giving a slight smile.

"Hamp said I'd never make twenty if I didn't change my ways."

"Mama Tried," Wesley said. "Your uncle was a good man, Quinn. I sure am sorry."

"You know anything about him having a dog?"

Wesley finished up on the last wheel and roped up the hose and turned off the motor, pushed the washer back to the department garage, and locked the gate. He nodded and said, "I hadn't seen Hondo all week. Went out last night trying to call him."

"You making much headway with this?"

"With what?"

"Finding out what happened."

Wesley, tall and as thick-necked as when he'd played football with Quinn in high school and then for two years at Ole Miss, wrapped his arm around his buddy and steered him on into the sheriff's office. "There ain't much to find out."

"No chance something went wrong?"

"He wasn't exactly a hated man, Quinn."

"He was sheriff. People can hold a grudge."

"You're welcome to look for them. But I

43

was there, Quinn. He'd planned the damn thing out. I know you saw Lillie and I know she got her mind chewing on things."

"Was there a note?"

"He got his point across."

Quinn nodded before they stepped inside, where he could see people walking around, deputies and a secretary tending to the business of drinking coffee and taking phone calls. He saw Leonard and George, two of his uncle's deputies who were there when Quinn had left a decade ago. Leonard, square-headed with a buzz cut, looked up from across a desk and gave Quinn a two-fingered salute.

"How's Meg?" Quinn asked.

"Left me for an insurance man in Jackson."

"And your son?"

"See him on the weekends."

"You look fit."

"Hell, I look fat," Wesley Ruth said, rubbing his shaved head. "You look like you don't weigh a hundred pounds."

"Y'all running tests on all this?"

"We are."

"What a mess."

"It's good to see you, Quinn," Wesley said, wrapping his arm around him again and gripping his neck. "How 'bout we get shithouse drunk tonight?"

"I got lots to tend to. I just learned that my uncle borrowed some money from Johnny Stagg."

"That doesn't sound good."

"And put up the farm against it."

"Forget that shit. Let's go out to the bottomland and shoot armadillos."

"I heard he was broke. Does that sound right?"

"When the man wasn't here, he was hitting every casino in Tunica," Wesley said. "Let's leave it at that."

Quinn nodded. "I'll call you."

"You see Anna Lee?" Wesley said, smiling like he had the punch line to some dirty joke.

"High school is long gone."

"You want to see Boom?"

"Headed there next."

Wesley shook his head and thumbed behind him. "One-stop shopping, brother. Boom got himself picked up two days back. Giving him some time to cool down a bit."

"What'd he do?"

"What does Boom always do?"

"Tear shit up."

4

Boom Kimbrough sat in a kid's plastic school chair, almost crushing it with his massive size, as he looked at nothing in particular in the jailhouse yard. The small bit of property had been corralled off in chain link and concertina wire, and there really wasn't much to look at besides bare trees and rolling brown hills down to the sluggish water of the Big Black River. He didn't even seem to hear Quinn approach after Wesley unlocked the gate and let him inside, but when Quinn was two feet away from his shoulder, Boom just said: "What up, Quinn."

Quinn looked down at his friend's massive shoulders and the back of his head. His hair had grown nappy and uneven around a puckered scar at the base of his skull. Despite it being about thirty degrees, he wore only a dirty white undershirt and the bright orange pants of a prisoner. Last time

Quinn had seen him, he'd been coaching linebackers for their old high school and was proud to be bringing in an extra paycheck with the National Guard. Boom had been sent to Iraq a few years back to guard convoys, and then there was something about an IED and some time at Walter Reed.

When Quinn circled him, he noticed only a left arm and another pink puckered scar across Boom's black cheek. His eyes were sunken and tired, and his Army boots were unlaced.

"I'd shake your hand, but you got to do it with your left."

"What'd you do?" Quinn asked.

"Knocked down parking meters with a sledgehammer."

"With one arm?"

"How else am I gonna do it?'

That one arm was even more massive than Quinn remembered, the thick forearm and bicep twisted with big veins. Quinn figured that arm must've grown, taking on double duty.

"You want to get out?"

"Shit, I can't make bail."

"I paid it."

"You know, this used to work the other way around," Boom said. He looked up from the river and met Quinn's eyes, searching for something and kind of suspicious, as Boom was known to be.

Quinn offered his left hand.

"Can you believe Wesley is sheriff?" Boom asked.

"Acting sheriff."

"Who's gonna run against him?" Boom asked. "Lillie?"

"Said he didn't want it. Someone will step up."

"God helps fools and children."

Quinn drove north and hit 9W, following the river and then breaking away west into pastureland and the big fuming expanse of the pulp mill and past Varner's Quick Mart, where he bought Boom a couple sausage biscuits and a Coke and asked about the break-in, and then kept on driving till they hit the county road heading to the old farm. The trees looked black and skeletal and cold far across the wide spaces of fallow land.

"How was Afghanistan?"

"The Garden of Eden," Quinn said. "The base had a pet monkey."

"You know, every goddamn day I wake up and think I'm still over there."

"I have dreams in night vision green. Isn't that sick?"

"Pretty damn sick," Boom said. "When you headed back?"

"Maybe never," Quinn said. "I either jump into the regular Army or become a Ranger instructor."

"While your boys storm the castle."

"Yep."

"You gettin' old, Quinn."

"Old man at twenty-nine."

"Does your dick still work?"

"Last time I checked."

"Well, you got that goin' for you."

Boom nodded and smiled as Quinn downshifted and slowed into the gravel drive of the old farmhouse, looming white and ramrod straight, with the tin roof shining. They both crawled out of the truck, Boom tossing the wadded-up foil of his biscuit into a massive pile of junk and garbage by the old house's front steps. "Whew."

"Got bad after my aunt died. My mom says Hamp stopped caring."

"This is just plain nasty."

"Inside it's even better," Quinn said.

"Why am I here again?"

" 'Cause I said I'd pay you if you'd help."

"You did?"

Quinn pushed open the door to find that same sickly scent as last night, the same smell that had driven Lillie and him out into the yard, locking the door behind them. They decided to take one room at a time. The parlor was loaded with rat-eaten furniture and boxes of old clothes and rags, absolutely nothing of value. Musty clothes and ragged suits decades out of style. Leisure suits of denim, white dress shirts yellowed with nicotine. There were stacks of newspapers and scrap wood, piles of drapes and rolled carpets without any purpose. He and Boom made a pile in the back field, and Boom walked to one of the old barns to hunt up some kerosene or diesel to start burning the whole mess of it.

Quinn found a suitcase filled with old family photographs and placed it on the kitchen table. And then there were the guns, damn guns, all over the house. Hampton had squirreled away pistols in the folds of his sofa, behind doors, high on bookshelves, and even a .38 on the lid of his toilet. More boxes of ammunition, souvenirs and medals from Korea, and tarnished awards from decades in law enforcement.

Boom had the bonfire in the back field stoked, and twisting gray snakes of smoke rose far up into the reddened twilight. Quinn had already found twenty-four guns, a pocket watch that had belonged to his great-grandfather, broken crystal and broken china, mountains of old books, tools that would be useful to get the property up to speed, and record albums he'd sort out later. There was gospel and plenty of George Jones and Charley Pride. Charley Pride always made Quinn think about his uncle, the music always playing when they'd come over for supper.

He also found two bottles of aged bourbon that Hampton had kept for much better days or perhaps just misplaced in the piles of shit. One of them had a tag reading MERRY CHRISTMAS FROM THE STAGG FAMILY.

Quinn uncorked the bottle with his teeth and reached for a tobacco brown ranch coat he'd found in his uncle's closet, the same coat Hamp had worn the day he'd found Quinn lost in the woods. Boom was a hulking shadow by the fire, holding a shovel in his one hand and watching the decades of memories and clutter crumble to ashes. Quinn handed the bottle to Boom, and Boom examined the label in the firelight, nodding his approval.

"You know, my parole officer says this stuff is the root of all my problems."

"You got the shakes."

"Appreciate you not judging me."

"Long as you reciprocate."

A biting wind separated them and whistled in Quinn's ears as Boom took a long swallow and passed the bottle back. They drank for a while as the night came onto the farm. The temperature dropped hard and fast, and Quinn was grateful for the coat and the fire his uncle had provided. A tattered piece of an old flowered dress that he clearly remembered his aunt wearing to one of his birthday parties caught and sputtered, bursting into a blue-and-orange flame, and then it was gone.

A large truck rambled down the gravel road an hour later, and the beams of the headlights swung onto the house and the back field. Two men got out, and Quinn and Boom exchanged glances. Quinn handed the half-empty bottle back to Boom and walked toward the headlights.

As the two figures stood there in the glow, a familiar feeling of being exposed out in the open and naked and vulnerable passed through Quinn — he wished he had a weapon, preferably his M4, but was then embarrassed by the thought. One of the figures stepped forward, and even in the distance, and through all the years he'd been gone, he recognized the craggy, comical face of Johnny T. Stagg.

"Good to see you, boy," he said, stepping

forward and offering his small hand. "I guess we need to talk about this situation here."

Johnny Stagg came from a family of hill people, moonshiners and dirt farmers who were unfit for society. They all possessed that same bright red skin, even in the winter, and crooked teeth stained brown from muddy well water. Stagg was a slight man, not even coming up to Quinn's shoulders, and kept a permanent smile on his face like a man who enjoyed every second of living or found the world a humorous place. Quinn shook his offered hand out of manners, waiting for Stagg to drop the bomb on what he really wanted. His hair was oiled back, as had been the fashion in his day, and he smelled of cheap aftershave and cigarettes. His suit was ill fitting and dark, and he wore an American flag pin on his lapel. He introduced the older man with him as Brother Davis, the pastor at his church.

"Brother Davis was at Hamp's funeral but didn't have a chance to speak," Stagg said. "He thought he'd have a moment with both of us now. Maybe a short prayer."

Brother Davis had wrinkled skin and a gold tooth. His eyes looked confused behind

53

the dirty lenses of his glasses.

"Y'all want a swig?" Boom asked, holding up the bottle.

Stagg bit into his cheek, the smile fading and then returning. "Naw, I don't touch that stuff anymore."

"What are you serving out at the truck stop?" Quinn asked. "Kool-Aid?"

"I don't have nothin' to do with that place anymore," Stagg said. "I sold it two years back."

Stagg smiled some more. Brother Davis smiled, too.

"God love you," Quinn said, walking to another junk pile in the front yard and tossing more into the bed of his truck. Stagg followed him, continuing to talk, as if he didn't find any insult in Quinn turning his back. This pile was mostly Hamp's old worn-out shoes and coveralls, issues of *Field & Stream,* and torn pieces of flannel he'd been using to plug holes in the walls.

"I didn't want you hearing this from a lawyer," Stagg said, still grinning. Quinn tossed more tattered rags into the pickup and waited a beat to hear him. "Your uncle owed a mess of money up against this old house. I helped him out awhile back with some work, but he never did repay me. I'm sorry, but I can't go broke on this here deal."

"Did he sign over the land?"

Stagg looked over at Brother Davis, and the country pastor smiled, showing off a couple of gold teeth.

"I got papers with me," Stagg said, handing them to Quinn, Quinn holding the papers into the glow of the headlights and scanning a legal document that looked as if it had been typed out by a monkey. Maybe three paragraphs, and Hampton's scrawl at the bottom.

"This loan here," Quinn said. "You're going to have to prove that it wasn't paid."

"I'd hoped we could settle it without all that mess," Stagg said. "Lawyers ain't gonna do nothin' but leach off what's left. Can I have them papers back?"

"Nope," Quinn said, folding them and tucking them into his coat pocket. "I'll take this to my attorney in the morning."

Stagg's face lit up like a jack-o'-lantern with a crooked-tooth grin. "Just the same, please hand those back."

"You come out to my uncle's place the day after he's buried with some two-bit preacher to steal land that's been in my family for generations, and you expect me to sit here with my thumb up my ass and pray? Get the hell out of here."

"This was a business affair between us,"

Stagg said. "And this man here is a reverend."

"I know who he is," Quinn said. "He used to drain our septic tank when I was a kid."

Brother Davis scowled and sucked at a tooth.

Boom walked up beside Quinn, standing a good head taller than everyone, and didn't say a word, just loomed there over all the garbage and refuse in the headlamps and faded light. "C'mon, Quinn."

"You can handle this deal any way you like," Stagg said. "Paper or no paper, your uncle owes me a lot of money for use of them machines and personal loans. You don't believe me, you just call up my competition. That Cat 320 alone goes for two grand a week."

Quinn nodded and went back to work. Stagg shuffled back to his car, the preacher followed wearing a cocky grin, and Quinn went back to the cab to start up the truck and load more onto the fire. Boom didn't even look up until that pile was gone.

"We gonna be here all night?" Boom asked.

"Looks that way."

"Your uncle got another bottle?"

"We haven't finished this one yet."

"Just thinking ahead. Don't you Rangers

lead the way?"

Must've been way past midnight by the time the bottle was gone, most of it going into Boom, who'd stretched out by the heat of the fire, lying on his back in the dead cold and looking skyward. They hadn't talked in a long while, Quinn being used to long periods of silence and waiting, just getting used to the difference in the sounds, the familiarity and quietness. The last few years had played hell with his hearing, and when it got very quiet, he could hear a piercing electric pitch, his ears waiting for more gunfire and explosions, the big revving hum from a Chinook or Black Hawk right before it would lift off the sandy ground and drop them up in the mountains or the edge of a village made of rocks.

He tossed the empty bottle into the fire, squatting down and poking at the embers with a stick. Boom spoke; Quinn was surprised to hear his voice.

"You want to tell me about it?"

"You asking?" Quinn asked.

"I'll just say I never expected you to step foot back in this town again."

"Unless someone died."

"Even then."

"What do you want to know?"

"What's been souring you?"

"I'm not soured."

"Okay. You want to play it like that."

"I'm not playing," Quinn said.

"I see you got that Purple Heart, too."

"I got hurt. Wasn't a big deal. My problems with the Army don't have a thing to do with that. My wounds were nothing, man."

"What was it?"

"The Regiment thinks I'm too old to be storming the castle."

"You don't have to be a Ranger."

"It's the only thing I ever wanted to be. I could give a shit for regular Army."

The last few sticks on the fire toppled over in the mound of ash, and Quinn found some more fallen branches and cedar logs to add to the pile. He warmed his hands and sat back on his haunches.

"How'd you get hurt?" Boom stretched out his legs.

"Hand-to-hand with the devout, hiding in some rocks near our LZ. He was on my back, yelling about Allah, me reaching for my M4 to neutralize the bastard when he yelled, 'Bomb!' "

"In English."

"Plain English."

"Funny how we use the word *neutralize.*

58

Sounds kinda nice."

"Yeah."

"Did you?"

"What?"

"Neutralize his ass."

Quinn poked at the fire and shook his head. "Yep, but he shot me, too, while we scrambled for that bomb. And you?"

"My world got rocked on a convoy outside Fallujah."

"That's it?"

"All there is to tell. Hell of a thing when you see your goddamn arm lying down the road from you. Puts you in a different frame of mind."

Boom started to laugh.

"Damn, Boom. I'm sorry."

"Don't be," he said. "You know what I miss most?"

Quinn waited.

"Neutralizing all those motherfuckers," he said. "I was pretty good at it. Riding convoy with that big-ass machine gun, protecting my boys. I liked that."

"Performing what you'd been trained to do."

The men didn't talk for a while. You could hear coyotes up in the northern hills, and the sky was bright and clear. Quinn sat down and fell asleep watching the fire, a hot, even glow of red ashes. When he awoke sometime later, Boom had passed out on the ground. Quinn tried to wake him. But Boom wouldn't stir, Quinn stepping down and lifting his friend's massive weight up with his legs.

He tossed his friend over his shoulder, the weight crushing, and carried him up the hill just as first light burned weak and gray over the dead trees. Down the gravel road, a rangy cattle dog padded its way up to the front porch and waited for Quinn to open the door.

The dog cocked its head, studying him with two eyes of different colors.

"Howdy there, Hondo."

5

Judge Blanton lived toward the northeast corner of Tibbehah County, right around the hamlet of Carthage, about five miles or so from the Rebel Truck Stop. This part of the county had once been far removed from Jericho and the highway traffic, but now the county road toward his house was clogged with trailer homes filled with Mexican laborers and poor blacks and poorer whites. Junk cars and garbage littered the road Quinn had remembered as pristine when he'd come to ride horses as a kid. He'd once felt like he'd entered a secret part of the county, miles and miles of virgin woods that belonged to the judge stretching far out into the northern hills where he'd been lost during that time as a boy, separated from the hunt camp and left to wander into what had felt like endless forest and backtracked trails and black nights filled with coyotes and copperheads. But then accepting the situation, owning it, and killing off any fears he'd had.

You used to could drive into the judge's land straight from the road, but now Quinn had to stop at a locked cattle gate and unlatch a chain, closing the gate behind him, knowing the old man must lock up at night with his pistols and shotguns. As he drove closer to the simple one-story home, noting two trucks and a car in the drive, two pit bulls ran out to greet him, circling Quinn as he stepped out, growling and bristling until the old man emerged from the horse barn and whistled.

Judge Blanton was a short, wiry man who probably didn't weigh much more than a hundred pounds. But he'd had the reputation as being one of the toughest figures ever to sit on the circuit bench, later serving on the state supreme court before retiring. He'd been a Marine in Korea — seen lots of action at Chosin Reservoir — and had been a mentor to Quinn's uncle. His skin sagged a bit from his chin, but he still kept that same white crew cut he'd had since forever.

Mr. Jim and Luther Varner walked out onto the front porch and waved to Quinn while Quinn shook the judge's hand. All the men wore heavy jackets and boots and were drinking coffee and smoking cigars. Luther

Varner, lanky and angular with long, bony fingers, handed Quinn one wrapped in cellophane, and Mr. Jim fiddled with an old Zippo to light it.

Mr. Jim kept a well-worn Bible under his arm, Quinn figuring he'd interrupted some kind of meeting between the men, a regular Saturday routine where they argued politics, religion, and women.

"Had a visit last night from Johnny Stagg," Quinn said.

"What a pleasure," Blanton said.

"He claims he owns my uncle's land."

Varner asked, "Can he back it up?"

Quinn unfolded the amateur document Stagg had given him, and Blanton pulled some reading glasses from his weathered plaid mackintosh jacket and read through the piece quickly, folding it and handing it back. The smoke on the porch was heavy but blew away with a sharp chill of wind.

"I know it's not what you want to hear, but I've seen shittier things than this hold up in court."

Quinn nodded, getting the plug of the cigar going in the cold, adjusting his feet, as the judge looked up squinting into the white light.

"He could fight you for it," Blanton said. "Even without a contract. Everyone knows your uncle played around with those machines like a kid in a sandbox."

"Son of a bitch," Mr. Jim said, settling his portly body into an old rocking chair and tugging down his Third Army ball cap over his bald head. "Y'all know about that deal?"

Blanton shook his head.

"Hell, he kept those bulldozers and backhoes at the farm. In exchange, Stagg said he'd let Hamp use 'em whenever he wanted. Hamp used 'em to dig that bass pond last summer, bulldozed a bunch of deer trails through the woods."

Quinn said, "Stagg says my uncle rented them."

"That's a black lie," Mr. Jim said, shaking his head, cigar clamped down in his teeth. "No other way to put it."

"So these were just personal loans," Quinn said. "Y'all know about some casino trips?"

Every one of the men nodded and mumbled but still kept on calling Stagg a son of a bitch for lying about the use of those earthmovers.

"He claims to have gone straight," Quinn said. "Said he sold the truck stop and titty bar."

Varner laughed and leaned against a support beam, smoking and coughing at the idea. Mr. Jim just shook his head, standing up from the chair for a brief moment and spitting over the railing before settling back down.

"Not long after you left," Blanton said. "He sold that filthy place, but I have my doubts. Same ole place, with its backroom whores and card games. It may have exchanged officially, but I have the feeling he's still got a piece of it."

"And got himself elected. He's running the county board of supervisors."

"Everything in Tibbehah County is for sale," Mr. Jim said. "Most folks who kept things straight are dead."

"Or retired," Blanton said.

"Well, I'm not handing it over," Quinn said.

"You could get a decent price for the property," Varner said. "It's the land he wants, not trouble."

"I'd rather burn the house and timber," Quinn said.

Varner smiled and looked over to Mr. Jim, who cracked a grin, smoke leaking out from his old lips. He crossed his legs at the ankle and smiled with pride at Jason Colson's kid, although the men had never really accepted Quinn's father, always seeing him for what he'd become, a drunk who ruined about everything he touched.

"Want some coffee?" Blanton asked.

Quinn nodded, placing his smoldering cigar on a large ashtray, and followed Blanton to the back door of the old house and into the kitchen, where he had a pot of coffee plugged into the wall. Blanton poured them both a cup and headed into a sitting area filled with fine antiques, foxhunt paintings in oil on canvas, and an enormous old grandfather clock that ticked and whirred, filling the silence until the time changed to eight, clanging and gonging, then only the slow tick between them.

"So you're going to stay awhile?"

"I got five more days."

"Can I recommend a good lawyer?"

"I was thinking of you."

"I'm retired."

"But you're the only one I trust."

"I guess I could file a few things in town to keep Stagg off your property. Sooner or later this thing'll end up in front of Purvis Reeves."

"He's the judge?"

"Even if Stagg hadn't been the one who put him on the bench," Blanton said, "Purvis'd likely look at both claims and seek to split the difference. That's his idea of justice. I might could whittle Stagg down some, though. That I can promise you.

Maybe you keep the house and a good hunk of the property. You're apt to lose some road front, though."

"I hate that bastard."

"He's not worth that," Blanton said. "Hate's too powerful an emotion to waste on turds."

Quinn tested the coffee and it had cooled a bit. Blanton walked to the fire in the small chimney and poked at it, the air smelling of burning cedar, pleasant and warming on a cold, gray morning. He looked through the glass panes in the front door and watched his friends, sitting comfortably and smoking. "Don't let that cigar go out on you."

"Do you know what happened to my uncle?" Quinn asked.

Blanton placed the fire poker back into the metal rack and turned back to him.

"Lillie Virgil doesn't believe he'd kill himself."

"That little ole gal likes to create problems."

"You must've seen him before it happened."

"None of us had spoken to Hamp for nearly a month," Blanton said. "He wouldn't return our calls. If we stopped by the jail, he'd find something that needed to be done."

"But you were his friend," Quinn said, leaning in from his chair. "Just what was it that hit him so hard and fast?"

"This county," Blanton said. "His job, the way most everything he'd known had been tainted and ruined. He'd become obsessed with taking the blame for things he couldn't control. He was too old and too experienced to take his work so personally."

"Is it that bad?" Quinn asked.

Blanton began to rebutton his mackintosh coat and motioned his head toward the porch. Quinn followed him to the front door, the daylight coming on strong but not seeming to break the brisk cold. Blanton put his arm around Quinn's shoulder. "Do you know I have to sleep at night with my doors locked and a pistol under my pillow?"

"And two mean dogs."

"Around here, I wish they were meaner," Blanton said. "People will steal anything not chained down."

He gripped Quinn's shoulder and led him back to the front porch.

Outside, Mr. Jim handed him the cigar and his old Zippo to get the damn thing going again.

Lena didn't get to see the man called Charley Booth till Saturday morning, dur-

68

ing what the acting sheriff called "family time" outside a chain-link fence where prisoners got to kiss through the wire and accept packages of food and cigarettes, some sly groping between the slots. A guard watched all the time, seeming to be more concerned about pot or pills than weapons. But Lena saw Jody right away, knowing it was him from the way he stood, too cool for everyone, smoking a cigarette, with shorter, spiky hair now, but looking skinnier and more pimply than when she'd known him in Alabama. He was talking to a black guy in a far corner, both laughing, Lena noticing for the first time a tattoo on the side of his neck and wondering just when he did that to himself.

She called for him. The tattoo was of a flower or a wolf head.

He turned to her but looked away as if he didn't recognize her. She'd worn her best clothes, a sparkled Miley Cyrus matching outfit she'd bought at the Walmart outside Tuscaloosa where she'd stopped hitching for a day or two and spent her last forty dollars on a cheap motel. That's where she'd learned Jody had left town for this nowhere spot called Jericho, Mississippi, and she'd had to make the choice whether to go back home or see the thing through, and that little kick in her stomach made that decision all the easier.

Jody finally got the idea that his eyes weren't playing tricks on him and bugged off the black guy and walked over to the fence separating them. She hung her hands up on the little diamond of wire and smiled at him, but he just shot her a glance and said in a low voice, "What the fuck are you doing here?"

She couldn't answer, her voice seizing up in her throat.

"You need to get your ass back home, girl. I'll call."

"Hell you will."

He looked away, and she noted the leanness of his jaw, his teeth looking looser and more askew in his mouth, almost as if he'd aged a decade in months. He rubbed his sweating neck and bristly beard on his skinny face. He spit onto the concrete and breathed hard out his nose.

"I have your baby in me."

"How do I know it's mine?"

"Goddamn you to hell, Jody."

"Hush."

"Just who the hell is Charley Booth?"

"You don't understand," he said. "Just go."

"You don't believe it's yours?" she said. "You should know I come for you with a

70

gun. Guess I don't need it now you're locked up."

"You need to shut up."

"Listen," she said, reaching through the fence with her skinny fingers and grabbing his orange coveralls and pulling him close. "I don't care what they say you done."

"I ain't done nothin'."

"We'll get through this. All of us."

"Oh, hell."

And she believed for a moment he was still speaking to her but then saw the glint in his eyes as he followed some movement behind her, back along the parking lot by the long, winding railroad tracks. She turned to see two men crawling out of an old black Camaro, both of them lighting up cigarettes, one of 'em as skinny as Jody and the other thick and muscular. They were dead-eyed, wearing T-shirts cut off at the shoulders and jeans so tight it was obscene.

"Who are those men?"

"Alpha dogs," he said, moving away. "Go. Get lost. I don't want you or that damn baby."

"I thought you'd quit messing with all that shit? Jody? Listen to me."

But he'd turned and walked up to the guard, who nodded him back inside out of the cold, where she was left shivering in a glittering shirt and ruffled dress that hugged her expanding butt. As she backed up, the sadness feeling like an animal clawing her chest, she passed by the two men. Her eyes met with the thicker of the two, black-eyed and scruffy-faced, with hollow cheeks and corded animal muscle on his skinny frame. His hair was buzzed down to the scalp, and the T-shirt he wore had the U.S. Capitol on it topped with a Rebel flag and read I HAVE A DREAM, TOO. The man eyed her and tugged at himself between his legs, smiling at the other, leaving her with his sharp odor lingering long after he'd moved away. On the back of his neck was a tattoo similar to Jody's, a crude — almost childlike — image.

He flicked his cigarette into the weeds and called out to the guard to get Charley Booth's ass out there.

She froze, and he turned back to stare, licking his cracked lips.

Lena ran for the tracks and followed them till she was back in town, broke, busted, and nowhere to go.

"Honey?" Jean Colson said. "I said cream of mushroom. Not chicken noodle."

Quinn's mind had drifted as he followed that shopping cart up and down the aisles of the Piggly Wiggly, nodding to what his mother was saying but not hearing half of it.

"Quinn?"

Jean Colson looked at Quinn as if he were still a twelve-year-old boy who'd get a quarter for the bubble-gum machine if he didn't act up. Caddy's baby sat up high and attentive in the cart, trying to reach for everything they passed.

"Wasn't there," he said.

"Look again."

"Didn't you go to the store last night?"

"This for Sunday," she said. "We got some folks comin' over after church. People want to see you, honey. There's going to be a ceremony. You got to feed those people who are coming."

"I'd rather have catfish."

"We'll go to Pap's before you leave."

"Who are all these people anyway?"

"Friends."

"You look. It's not there."

She handed over the grocery cart with a huff. Jason held on to a box of animal crackers as Quinn headed down aisle 8, cake mixes and spices and syrups and things. He stopped to pick up some Aunt Jemima pancake mix, his momma never having breakfast food, and was thinking that a

73

pound of good coffee would be nice when he spotted Lillie Virgil striding down the aisle, one hand on her gun, lithe and hard in a tan uniform, until she reached the cart and grabbed hold of it in midroll. She smiled at Jason and called to him, tickling his chin with fingers and talking baby talk, telling him he sure was a handsome boy, before lifting her eyes at Quinn and asking, "You think your momma will let you out tonight?"

"Come again?"

"There's someone you need to talk to. Says he'll only talk to you."

"I can't right now. Can't you see I'm grocery shopping? We have people coming over after church and you need some cream of shit to make the casserole."

"He sure is cute." She leaned in again, face softening, and said, "I'll pick you up."

"What's this about?"

"What do you think?"

"I'm not hearing a lot of what you're telling me."

"Good soldier, believing what you're told."

"What time?"

"Give me thirty minutes," she said. "I got to change out of this uniform."

Quinn smiled at her. "Don't get yourself

in deep on my account."

"Who said I'm doing this for you?"

Quinn kept pushing the cart, running his hand over his clipped hair, Jason growing upset because the last animal cracker was gone. He searched down the aisle of flour and spices, the kid now crying like crazy, till he was able to make it three rows over to the cereal aisle.

He found the first box he saw, some kind of sugary -O's, and opened the box. His nephew was pacified and smiled up at Quinn, a big old thank-you smile, and Quinn leaned into him and grabbed his ear, noticing his father's eyes for the first time, and the thought startled him.

6

There were three trailers at the bottom of a dead-end road that didn't even have a number, just another knot in this little enclave called Chance's Bend, which was mainly white and broke-ass, on the outskirts of a hamlet called Fate. Quinn got out of his truck followed by Lillie, Lillie looking better than he could recall, in a black V-necked sweater with dark jeans and boots, smelling and looking very nice. Quinn had joked with her about her dressing up for him, and the comment didn't sit too well with her, Lillie trying out the silent treatment, almost embarrassed, for the last ten miles.

She followed behind Quinn as he knocked on the door, seeing a large couch laden with a pillow and sleeping bag through the glass. A toilet flushed, and a fat man with a ponytail walked back into the room wearing an open bathrobe and boxer shorts, scratching himself.

Quinn knocked again, and the man made his way to the door and cracked it, trying to keep some privacy, although the door was glass and there wasn't much to hide.

"Heard you were lookin' for me?" Quinn asked.

The man was slack-jawed, with a pitiful goatee on his weak chin, more salt than pepper, and he had smallish eyes that looked like pinholes. "Get in here, boy. Damn, someone's gonna see you."

"What's up, Uncle Van?" Quinn asked.

"Don't you know I got shit to do?"

"You could've stopped by my mother's house."

"Shit."

"Or called."

"Lillie stopped by and was asking me questions, and I told her some of what I know'd and left out a few things I didn't. I told her I had some things to share but would rather share them with my own people. You understand?"

Uncle Van was the youngest of the Colson brothers; Quinn's dad, Jason, was the oldest, and the middle brother was Jerry, a good man who made a decent living working as a long-haul truck driver. But it was Jason Colson that everyone knew. He'd made a name for himself in Hollywood as a stuntman and drank all his money away back in Jericho. He'd been gone since Quinn turned twelve, no one hearing where he'd disappeared to or what he was doing. Not so much as a birthday card.

Van was the last one left in Tibbehah County, wandering his way through professions as diverse as coyote trapper to tree surgeon to housepainter. He kept scratching and readjusting himself on the couch, reaching for the remote and killing the television, the channel tuned to an infomercial about a religious enema called the Almighty Cleanse.

"That man on TV says everyone has backed-up shit," Van said. "That's the trouble. He says everything from headaches to cancer to personal relationships can be fixed. You believe that?"

Quinn shook his head.

Uncle Van shrugged and massaged his chest, reaching for his pack of Vantage cigarettes and some matches. "If I had the eighty dollars, I'd at least try it. Wouldn't that be something if you could just shit out your problems? Damn, I'd be on the toilet for a week."

"Van," Lillie said, not sitting or taking off her leather jacket. She just stood there with her arms across her chest, looking down at his uncle. "Tell Quinn what you were telling me, about seeing Hamp last week."

"I saw him Friday."

"Day before he died," Quinn said.

"I'd seen him a few times before that."

"You said Quinn might want to know," Lillie said.

"I don't want to be involved with this shit."

"You're already involved with this shit," Lillie said, moving in a bit, blocking the television as Van was trying to turn it back on to learn more about the Almighty Cleanse system. "Tell Quinn."

"I seen your other uncle a couple times out at the Rebel Truck Stop," Van said, putting down the remote, leaning into the thick cushions of the beaten couch. "Okay?"

"So what?" Quinn asked.

"Do you mind?" Van said, turning to Lillie, who still stood over him. Lillie looked to Quinn and shrugged and made her way out of the trailer, the door slamming shut behind her.

"I'm not pleased to admit this, but I do on occasion like to head down there for some companionship. When I have the money."

Quinn waited.

"I talk to the girls, watch 'em dance a little. There was one I used to bring flowers from the Piggly Wiggly. But she wasn't worth it. When the money ran out, so did the companionship. You can get the full treatment out with one of them lot lizards. You know what I mean?"

Quinn kept waiting, not saying a word, seated across from Van in a rickety metal chair, the room smelling of stale cigarettes and Lysol. An open Styrofoam box sat on a barstool, a half-eaten portion of barbecue and baked beans.

"Both times I seen him, he was with the same girl," Van said, finishing the cigarette and burning into a new one, perched there like a redneck Buddha. "She and Hamp were doing some serious talking in his personal vehicle. Just made me think of all the times he looked at me like I was the shit off his shoe. Here I am, getting worked on, and across from me is the damn sheriff of the county with a woman in his car. That's what I would call a complex sitiation."

"But they were talking," Quinn said.

"Ain't but one reason to talk to a woman like that and that's to haggle over the price."

"Maybe he was going to arrest her?" Quinn asked.

Van shook his head.

80

"You've seen the girl? You know her?"

"They call her Jasmine. Like the plant. I know'd 'cause I kidded her about it."

"That's it?"

"Just leave me out of this. Okay? I'm trying to get a job with a road crew."

Quinn stood up and checked his watch, noting it was coming up on five. He saw Lillie on the other side of the glass door, leaning against the handmade railing and smoking a cigarette, checking her watch, too. Quinn offered his hand to his uncle and thanked him for getting in touch.

"Hey, Quinn. Listen, since the plant closed, things been a little rough. Wonder if you might give your old uncle a loan till I get straight?"

Quinn reached into his pocket and pulled out forty dollars, mashing it into Uncle Van's hand. "Will that hold you?"

"You were always my favorite," Van said.

The Rebel Truck Stop had occupied the same piece of property since the late fifties, not a half mile off 45, the old highway that runs from the Gulf of Mexico up to Lake Superior, cutting through the eastern edge of the state of Mississippi and along the eastern border of Tibbehah County. The station used to be known for the billboards advertising a pair of Bengal tigers caged by the pumps, a sign above them reading DO NOT TAUNT OR FLICK CIGARETTES ON THE ANIMALS. But by the time Quinn was a child, only one of the tigers was still alive, slow and toothless, rottenly depressed and living in filth, dying a little while later.

That was about the time Johnny Stagg got the idea to open a truck stop strip club, a little shack called the Booby Trap. The county tried to shut him down dozens of times and failed, with Stagg lining the pockets of the supervisors, thriving for years until someone set fire to it, most believing it was Stagg himself. Stagg rebuilt bigger and bolder, with a place for truckers to get showered and fed, buy spare parts for their eighteen-wheelers, or rest for a while in a big-rig parking lot that stayed full most nights. Maybe a hand job before they got back on the road.

Quinn parked up toward the restaurant. The strip club was housed in a separate building visible from the highway, a big neon sign plastered on the broad side with a Confederate flag and the outline of a curvy woman, the kind you see on mud flaps.

He waited with Lillie in the truck about twenty minutes until they saw what they were looking for, a girl in a short plaid skirt, cowboy boots, and a pink ski jacket jumping down from the cab of a big rig and counting the cash in hand.

Quinn nodded to Lillie and followed the girl into the truck stop, bustling with tired folks cutting into leathery steaks and wilted salads. The girl asked a cashier to break a twenty and found a spot at the diner's counter, ordering a slice of pecan pie and a chocolate shake.

The girl was black-headed and very pale, with pockmarked skin and skinny legs. She ate the food fast and went back out into the cold, strolling through the long rows of parked big rigs, sometimes craning her neck up to an open window to talk, then moving on to the next row. Quinn caught up with her as she turned a corner, smiling and waving her down, dozens and dozens of trucks chugging around him in the cold, the air smelling of diesel. Parking lights almost looking like holiday decorations.

"Hey, I'm not hustling anyone. I'm looking for my boyfriend."

Her eyes were brown and strangely narrow, her nose stubby. Quinn offered her a twenty-dollar bill. She shook her head.

"I just want to talk."

"I don't go nowhere for less than fifty."

He paid her, tapping out his wallet for cash.

"Where's your rig?"

He led her back to the F-150, Lillie in the passenger seat. The girl not seeming to mind there was someone else in the cab, just hopping right between them while Quinn cranked the engine. "You can pull round back of the club," she said. "They don't open up for a few hours. And only one of you can touch me. Okay? Goddamn, it's cold."

"You know a girl named Jasmine?" Lillie asked, her face coloring.

The girl shook her head as Quinn drove to the back side of the strip club, parked by two overflowing Dumpsters, and killed the engine. The daylight was fading into a horizon of black, the pine trees inked cutouts, pools of stagnant water on a parcel of cleared land turning to ice.

"You sure?" he asked.

The girl shook her head. She looked scared.

"I think you're full of shit," Lillie said, letting down a side window and lighting a cigarette.

"You the law?"

"Yeah, I'm the law," Lillie said, turning to face her, reaching into her purse and showing her badge. "How about you tell us where to find Jasmine, and we'll set you right back where we left you? If not, we'll get you for solicitation."

"I don't give two shits."

"Don't act like you haven't got any sense," Lillie said. "We just want to ask her a couple questions."

"I've only been here a week."

"That's a lie," Lillie said. "You got busted for trying to peddle pussy on the town Square this summer."

The girl didn't say anything.

"You're from Florida," Lillie said, blowing smoke through the cracked window. "You got priors. Your name is Kayla."

"She hasn't been around in a while. Okay? Y'all leave me alone."

"Are y'all friends?" Quinn asked.

Kayla studied her hard-bitten nails, her knee jumping up and down like a piston. "Can I have a cigarette?"

Lillie handed her one with her lighter.

"You know where she lives?" Quinn asked.

"She got real fucked up. She ain't coming back. What'd she do anyway?"

"She knew a man who got killed," Quinn said. "We think she may have seen something or known something about it."

Kayla looked out at the blackened horizon

over an endless row of pines bordering the highway, looking like a high wall to Quinn. Lillie let out a long breath, patience waning, reaching for the girl's arm and pulling her attention toward her. "You know her real name?"

Kayla shook her head.

"You know where she's from?" Lillie asked.

"Said she was from Bruce."

"What's she look like?"

"I don't know."

"She's white?" Quinn asked.

"Sure she's white."

"What color's her hair?" he asked.

"Brown. Hell, you could look right at her and then forget her face. She looks like half the people I ever met."

Lillie let go of her arm. "What else do you know about her?"

"I know she's got a kid. Showed me pictures on her phone."

Quinn looked to Lillie and Lillie asked, "She say the kid's name?"

Kayla didn't say anything, just looked down at the cigarette in her hand. Quinn repeated the question.

"Said her daughter's name was Beccalynn. She said it like that, all one word, because I asked her if she'd call her Becky, you know, just to talk. But she said no because it was one name."

"That's a start," Lillie said. "If she's in school. How old do you think her daughter would be?"

"I don't know," Kayla said. "Six? She didn't say."

"Can you ask some of the other girls for us?" Quinn said. "I pay cash."

Kayla shrugged. "I think that girl is long gone. Y'all ain't gonna find her."

"How d'you know?" he asked.

"If she wasn't, she'd be out here with me in the cold, peddling pussy and trying to scrape up some money. What the hell else is there to do in this shithole?"

Lillie stared out the windshield, nodding. "You mind giving me that lighter back, sweetheart?"

7

Quinn checked out of the Traveler's Rest
and headed to his mother's house at about
eight, parking on Ithaca Road, an unfamiliar
Honda in the drive. When he knocked on
the door, he found it partially open and the
television switched on. The sound was
muted, and he heard footsteps, before a
woman holding Caddy's child opened the
door. It took a few seconds to refocus on
Anna Lee Amsden's face, ten years of his
life, twelve to twenty-two, and now Mrs.
Luke Stevens. Quite a thing. But things go
like that, he thought, not having to force a
smile on her, thinking she looked older, of
course, but better with those sleepy brown
eyes and dark blond hair tied in a ponytail.
She was neatly dressed in a white T-shirt
and jeans, shoes kicked off by the front
porch, all casual and loose as she had been
as a teenager, with her crooked nose and
long legs jumping into creeks and into

Quinn's waiting arms.

"Did the Army take your ability to talk?" she asked.

"Guess I didn't expect you."

"Your momma had to run back to the Piggly Wiggly. I told her I'd watch Jason."

"It's good to see you."

Quinn removed his baseball hat and walked past her, Anna Lee following and plopping Jason down in front of the television, where a cartoon kid was spelling out the words *cat, hat,* and *rat.* He turned back to look at Quinn, smiled, and then back to the television.

"She said you were staying at the motel."

"I'm gonna stay at my uncle's place a few nights."

"Heard it was yours."

"That's up for debate."

"It's good seein' you, Quinn," Anna Lee said, smiling, but in kind of a ragged, eye-rolling way, twisting her red mouth up and walking into the family room, reaching for the ponytail and letting her hair spill down to her shoulders. She had nice muscles in her back and lean arms, and a tall, delicate neck. Quinn pretty much liked all of it, knew that feeling wouldn't change, expecting it, and forgiving himself for it.

"Your momma hoped you'd stop by," she

said. "She even got beer."

"Praise Jesus."

"They sell it in town now."

"I would've come back sooner."

"Hell of a fight with the Baptists, but it passed. We even have a bar downtown."

"Civilization."

"Luke's down there now. He said he had something important to talk to you about."

"He say what it was?"

"Figured it was something about your uncle."

Their eyes met, and Quinn smiled at her some more. She reached over to Jason and pulled him into her lap and hugged him close, the boy intent on the television screen, the cartoon kid now counting to ten. All the basics being covered in a single episode. He thought about Caddy, wondering what she'd gotten into now, and knew whatever he or his mother did, it wouldn't make a damn bit of difference.

"Your momma is worried you're mad at her."

"I'm not mad."

"You could've stayed here. She can't understand why you stayed at that roach motel."

"I get up at all hours. I'd wake everyone in the house. And with a child here —"

"Maybe you can stay for dinner. Jason doesn't bite."

"What's the name of that bar?"

"The Southern Star."

"Maybe I'll get a few drinks first."

"You might want to get over whatever's eatin' you."

He walked back to the kitchen and fetched a Budweiser, noticing the photo he'd brought home of his platoon outside Camp Phoenix now under a magnet, next to several photos of Jason and several clippings of Elvis Presley. Quinn walked back and took a seat on the sofa, Jason turning around, staring at Quinn and not finding much interesting, turning back to the beginning of *Curious George.*

"When I was a kid, I used to think we were related to Elvis."

"Your mom says she met him once."

"She touched his hand when he played the Mid-South arena," Quinn said. "It was during 'I Can't Help Falling in Love with You,' and she kept the scarf he handed her. She keeps it in a specially made cedar box."

Anna Lee adjusted Jason on her lap, stretching out her long legs and wiggling her bare toes, having to crane her neck back to look at Quinn, and Quinn feeling embarrassed, noticing that the blue carpet, the Elvis knickknacks, and even the goddamn old console television, hadn't changed. They'd lay there, watching television, curfew coming up like a son of a bitch, waiting for his mother to finish that last white wine and turn in, and then rolling around on the floor, crazy and wild, sneaking back to his bedroom, so damn hungry for each other that they barely could catch a breath. It was the quietness and stillness of it that had made it.

"You still with me, Quinn?"

"What's that?"

"Like I said, you seem like you've again lost your ability to speak."

"The Southern Star?"

"Stay for dinner," Anna Lee said. "You'd make your mother's night. Luke's off. We'll be out late."

Quinn finished off the Budweiser and reached for his truck keys. "It's good seein' you, Anna Lee."

"Yeah, let's do this again in another six years."

The Southern Star stood on the north part of the town Square between a check-cashing business and a tired old beauty shop. The idea of it, having a bar in Jericho, was such a novelty that Quinn felt a bit self-conscious ordering a beer, and even more so when the bartender, a tiny girl of less than five feet who couldn't have been much past twenty-one, rattled off a list of what they had on tap and in bottles. Quinn ordered a Reb Ale, spotting Luke Stevens down the counter near the jukebox as the bartender cracked off the top.

"Hoped you'd see Anna Lee," Luke said, shaking his hand.

"She said you wanted to talk."

Luke was a little shorter than Quinn, thin, with shaggy brown hair, and wearing a dress shirt with a V-necked sweater. He'd known Luke since first grade, but he never really considered him a close buddy. There had been a time, second grade, when Luke's dad had told Jean that it was best that the kids didn't play together anymore. That was after a fight over some action figures and some flying fists left Luke with a black eye.

"What're you drinking?" Luke asked.

Quinn showed him the Reb Ale and took a seat.

The silver jukebox, a real authentic one that played 45s, pumped out Charley Pride's "Kiss an Angel Good Morning."

"Tibbehah's hell-raiser is back in town."

Quinn smiled, thinking how Luke made the honor roll and might have been class president. He was the kind of teenager that the cops didn't tail every time they saw his truck circle the Square and that wasn't put on the prayer list at church every other week even though he hadn't been sick.

"A real live drinking hole," Quinn said.

"We're big-time. Even got a coffee shop out in front of the tanning salon."

"Is that what brought you back?"

"Nope," Luke said. "I just love the high pay and easy work."

Luke grinned at him, but it was a cutting grin, and it made Quinn remember Luke Stevens in high school, that attitude he'd had, knowing he'd be the one who'd get out of town before anyone else. He always figured boys like Quinn, and Wesley and Boom, would be the ones checking his oil at the filling station. But how in the world can you slight a guy who returns to take his father's place as the only decent doctor in town, starting a medical clinic for the poor when he could be living it up in Jackson or Memphis or staying down in New Orleans, where he went to med school.

"How's your mother?"

"Fine," Luke said. "She and your mom have gotten to be pretty good friends, both of them widowed and all."

"My mom isn't widowed," Quinn said.

"She just tells people my daddy's dead."

"You're joking."

"It's a sad fact," Quinn said. "She's been doing that since I was twelve."

"What happened to him?"

"Don't know and don't care."

"I remember how all the kids used to look up to him," Luke said. "I still think about that time he brought that actress home with him and they rode in the Christmas parade. What was her name? She was on that sitcom with Burt Reynolds. She had huge tits."

"That didn't make for a holiday special at the Colson house."

Luke leaned over the bar and called the short girl, the jukebox clattering and stopping, whirring and slapping on some more vinyl, this time playing Patsy Cline, "Walkin' After Midnight," and that steady drumbeat just kind of held Quinn there in that open space, thinking of Anna Lee out back of the football stadium, she and him buck-ass naked and kissing, hands all over each other, when the headlights of her father's car lit up his rearview.

"Quinn?" Luke said, handing him a fresh beer. "Here you go."

"Appreciate it."

He patted Quinn's back and told him how sorry he was and how much he respected his uncle. He said he'd gone quail hunting with him last year and even did a little fishing in late summer, saying he never saw any signs of depression. "But most of them hide it well. Your uncle put on a good act."

"Could he have been sick?" Quinn asked.

"Didn't see any sign of it."

"Were you his doctor?"

"I'm lucky enough to be the town coroner," Luke said. "But that's not the same."

"You see anything strange about the kill shot?"

"You mean the wound?" Luke shook his head and drank some bourbon.

"Lillie said the entry point didn't make sense."

"Makes sense if you're that drunk."

A couple women from the nail salon, spray-tanned orange, saddled up next to them at the bar, and Luke introduced Quinn as his old buddy, a Ranger and a national hero. Quinn couldn't tell if the last part was praise or sarcasm.

"If you're asking did anything look strange," Luke said, "I'd have to say no."

Quinn turned back to his beer, and after a few minutes asked, "So what'd you want to see me about, Luke?"

The two of them sat side by side, the bartender putting down a couple more drinks for them, no one asking for another round but appreciating it.

The jukebox clicked onto some Loretta Lynn, telling ole Doo not to come home drinkin' with lovin' on his mind, and just about halfway through Anna Lee walked through the door, getting stopped by a couple of women playing darts.

She'd changed into heels and nice jeans with a sequined tank. She waved over to her husband.

"I guess I don't want you to feel weird about the situation with Anna Lee."

"What's the situation? She's your damn wife."

"It'd be nice if we could all have drinks while you were at home."

"Isn't that what we're doing?"

Luke smiled, and Quinn realized his voice had some edge to it. No one could think of anything to say, Anna Lee getting stopped every few feet, talking to everyone in town, Quinn not knowing almost anyone, wondering who in the hell they were. The Southern Star was elbow to elbow, lots of laughter and loud drunk talk. Quinn usually tried to stay out of bars because bars are where all those fights had started.

"If you were the coroner, you worked with my uncle a lot."

Luke nodded.

"I heard the job had run him down."

"I know he needed help with all the drugs."

"I don't remember a lot of drugs." Quinn grinned, taking a swig of beer. "Besides some of that dope I smoked."

"Most all the problems I get as a physician are connected to meth," Luke said. "I mean, it could be neglected or abused kids, or a woman being beaten up. Your uncle had to deal with the other side of it, people robbing Mr. Varner or the Sonic for fifty bucks, or people jacked up on that shit taking shots at his deputies. You know they call it the workin' man's cocaine? Sometimes I wish someone would put me in a padded room and let me try that stuff. It must be some kind of high, to sell your soul away."

"They grow poppies in Afghanistan like we grow cotton. And the Army was under direct orders to leave it alone. No one wanted to offend the warlords."

"You see much action?"

Quinn shrugged, Anna Lee weaving her way between them and picking up Luke's glass of bourbon and downing the rest of it. Luke laughed at her and reached behind her, gripping her ass hard. "Ain't she a pistol?"

Anna Lee squealed and knocked his hand away.

"I better be goin'," Quinn said.

Luke excused himself and stumbled his way to the toilet while more sad country music played on the jukebox. Anna Lee elbowed Quinn in the ribs, a soft smile on her lips. "Quitter."

"What's that supposed to mean?"

"What do you want it to mean?"

"Good night, Anna Lee."

Quinn got to the Dixie Gas station before they closed up for the night, reaching for a six-pack in the WELCOME HUNTERS display, paying cash, and then hitting the back roads and sites. They used to call it lowriding, although all of 'em had jacked-up trucks, but it was all slow and cool, prowling the unpaved roads, popping one beer after another, keeping clear of the main roads where you'd find the law. You might stop at some country cemetery to get out and smoke or take a piss, then get back in your automobile, just rolling with the curves and twists, heading out to the very spot you wanted to find, that spot where you found yourself absolutely lost, maybe ducking into that next county.

Quinn couldn't get lost.

He tried his damnedest, but even after the third beer all of Tibbehah County seemed as clear as a road map. He headed up near the Trace, thinking of following it awhile, just as he popped open a fresh beer. This was the first time he'd been able to get a little loose in several years. As the platoon daddy, he had to pretty much hold it together while his boys could go out and raise hell, Quinn being the one on call to break up fights or raise money for bail. He had to stand tall and be responsible when sometimes it was the platoon sergeant who craved a drink more than anyone.

Not that he didn't have his fair share of hell-raising as a private. Privates were always into stupid shit, and he hadn't been any exception. Not long after earning his tab, the 3rd Battalion found itself waiting outside an airstrip in Oman with some of the most elite Special Forces guys in the world. Most of these guys were battle-hard and older than Quinn was now, working with Rangers who weren't even old enough to drink.

After a few days, one dumb Ranger decided to slip into some black cold-weather gear and don a black balaclava and carry throwing stars made out of Copenhagen cans and nunchucks fashioned from duct tape and 550 cord. While the Delta guys sat in their tents discussing dangerous secret missions, this Ranger private, dressed all in black, was throwing Copenhagen tins at them and yelling, *NINJA!,* before hauling ass.

The officers never found out the identity of that man in black. But whoever he was, he's still a legend in the battalion.

Quinn smiled to himself and took a hard turn over the creek and down the gravel road and up into the farmhouse driveway, slamming the truck door behind him and using the front fender to steady himself while he took a leak. He kept on smiling and laughing at that ninja. He enjoyed the way the big oaks and pecans in a distant cattle field had many different branches.

As Quinn finished up, he saluted the moon, and reached into the truck for the last two beers, popping one, saving the other for a nightcap. About halfway to the dark house he heard a dog barking, his first thought being that Hondo had treed something, and the last thing he wanted to do was walk half a mile to save a scared raccoon.

The bark was quick and popping. And then he noticed the sounds of the cows.

And the voices of men in his uncle's pasture.

Quinn moved into the house and retrieved an old Winchester .45 lever-action, then followed the road, a long dark tunnel with nimble, wiry branches overhead. The cows' crying growing closer, Hondo's barking. Men yelling, and then the dog's yelp.

He levered the gun, put a .45 in the chamber, and continued to walk. Hondo zipped under the barbed wire and walked at his side under the moon. A cold wind shot down from the foothills.

At the fence, he could make out three men, and then five, kicking and swatting at the cows and loading them onto a long rusted trailer. Quinn moved along a ditch, then steadied his hand on a cedar post, staying there for maybe a good five minutes, rubbing Hondo's ears, before one of the miscreants spotted him and nudged another in the ribs.

They weren't ranchers. Three of them were nothing more than kids with shaved heads and wearing ragged jackets, another was a fat man with a shaved head, wispy red beard, and a scrawled tattoo on his neck. Quinn took the last fella to be running the show, from the way he was bossing everybody around. He was older, tall and skinny, with hollow dark eyes, and was shirtless under a camouflage jacket with all matter of patches and symbols.

Quinn's hand left Hondo's head and waved to them. "Hello."

The skeletal man broke away from his group and walked to a midpoint between them and Quinn.

Quinn walked toward him, seeing himself and the dog as moon shadow. He held the rifle loose and easy in his left hand.

"Evening" was all that came to Quinn's mind.

8

The skinny guy didn't say a word, just kind of stood there. He was a little shorter than Quinn, sporting a shaved head with short black mustache and goatee. He had vacant black eyes and a bulging lower lip packed with snuff, spitting every few seconds. Quinn guessed the guy was trying to stand tough, but he looked more confused than anything, other men now surrounding him in the moonlight like trained dogs. He didn't break his stance as Quinn walked around to the open cattle gate, some of the cows scattering from the herd and heading back to pasture.

"You boys lost?"

The skinny man — Quinn seeing the jacket patches included both the American and Confederate flags — smiled a row of very uneven yellowed teeth. A tattoo crept around the side of his neck. He looked to be jail-hard, moving slow in speech and eyes. A gun at his waist. That fat man with the wispy red beard carried a 12-gauge.

"Let 'em out," Quinn said.

The skinny man kept grinning.

Quinn walked right through the center of the group, elbowing one boy out of the way, and to the cattle trailer. He opened the gate, whistling and calling out the cows. Hondo hopped inside and nipped them along.

A half ring of men moved toward Quinn as he stepped back and let the flow of cattle pass him. He saw two more guns, the boss yet to pull his pistol, and Quinn kept his rifle by his side, finger on the trigger.

The men shuffled and stared, a couple of them looking to the boss and toeing the ground.

"You need me to call the sheriff's office?" Quinn asked. "This place isn't abandoned."

The skinny man nodded to a couple of the boys and they made a run at Quinn, Quinn stepping right for them, busting one in the skull with the rifle's butt and punching the other in the throat, not even breaking stride until he got within maybe a foot of the boss man's face and smiled at him. The man smelled of sharp body odor and old cigarettes.

The man pulled his pistol, and Quinn reached for his wrist, twisting it back until there was a sharp snap and the man fell to his knees. Quinn kicked him in the body twice as he fell and the gun dropped. Quinn picked it up, emptied the cylinder of the cheap .38, and slid it into his pocket.

"Gather your shit and get gone," Quinn said. "I'm in my legal right to shoot every one of you shitbags."

Hondo barked and nipped at the fat man's heels. He kicked at the dog.

Quinn said: "Do that again."

He walked straight away, not looking back, not hearing that telltale click of weapons until he reached the gate. There were two clicks, but Quinn didn't really give a damn, as if he'd heard the buzz of a mosquito.

Quinn called Wesley Ruth, but five minutes later the rusted trailer drawn by a King Cab truck ran down the road, bumping over potholes and ravines, Quinn standing on the porch, watching the face of the skinny man behind the wheel but not getting a look in return. With the trailer in the way, Quinn couldn't get a read on the tag.

The fat man remained in the empty cattle hold like a fattened hog, pointing a pistol up at Quinn and smiling, wild-eyed and happy, giving a jailhouse wink before they turned onto the main road.

■ ■ ■ ■

Quinn made coffee in an old speckled pot on the propane stove, and he and Wesley sat on the porch rocking chairs — just as cold inside the house as outside — drinking and talking. Quinn had a couple cigars in his truck, and they fired them up, Hondo now at his feet.

"So you found the dog," Wesley said, studying the tip of the cigar like he was surprised by the glow. He wore a flannel shirt under his old Tibbehah High letter jacket, occasionally taking off his ball cap and rubbing his head.

"He found me."

"You say there were five of them."

Quinn described all the men.

"You think your uncle may have sold the cattle?"

"You know a lot of folks who work cows in the middle of the night?"

"I put out word to look for that King Cab and the trailer."

"I guess I need to do something with those damn cows," Quinn said. "Anyone caring for them?"

"I heard Varner was tending to your uncle's business."

Quinn nodded, and the men sat in silence for a while. "I saw Anna Lee tonight."

Wesley cracked a grin, the cigar clamped in his teeth. "That didn't take too long."

"She was babysitting Caddy's boy, and I stopped by."

"Your momma is a saint for helping out Caddy."

"I don't think she had much choice."

"Caddy was a wreck when she finally left Jericho," Wesley said. "I picked her up twice for driving drunk and high. Took her straight home."

"Can we discuss the matter at hand?" Quinn asked.

"Does Anna Lee still make it hurt?"

"How old are you?"

"You know, every time I see Meg I still want to take her to bed."

"We weren't married."

"But it still hurts," Wesley said as he walked to the porch edge and tapped the ash. "Even when she's chewing my ass out. I'd even say especially when she's chewing my ass out."

"What happened?"

"Let's not share a special moment. Okay, Quinn?"

"Just asking," Quinn said.

"I think she got something different than

what she signed up for," Wesley said, a hard flash in his eyes. "She was counting that NFL money before my junior year."

"She wasn't like that, man. Not that I recall."

Wesley just looked at Quinn, smoking down the cigar, dropping it to the front steps, not even half spent, and crushing it out. "Shit."

"Can I show you something?" Quinn asked.

Quinn found a kerosene lantern in the shed and set it on top of the kitchen table, which was covered in checked oilcloth. He pointed out the patterns of blood that he'd seen on the wallpaper, careful not to touch any of it. The spatter — which someone had tried to blot away — looked like an enormous halo, flecks of dried blood across the flowered print.

"What's this tell you?"

"That Leonard didn't clean up what I asked him to clean up."

"But all this was examined with whatever you people do?"

Wesley nodded. "We do have a little sense around here."

"How long does that take?"

"Could take several weeks. Maybe a month. State lab is backed up."

"You know what happened to the gun?"

"You want to tell me what you're thinking?" Wesley said, holding on to the edge of the table.

"Johnny Stagg says he owns all this land," Quinn said. "He's putting a lien on the property."

"I know you don't like the idea of Stagg finding the body, but they'd been friends for the last few years. Stagg would come over just to check on his equipment."

"And make loans."

"I wouldn't be telling folks about your uncle's gambling problem," Wesley said. "What good would it do?"

"Since I've been back, everyone seems to want to tell me my uncle was a great man before they whisper secrets in my ear."

Wesley shrugged, every movement in the old house magnified in the emptiness. The men turned down the hallway back to the front door, moving back outside, the screen door slamming behind them.

"No ideas on those shitbags tonight?"

"The cattle rustlers? I'll think on it."

"No offense," Quinn said. "But you don't seem to know a hell of a lot."

Wesley leaned on the door of his patrol car and nodded. "Oh, I know who they are. I just don't think it's a good idea to tell you.

We got it, Ranger."

"Nice jacket."

Wesley looked down at the old letterman's jacket and all the gold pins that covered the big *T* and smiled. "I earned this son of a bitch. And hell, it was the first thing I could find when you woke me up. You mind if we both get some sleep?"

Quinn got to sleep for ten minutes before he heard a car roll into the drive. He checked the window, seeing a sheriff's cruiser, thinking that Wesley had changed his mind.

But when Quinn went to the door, he found Lillie Virgil, dressed in uniform and holding a flashlight up into his face.

"I thought you were Wesley."

"Do I look like Wesley?"

"Nope."

"I got a lead on the lot lizard. We gotta head up to Bruce. Are you sober?"

"I've been drinking coffee for two hours."

"Good," she said. "If we leave now, we can make it to church."

9

Bruce was about thirty minutes out of Jericho in the northern part of Calhoun County. A lumber mill dwarfed the small downtown — a road sign reading WELCOME TO BRUCE WHERE MONEY GROWS IN TREES — and even at dawn the metal buildings were lit up, with mountains of logs waiting in piles to be cut down into planks, plumes of steam rising up into the cold air. Lillie pulled into a service station and grabbed a couple more coffees; they'd arrived in town thirty minutes early and were supposed to see the minister at his church at seven. Quinn and Lillie sat in her Cherokee for several minutes, watching the logging trucks bumping their way down a gravel road and leaving the mill's chain-link gates. The light turned from slate gray to a brilliant purple while Lillie, making a face at the weak coffee, confessed to not stepping foot in a church for ten years.

"The only people who are brave enough to pay me a visit are the Jehovah's Witnesses," she said.

Quinn blotted a napkin at the busted skin on his knuckles.

"You should wrap that up," she said.

"I will when we get back," he said. "Do those men sound familiar?"

"We'll look at some photo packs back in Jericho," Lillie said.

"Wesley said he knew 'em but won't tell me."

"Wesley is often full of shit."

"You think Stagg sent 'em?"

"What do you think?" Lillie started the cruiser, and they made their way through the old downtown, not all that different from Jericho, and along a small street to a Baptist church with a parking lot that was empty except for a Buick parked in a space reserved for the minister. After Lillie had left Quinn at his mother's last night, she'd made some calls to people on the Calhoun County school board, finding two girls named Beccalynn younger than ten. She'd spoken to the first girl's mother, finding the woman at home with three other children. The second call yielded the Bullard family, and a long pause when Lillie asked questions about young Beccalynn's mother, whose real name, it turned out, was Jill. The man, a pastor, asked if they could meet in person.

"How long has it been since her family saw her?" Quinn asked.

"Three months," Lillie said.

"How long has their granddaughter been living with them?" Quinn asked.

"More than a year."

They found Reverend Bullard in his office with an open door, the church offices smelling of musty old Bibles and cleaning supplies, that familiar church scent. He had them sit in a little grouping of four chairs, where Quinn assumed he did counseling. Lots of brochures on alcoholism and domestic violence on a table between them. He offered them coffee and they took it, pretty weak, but they couldn't complain, waiting for him to come to the point as he made polite conversation, talking about losing his sermon and having to retype the whole piece last night.

He was in his early forties, slight and graying. He had a soft, gentle voice and wore a basic blue suit and red tie. A piece of toilet paper had been stuck on a cut on his chin. "Did you find her?" he asked.

Lillie shook her head. "Your daughter, Jill, was in Tibbehah County last month. We want to talk to her in regards to an ongoing investigation."

Quinn could tell Bullard assumed he was a deputy, too, and Lillie did nothing to try to set him straight.

"What's she done now?"

Lillie shook her head. "Nothing. But a man she was seen with was killed. We just want to know more about him."

"I figured she was dead," the pastor said. "We've been expecting that call for four years. I pray for her every day, but she has to make decisions on her own."

Lillie nodded. Quinn felt himself start to sweat.

"Beccalynn was Jill's second child," he said. "She aborted the first. We didn't know until later. There has been nothing but drugs and men ever since. We only have one child now and that's Beccalynn, and we pray that her mother never again enters her life."

"Do you have any idea where she could have gone?" Lillie asked, her hands held tight in her lap. Quinn shuffled in his seat and put down the coffee, feeling hot in the small room with all its plaques and religious posters, a purple robe hanging on a hook by the door with two umbrellas and a baseball cap.

Bullard shook his head and looked at his hands.

There'd been a time when Caddy had gone down to Panama City with some friends and had disappeared for about eight days. Quinn's mother about lost her mind, and Quinn had to get a special pass to leave Fort Benning. He and another Ranger who wanted to come along had searched in and out of every shithole along the Miracle Mile until they found her passed out in a daiquiri bar, two boys from the Navy base trying to ease her back to their car.

He and his buddy nearly ended up in jail for whipping the shit out of those sailors. Four months later, Caddy disappeared again.

"She used to call and ask for money," the preacher said. "I didn't even know that she'd been in Tibbehah County. I figured she was still in New Orleans."

"Does your wife know we called?" Lillie asked.

"No."

"You think she might know something?" Quinn asked.

"She knows less than me," he said. "The last time I saw her was in New Orleans. I had wired Jill money at a grocery store on Royal Street. I waited till she came and picked it up, and followed her out. She looked just wild, with her clothes and hair. She didn't seem to know me at first. When she did, she made wild accusations and said very hurtful things. She's not my daughter. I don't know who she's become and would never want my wife to feel what I had felt."

Quinn stood, feeling like he could not breathe.

"Now we have a name," Lillie said, still sitting looking up at him. "We'll try and run her through the system."

"You understand if I don't want to be notified," the preacher said.

Lillie laid down her card and wrote her cell phone number on the back. "If you hear from her, please let us know."

Quinn shook his hand with speed and left the building, finding some comfort out in the chilled early morning air. He wanted to punch the shit out of something but tried to calm his thoughts with breathing.

They always said that shit worked, and sometimes it did.

Lena had spent the last three days at a women's shelter in Jericho, where they fed her three meals a day and gave her a bunk in the basement of the Baptist church among rows of folding chairs, golden choir robes, and two Ping-Pong tables. The fat wife of the preacher had taken particular interest in her, coming down the steps late at night with cake or pudding, high on the glory of the Christmas season, reading tracts of Bible stories from old *Guidepost* magazines and comparing Lena's plight to that of the Virgin Mother. She told the fat lady she hadn't been a virgin since she was thirteen, thank you very much, but she did appreciate the pudding. The woman would smile at her and pat her on the head, and for most of the day Lena was free to help out with dishes in the kitchen after prayer breakfasts and fold laundry of the other gals who were there, including a woman in her forties with a busted lip and a black girl about her age who was just about as knocked up and said she wasn't no virgin, either. On that Sunday afternoon, after a supper of baked chicken and peas and sweet tea, Lena took a walk, promising the local counselor that she only needed some air and would not smoke, drink, or do intentional harm to herself or the baby.

She found herself in downtown Jericho, the sun headed down not long past four. The bare trees and old rusted tower looming over the squat buildings were dark and shadowed, as if they'd been sketched in pencil. With the four dollars left in the quilted coat she'd been given, sewn by the good sisters of the church, she ordered a hamburger and small milk shake at the Sonic Drive-In, sitting at a table up by the kitchen window, while the slots were filled with white boys' muddy trucks and black boys' sporty sedans jacked up on high silver rims.

The milk shake was what she needed, and, with less than a dollar left, she asked the waitress for an order of fried pickles. The woman set them down and didn't even ask to be paid, Lena left somehow thinking that she'd been in a similar spot at one time or another.

Visiting hour was tomorrow, and if Jody, or Charley Booth or whoever he really was, didn't want to see her again, she guessed she'd hand-crawl her way back to Alabama and ask for some forgiveness from her father, although her daddy had made it pretty damn clear she was not much use to their family as a common whore. She figured maybe she could stay at the church and work, but the ladies had already tried to place her with a program in Jackson that sounded like a place that a girl left without her child.

If she could just have the kid and get back

on her feet, she could take care of it. She had a sister in Birmingham who could watch the baby if she could find work. Her momma could help if she could find where she was living, the last place being Tampa, where she'd been working as a dancer. She figured she just needed to settle this thing with the boy since it was him who'd told her that he'd loved her and that she sure made him whole, and all of that had sounded pretty solid over some cold beer and weed, but sober, rattling around her head at the Sonic, it sounded pretty much like horseshit off a greeting card.

She tried to keep the last few pickles, them cooling off fast in the wind, when she saw the black Camaro, the one from the jail the other day, whip into the parking lot and slide right into a slot by an old Ford.

That muscled guy with the shaved head and the stubble mustache and goatee leaned out the window and pressed the red button, calling out what he wanted just as if they didn't have an intercom and kind of laughing about it to some girl that sat next to him, shadowed in the front seat. The man said he wanted a country-fried steak sandwich, some tater tots, and a large cherry limeade.

"Oh, and a sundae with that cherry top-pin'," he said.

Lena watched him, noticing his large, veiny arm, lined with tattoos, and the way he turned out the window again and dug a lump of dip from his lower lip, flinging it down onto the pavement and turning his black eyes right on her.

She sucked on her milk shake, not backing down for one damn minute. She'd paid for her food and would enjoy it, even longer than she'd expected. She turned away and watched a man in white working the grill, flipping over patties and checking some fries in a grease trap.

Lena placed her hands in her little knitted coat, feeling the wind kicking up over her back.

"I love the look of a woman with child," a man said. "Y'all got that glow."

She craned her head.

He smiled at her, wearing a black T-shirt with no sleeves like it wasn't about forty degrees out, and reached out and grabbed her last two fried pickles and put them on his fat tongue, sliding into the seat in front of her.

"Don't look at me like that, girl," he said, scratching the stubble on his chin, his teeth yellowed. "You can forget that Charley

Booth. Right now, I may be the best friend you ever had."

10

Quinn bought a bag of dog food in Bruce and left out a bowl for Hondo at the farm before picking up his old truck and calling home, letting his mother know that he wouldn't be able to make that church service. He had to pull the cell away from his ear at her response. "It's important," he said. Words were said about the chickenshit casserole and the preacher dropping by and some kind of plaque that had been arranged. She made him promise three times to at least make the lunch and all three times he'd agreed.

"Okay," she said, finally.

"Okay?" he asked.

"Okay."

"Love you, Momma."

He headed east back to the truck stop, finding the lot pretty bare, maybe ten or so trucks chugging out those diesel fumes. The drivers catching some fuel and rest for a couple hours before heading on. The whole scene reminded him a bit of some staging areas in Iraq, when getting supplies down highways had been a major operation and strike teams were sometimes needed to clear the way. You could kind of feel the expectation in that silence.

Quinn walked the ground between the trucks, seeing no one. Even the cabs were empty, with the truckers sleeping or in the diner eating. He walked the rows twice and then walked inside the Rebel Truck Stop, ordering a plate of eggs and hash and black coffee. The truck stop was a massive operation, with an adjoining Western shop where they sold hats, boots, and big belt buckles with horses and bulls on them. You could buy Mexican blankets and bullwhips, and John Wayne movies on DVD for five bucks. Dirty movies for ten.

Quinn paid his tab and walked back out into the cold. The morning light shone hard and bright white across the blacktop.

He walked the rows again. A couple trucks pulled away, leaving only a handful, and it seemed to him that the night's action had probably picked up and left. Sunday, even for some hard-up truckers, wasn't the best time to get laid in Mississippi.

About halfway back to his car, he saw her.

At first he thought it was Kayla again. The girl using the pay phone was dressed in a jeans skirt and T-shirt, some black tights the only thing protecting her from the cold. She wore big black oversized glasses, but as he approached he saw it was the girl from the other night that he damn near hit on Highway 9.

She turned to him and then back to the corner of the pay phone, the wall scrawled with keyed crude drawings and biblical passages. He tapped her on the shoulder, and she turned and said, "What?"

He stood there. She hung up, the change rattling down in the return.

She scooped it out quickly.

"How you making out?"

"Fine," she said, hugging her arms up over her extended belly.

"You look cold," Quinn said. "Can I buy you something to eat?"

"I'm fine," she said. "I'm with a friend."

"Jody?"

She shook her head. "Another friend."

"You look like you're getting close," Quinn said.

She nodded.

"Don't you think you better put on a jacket?"

"I can round up the money for that motel

room," she said, shifting from leg to leg in the cold wind.

"Don't worry about it."

She nodded and turned back to the glass door of the truck stop. Quinn watched her move to a back booth, removing the glasses and showing off a nasty black eye. A waitress put a menu in her hands, the girl folding the glasses and then unfolding them, placing them back on like blinders. Quinn walked back inside and went to her table. He didn't say anything but leaned down and wrote out Luke Stevens's cell phone number on the back of a book of matches. Underneath he wrote QUINN and his cell number.

She looked at him and frowned, leaning into an open hand propped on an elbow. She didn't make a move to pick up the matchbook.

"This doc is a friend of mine," he said. "You get that baby checked out. I'll make sure it's paid for."

"I don't know you."

"What's that got to do with anything?" Quinn said. "You want to tell me what happened?"

"Not really."

"My name and number is written there, too."

"Why are you doing this? You want some-thin'?"

"Don't be so tough that it makes you stupid."

"You go to hell."

Quinn tipped the edge of his baseball cap and left.

He sat in the cab of his truck for a long while, getting a nice view into the diner, the place like the inside of a fish tank. The girl sat alone, drinking a Coke, until a man entered from a side door and took a seat across from her. He was a decent bit older — or looked older — with a shaved head lined with black stubble, the same length as the hairs under his nose and on his chin. He had a lit cigarette in hand and kept his arm around the back of the booth while he made rapid, wild gestures and pointed. The girl just looked down at the tabletop, reach-ing for some sugar and putting it into her glass, finding some kind of interest in the way it dissolved.

The man wore a sleeveless T-shirt, his arms thick with veins and muscle. Every few minutes he'd reach for his phone, talk for a bit, then slam it down. He kept pick-ing it up, looking at the face of it, and typ-ing on the keys.

He didn't speak to the woman as he ate,

and then he moved for the back door, Quinn cranking the engine and driving slow to the diesel pumps, where he saw the man, short but powerful-looking, approach a dually Chevy with the back window obscured by a large decal of an evil clown's face.

Quinn kept driving to a decent vantage, no one even looking at his truck, and he killed the engine. The man leaned into the open window of the truck, revealing a .45 tucked into the back of his tight ragged jeans. When he turned back, he was still laughing, walking along with a rotten smile on his face, his breath clouding in the cold, a fat green shamrock tattoo across his neck.

The dually Chevy cranked to life and worked a fast U-turn, passing Quinn.

The driver was a skinny fella who wore a homemade splint of silver duct tape on his left wrist.

Jericho had always been a lonely town on a Sunday. About the only place open was the truck stop; the Fillin' Station and all the downtown was closed. There was a new storefront church in the old town movie theater where a hand-painted piece of plywood advertised the services of Brother Davis. Only two movie posters were under the glass; one for a film starting Kirk Cameron about saving your marriage and another showing a large airliner advertising the LAST DAYS OF MAN. Half that parking lot was filled, and with the windows cracked Quinn could hear the singing and electronic-piano music inside. He drove east, knowing he had to be back by one to his mother's, feeling like he didn't want to face the farmhouse alone and hear those dull, empty spaces when he talked and shuffled, feeling like the cavern needed to be filled up with something new, pushing out the dead and hollow.

Ribbons and ribbons of country highway opened up under him, splitting off Main and heading up toward the town cemetery, Quinn half thinking he should visit his uncle's grave but not really wanting to stop, just driving past a volunteer fire station and an old cotton gin that had been closed for years. He passed the old ammunition factory and a transmission-repair shop, and everything kind of ended there, past the original town cemetery, where Civil War soldiers had been buried when Jericho had been a hospital during the war, Quinn recalling all the stories and visits with his uncle while his father was away, chasing another business scheme or shooting a movie.

Where the paved road ended, a gravel path grew under his tires, curling up to the north in a single lane of more dirt and gravel, signs for PRIVATE LAND and hunt clubs and logging companies nailed onto pine trees. This was the place where people came to dump their old refrigerators and washers and car parts, in the long ravine choked with last year's pine straw and faded beer cans and diapers and old plastic dolls. Quinn wished he had a beer right now as he drove, searching for music on the radio but finding only messages of salvation and digs at the sinners of this world. He checked in with the old rock 'n' roll station out of Tupelo but found that it had become nothing but the yelling voice of talk radio. He wished he'd brought some music with him. Keeping the windows down, the cold air feeling good on his face and in his lungs, he reached into his jacket for that extra cigar that Judge Blanton had given him the other day and lit it. As he circled the bend, he found himself on blacktop again as the road headed back to join up with Highway 9, a few trailers off to the north over some cleared land.

A lone figure walked far in the distance, a big, hulking shadow keeping up high on the shoulderless road, wearing an old Army coat and ragged pants tucked inside flopping desert boots. Quinn slowed behind the man, honking his horn.

Boom Kimbrough turned.

"Get in," Quinn said, reaching for the passenger-door handle, cigar clamped in his teeth. "Where are you goin'?"

Boom shrugged.

"You're coming to lunch," Quinn said. "Don't think you're leaving me alone with my momma's church friends."

Boom smiled at him, and Quinn gunned the motor just like when they went riding in high school, trying to stay one step ahead of the law, knowing every back road and fire trail in the county. "You remember when we smoked ole Deputy Frank? He about shit his pants, trying to prove we were the ones who outran him. I wonder what happened to him."

"He's dead."

"He always reminded me of Barney Fife."

"Where you been?" Boom asked.

Quinn told him about the meeting with Uncle Van and the truck-stop whore, the trip to Bruce, and then seeing the pregnant girl at the Rebel Truck Stop.

"You sure it was the same guy?"

" 'Less I broke another man's wrist."

"You do love to fight, Quinn."

"It was him."

"What'd the other one look like? The one with the girl?"

Quinn gave a description of the sleeveless muscle shirt and the shaved head, the bad teeth and the .45. "And he had a tattoo of a shamrock on his neck. Must be Irish."

"That or he's in the Aryan Brotherhood."

"That's their symbol?"

"Yeah. The peace sign was taken."

"Sound familiar?"

Boom nodded, adjusting his large weight in the cab of the truck, reaching down to roll back the seat and pulling at the seat belt with his left hand. "That motherfucker's name is Gowrie. His people moved in here about two years ago. He is bad news, man. He's plugged into the Memphis scene, cooks meth all around the county, and fucks with anyone who gets in his way."

"Why do you think Wesley wouldn't tell me that?"

" 'Cause he got a little bit of sense," Boom said. "And knows you."

"So what's in this for Johnny Stagg?"

"Here we go," Boom said. "Fuckin' with things. Quinn, you just can't help but fuck with things."

11

So he hit her. Lena wasn't all that surprised by it after she spat in the man's face, but she was surprised by him handing her a wad of twenty-dollar bills and saying for her to get cleaned up. He'd taken her back to where he lived, where they all lived, and she found out his name was Gowrie. She wasn't sure if that was his first or last name or just something folks called him. He and his boys had five trailers laid down in this big gully wash off some back road north of Jericho. He'd told her they planned on getting Charley out real soon — Lena still getting used to folks calling him Charley, or sometimes Slim — and that if she'd just stay put, they'd take care of her. They were Charley's family, and now that he'd planted his damn seed, they were Lena's family, too. The smack in the face happened only once, when she got kind of hysterical. She said she'd sit in the car, and then he just started to drive, taking her up and around the Square, and then flat out hitting it on the main road north. She'd reached for the handle of that black Camaro and, the next thing she knew, she felt like she'd been kicked by a mule.

They had electricity out at the trailers, something she was surprised about because it was so far off the main road. But she heard the loud humming of generators and saw a mound of red gas cans by the mouth of a leaning barn. The trailers were all rusted and worn, looking like they'd been picked up and set down plenty, the steps fashioned out of scrap wood, some just loose bricks laid down in the mud. A long sluicing ravine fed into the mouth of the old barn, that looked like something that had been there for a hundred years, and by midday she found this was a place where the men, about fourteen or sixteen of them she was pretty sure, would gather. Some of them brought their women and children. Some were alone. Most of them smoked weed or chewed tobacco, circling around Gowrie as he spoke to them, Lena waiting for a sermon but instead learning of a world that was about to collapse in on itself due to all the Mexes and niggers in their midst. And if they didn't get to work, get some money to buy more weapons, they'd be swept up in a darkness that would descend on the land like locusts.

Gowrie was geeked-the-fuck-out. She'd seen plenty of folks with their minds burning on that crank. But Gowrie was wild-eyed overtime. One time he just flat out kicked a boy from a folding chair when he thought the boy's attention had wandered. It was that kind of speech, Gowrie walking and spilling out all matter of hateful things, wearing a T-shirt reading WHITE PRIDE, WORLDWIDE over a Celtic cross.

Lena grew restless in the chair, wanting to get up, her feet hurting, growing hungry, but afraid to move. The damn thing finally broke up after what seemed like forever, and trucks and four-wheelers started, Lena noticing more shithole trailers up into the scrub oak and pine. They lit a fire and gathered around it, passing around whiskey, and crank to snort. The day was cold but bright.

No one spoke to Lena for a while, and she was afraid to move from the radiator in the barn. When she could, she'd get clear of these people and back on the road. She'd give ole Charley Jody Booth one more try and then she'd find her way back to Alabama.

She felt hands on her shoulders and she jumped. But it was just a dumb boy putting a jacket on her. The jacket was warm and smelly and about four sizes too big. But she was in no place to refuse it and thanked the boy, who was short and fat and had the face of a pig.

His hair was shaved down, like all the men in Gowrie's world. But his teeth seemed a mite better, and his voice was even and steady, asking if he could fetch her some food. She just nodded and followed, moving back to a row of freezers laid side by side at the back of the barn. A big Honda generator kept them going, and the boy opened the top of one of them to show food stocked like the cold section at a Walmart. TV dinners, sausage biscuits, even whole pies and ice cream.

The boy's T-shirt had a picture of Alan Jackson on it. His arms were covered with goose pimples in the cold. He smiled a lot as he lifted a whole chicken potpie into a microwave and sent it spinning. He poured her a tall Mountain Dew in a plastic cup and took her over to a card table piled high with books so worn they'd grown soft and spineless. *Weapons of the Middle Ages. Being White in America. The Coming Race War.* Several comic books featuring Wolverine.

"You know Charley Booth?" she asked.

He nodded.

"Are they really gonna get him out?"

"That's what Gowrie says."

"He creeps me out."

"Shh. Gowrie's got a lot on him. Everything we got here is on account of him."

"I think he's crazy."

"How's your eye?"

"How's it look?"

The bell dinged on the microwave, and the boy brought the potpie out to her. His jacket felt mighty warm. And she no longer noticed he had the face of a pig. She just saw a mess of freckles.

"My name is Pete. They call me Ditto."

"Why they call you that?"

"I guess on account of me agreeing with most folks."

You had to hand it to Jean Colson, she could sure put on a Sunday spread. Quinn and Boom stepped into the full house, barely noticed by all the people Quinn didn't know, piling their plates with boiled ham and fried chicken, potato salad, and collard greens. His mother had made biscuits and corn bread, two pies, and that damn casserole based on cream-of-mushroom soup. Quinn took off the rancher coat, hung his baseball cap on the hook by the door, and started the progression of handshakes and hugs, making sure Boom was included in the conversation when the conversation turned to war. Boom seemed not to give a damn, excusing himself to join the line for the food, Jean making him comfortable up at the long, polished dining-room table, filling his glass with sweet tea.

Sometime in the night or the early morning his mother had decorated for Christmas, lights across the mantel, garlands on the front railings, and candles around the kitchen. The house smelled inviting and warm. His mother brought him a plate, and he sat down next to Boom, his chair in the center of the table, the wide mirror in the hallway reflecting Quinn flanked by family and friends, an elderly aunt patting him on the shoulder, more potato salad passed from his left. Elvis, as always, played on the stereo, Jean choosing a nice mix of old-time hymns and songs from his movies. "Peace in the Valley." "Clambake."

Wesley Ruth and Judge Blanton stopped by but didn't eat. Luther Varner got loose from the Quick Mart for a few minutes. Mr. Jim stayed, taking an empty seat by Quinn and not saying a word but giving a polite nod before settling into a large piece of fried chicken. Boom excused himself and left with his plate empty, and that chair was empty all of ten seconds when Anna Lee sat down, wearing a bright red coat buttoned high, blond hair loose over her shoulders, giving a crooked smile and a roll of the eyes to Quinn. "We missed you in church," she said. "They called for you all of two times. Your mother said you were working. I thought you might have headed back to camp."

"I went for a drive."

"With who?"

"Myself."

Anna Lee cut her brown eyes over at him, her long fingers picking at her chicken, pulling the skin off, taking little bites. Quinn smiled at her and she looked away, another old woman coming over to him, a friend of his dead grandmother, handing him a greeting card she wanted him to open when he returned back home. Quinn wasn't quite sure where she meant.

He laid his hands on her old hand and thanked her, his eyes lifting up and seeing Lillie Virgil holding Jason upside down and swinging him from side to side like a pendulum. She was dressed up, long black pants, a nice silk top. Quinn noticed Anna Lee watching her and then looking down when

139

she saw Quinn was staring.

"People have seen you around with Lillie," she said, smiling. "What's going on there?"

"Nothing."

"Heard y'all have barely been apart."

What do you say to that?

Quinn messed around with the last few mouthfuls and put down his fork, looking for some sweet tea to clear his mouth. He took a deep breath, catching Lillie's eye and smiling. Lillie smiled back.

"She never dresses like that."

"Stop," Quinn said.

"What?"

"Needling me."

"Congratulations," Anna Lee said. "They sure missed you at church."

She cleared her plate and was gone. Quinn turned to the right, where Mr. Jim was working on a chicken leg and then wiping his mouth. He looked at Quinn and shrugged.

"What do you make of that?" Quinn said.

"I wouldn't have kept my barbershop open for forty years if I didn't know when to shut my mouth."

"I will never understand her," he said.

"Hell, men and women, we don't speak the same language," he said.

Quinn winked at the old man, gathered his plate and took it back to the kitchen. His mother, never one to have a good time, was already elbow-deep in the sink, suds spilling over the counter onto the floor. Jason was running wild, with Lillie running after him, running right into Quinn and then pushing him back with the flat of her hand.

"Y'all have a nice talk?" she asked.

Quinn reached for the coffeepot and poured a cup.

He rolled up his sleeves and started to help with the dishes, his mother trying to push him away. "Go talk to everyone," she said. "I can't be in there."

"Let me ask you a question," Quinn said, reaching for a wet plate to dry. "Was Uncle Hamp really friends with Johnny Stagg?"

"I know they did business," his mother said. "I don't know if they were friends."

"Stagg wants our land pretty bad."

"He won't get it."

"You're goddamn right."

"Quinn?"

"What?"

"Watch that mouth."

Quinn reached for a glass and dried it, setting it on the rack, Lillie wrangling Jason long enough to sit him at the little breakfast

141

nook, trying to get him interested in a coloring book. Over his mother's shoulder, he
saw Anna Lee in the foyer throwing a purse
over her shoulder and reaching into her coat
pocket for her keys. She looked at Quinn
and then turned for the door, Quinn knowing the move, knowing she wanted him to
follow her outside so they could argue a bit
more.

Quinn reached for another dish.

"Judge Blanton is going to keep his eye
on things after I'm gone," Quinn said. "I
don't want that land ever coming to that
son of a bitch."

His mother shook her head.

"Okay?" Quinn said, Lillie lifting her head
from the table and looking at him.

His mother nodded.

"Do you now see how he wasn't in his
right mind?" Jean Colson asked. "It
would've been just his mind-set to sell that
property to someone without telling me."

"He didn't sell it," Quinn said, "just
signed some stupid agreement on a scrap of
paper."

"I hadn't spoken to him since last Easter
Sunday, and here he comes in maybe three
weeks ago, knocking on my door and wanting to know if I could store some of his
boxes. This is a man with two barns and

three sheds. He had so much junk he needed me to watch his possessions."

Lillie stood up from the table. She looked to Quinn.

"What did he leave, Mrs. Colson?" Lillie asked, placing her hands in her pockets and standing on the balls of her feet.

His mother had turned his bedroom into a sewing/storage room but kept the walls as they'd been ten years ago. There were posters for the U.S. Army BE ALL YOU CAN BE, Rangers LEADING THE WAY, and a black-and-white of Tishiro Mifune from *Yojimbo* over a small bookshelf filled with all five of James Fenimore Cooper's Leatherstocking Tales, Hemingway's Nick Adams Stories, *Walden, A Book of Five Rings, Huck Finn,* and a volume on Bruce Lee's *Jeet Kune Do.* He'd nailed up ninja throwing stars and a bowstave, and all of the belts he'd earned as a kid taking tae kwon do. Everything hung on the wall leading him on the path to becoming a modern warrior. He'd wanted to be a Ranger since first seeing the film *Darby's Rangers* on late-night television during one of his father's rare long appearances. He became obsessed when he found some Ranger literature at the recruiter's office. The idea of a Ranger having to volunteer four times for service seemed ideal. He was prepared to volunteer for whatever was thrown at him, his teenage self traveling about a million miles an hour, fearless, but not really understanding what fear meant.

"I'd forgotten how intense you used to be," Lillie said, lifting one of the five boxes his uncle had left on a bed with a thin bedspread. She used a pocketknife to slit the tape, finding rows of manila files crammed inside, snapping the knife closed and back into the pocket of her wide-legged pants. The light was white and harsh through the curtains, and Quinn closed them, standing over Lillie's shoulder, his mother still in the kitchen cleaning up with some other women, Jason down for a nap.

Boom had disappeared an hour ago. No one saw him leave.

A prom picture of him and Anna Lee in a gilded frame stood on the bookshelf. Quinn looked stiff and posed in a rented tux, red flower on his chest, hands around Anna Lee's waist. While flipping through the files, Lillie said, "Damn, y'all look like kids."

"What do we have?"

"These are just tax records," she said. "Looks like he saved every damn receipt for the last five years. I don't know. You can look if you want. We probably need a CPA to go through all this. Maybe something he wanted you to see."

Quinn hefted up another box, this one containing fistfuls of family photographs going back maybe a hundred years, people from his family at the turn of the damn century, standing grim-faced in front of churches and sitting in rocking chairs holding rifles. "Yep, that's your people all right," Lillie said. "Look at that guy, he looks just like you. Same serious scowl, the way he's holding that weapon. Run for the hills."

Quinn flipped through a few pictures, photos of his mom and dad. Several of Quinn with his uncle, fishing, hunting. Quinn with the first big buck he'd killed, the one that won his second prize in the state for young hunters. The damn thing's head still hung over the mantel in the family room. He placed the photos back in the box, Lillie losing faith that any of this crap meant anything, lying back on the old bed in the room clogged with two sewing machines and unused exercise equipment. She flipped through a big wad of photos, Quinn noticing the way the silk top had hitched up on her stomach a bit, the tautness of her stomach as she shifted.

He turned away and reached for a fourth box.

"Y'all okay in there?" his mother yelled.

"Yep," Quinn said, slicing into the fourth, finding more rows and rows of tightly stacked manila files, expecting to see more stuff for the tax man but pulling out the first file and clearly seeing typed-up copies of crime reports. Each folder label noted the case. "Lillie?"

Lillie moved off the bed, leaving the old photos spread out.

She got near him, everything in the room so cluttered that it was hard to breathe. She was about his same height, and Quinn felt her pressed against his shoulder, breathing hard, and then setting down on one knee to shuffle through the piles. She split the files in two stacks and told him to start reading. She sat down Indian-style, flipping through the first file, and within seconds it was on the floor and she was on to the next.

Jean brought them fresh coffee, not saying a word while they read, and closed the door with a light click.

"What are we looking for?" he asked.

"I imagine you'll know when you see it," Lillie said.

"This is a file on a vehicular homicide," he said. "Some drunk ran over a fella out on County Road 389."

"Keep going."

"Why would he keep these here?"

"He'd have no reason to take these from the office, unless it was something active he wanted to work personal."

"He do many investigations himself?"

"When you got eight folks looking out for one county, everybody pitches in."

"And no police department."

"Jericho still can't afford to put anyone on the payroll. Let alone any of those hamlets."

"Here he's got five files all for some fire out in Carthage. Does that make any sense? I thought that'd be the fire marshal's business?"

"When was it?"

Quinn scanned the top sheet. "Looks like back in June."

"I know that fire," Lillie said, reaching for the file. "Two men were killed. A couple kids, too."

She stood up and moved to the edge of the bed, spreading the file out beside her. Quinn sat next to her, reading over her shoulder, Lillie pulling back her curly hair and tying it up with a band from her purse. She read for a long while, flipping through pages like crazy, reaching for the next file and tearing into it.

Quinn stood.

He picked up the photo he'd set aside of

147

him and his uncle with that prized deer. That had been the year after he'd been lost, about the time his dad had gone back to California and Uncle Hamp had taken him out every weekend during deer season, even letting him be late to school once or twice, walking up deep into his hundred acres of land and sitting in silence in the tree stand. Quinn holding that bow line taut, right over that buck without that buck getting wind of him, knowing that even some dirt off his boots should scare him away.

He'd taken a perfect shot, hitting that buck right through his heart. An instant kill — the animal running for a hundred yards without pain or even knowing it was already dead — the way you want all kills to be. Something he'd learned from his uncle.

They'd dragged it back to the house, hoisted it up, and gutted it.

"Here it is," Lillie said.

"What?"

"You got two folks who made it out of that hot box alive. A man and a woman."

Quinn waited.

"This one fella was airlifted to the burn unit in Jackson," Lillie said, still staring at the pages on Quinn's old bed, the springs and slats creaking under her. "I recall that, meeting the helicopter and the ambulance

148

out there. I don't know what happened to him."

"And the woman?"

She looked up and said: "The woman was Jill Bullard, the preacher's daughter."

12

Quinn and Lillie found the cutoff and cleared land through a thicket of pine trees and headed down the muddy road on foot, fearing getting her Jeep stuck. The thicket opened up onto the burn site just as it started to sleet, nothing left but a footprint of gravel and concrete blocks, the charred remains of the trailer heaped into three piles of dirt and shorn metal. The whole site had been scraped clean and neat, no power or telephone lines ever reaching this far off the main roads of Tibbehah County. Quinn squatted to the ground and sifted through some dirt, finding some blackened and twisted PVC pipe and a rusted screwdriver with a melted handle. Lillie kicked around the site, toeing at piles with her boots and walking toward the edge of the land, looking south toward where the gentle, deadened slope gave way to the highway leading back to Jericho.

She kept her hands in her pockets, a sharp cold wind kicking her hair up off the collar of her jacket.

Quinn threw down the pieces and joined her at the edge.

"Not much left," he said.

"I'll check the property records in the morning."

"You don't think they owned the land?"

"They could've been squatting," Lillie said. "Lots of trailers just set down where people won't bother them. Don't expect much."

"Is the fire marshal still Chuck Tuttle? He signed off on this deal."

"Yeah, he's still around."

"You don't like him?"

"I like him fine. He just is too friendly when he should be doing work."

"Maybe he talked to the Bullard girl. Or heard something."

Lillie shrugged, pulling the hair back from her eyes only to find them covered again. Everything down in the valley was gray and lifeless, mud up to their ankles. Wind cut through the pines, making sounds like an approaching train.

"Hamp's coat suits you," she said, smiling, sort of absent and loose, looking down into the valley. "He'd be proud you have it."

They spotted Tuttle loading wood into an old pickup just as they turned off the main road to town and toward his ranch house. He tossed a couple more sticks into the back of the truck and walked toward Lillie's Jeep, a teenage boy behind him continuing the work, Quinn figuring the boy was his son. Tuttle was in his mid-forties, stick thin but with an enormous belly that pulled at his flannel shirt's buttons. He walked slow, waving to Lillie, wiping his hands with a bandanna and greeting Quinn with a nice handshake, talking for a good bit about how sorry he was to hear about his uncle. Quinn thanked him, with Lillie following: "Chuck, we got a few questions for you about that fire that killed that family in June."

Tuttle's boy continued to throw the wood onto the back of the truck, the steady rhythm of it sounding like a drumbeat. Tuttle reached for his thick glasses, breathed on them, and cleaned them a bit with the bandanna and then blew his nose with it. "I can pull that report for you," he said, smiling at Lillie. "Can it wait till the morning?"

"We've seen it," Lillie said. Quinn stood beside her, watching Tuttle, Tuttle smiling

152

back. The wind came down through the hills and across his back, rattling their jackets and pant legs.

There was slow traffic passing the house, so close to town.

"My mother-in-law used up all her wood last week," Tuttle said. "Waited till tonight to call me and say she was cold. Now, how come it took her so long to let me know? I'd just settled down to watch the ball game and now I'm gonna be loading wood."

"Just a couple things," Lillie said. "Did you talk to the girl, Jill Bullard?"

"Don't recall," Tuttle said. "She the girl that got free of it?"

Lillie nodded. "There was a man who lived, too."

"Got burned up real good. Think he died down in Jackson."

"I saw the Bullard girl mentioned in your report, but the address showed the same trailer. Did you take her statement?"

"There wasn't much to this thing, Lillie," Tuttle said. "One of them left a skillet on the stove and started a grease fire. One of the men who died come in about one in the morning to fix some eggs. That's all I know."

Lillie nodded and looked to Quinn.

"I saw you at the memorial service," Tuttle said. "How's your momma?"

"Fine." Quinn nodded.

"Didn't see her there."

"She didn't go," Quinn said. "Mr. Tuttle, you think there could've been more to this fire?"

"No," Tuttle said. "There wasn't evidence of arson, if that's what you mean. Like I said, it was pretty clear to me."

"Reason we're asking," Lillie said, "it seemed pretty important to Sheriff Beckett. He'd kept the files separate from his office work. I think he'd really been studying on it."

Tuttle nodded and yelled for his son, who'd sat down on the rear bumper of the truck. "Be there in a minute."

Quinn shifted his weight.

"Your uncle took this one pretty hard," Tuttle said. "Two children got burned up. He talked with me a lot about it. He blamed the parents for squatting up there in the hills like that, no electricity, cooking on an open flame. I think he just had a hard time not being able to make a bit of sense of it."

Tuttle's truck started, his boy behind the wheel, slowly turning and heading down the short drive. The truck idled by them, Tuttle offering his hand to Quinn. "You think this could've been what was worrying him so?"

Quinn nodded. "Looks like it."

"But you don't recall anything more about Jill Bullard?" Lillie asked.

"Only met her once and that was the day of the fire. I made some notes, and she left. I never saw her before or since. She was a pretty gal. Not in a good state. I recall that."

"Sheriff Beckett had been talking to her," Lillie said. "Was he assisting you in any way?"

Tuttle shook his head, reaching for the door handle of the truck, the black exhaust wreathing his legs and face. "That must've been a whole other matter."

The sheriff's office didn't get the call till late that Sunday, but it didn't take long before the whole town heard the story of the twin boys on that first weekend of deer season, riding four-wheelers and raising hell through the eroded hills and woods of their daddy's five hundred acres. Both of them had on matching camo Mossy Oak gear and brand-new pairs of Cabela boots. They'd packed rifles and plenty of ammo, bottles of Mountain Dew, and beef jerky in case they got hungry, and a fresh can of Skoal that the older brother, older by a whole five minutes, kept in his own back pocket 'cause he'd paid for it.

This was their second time out that day,

heading out to hunt with their daddy at dawn and then out again after church, barely able to contain themselves as they kicked off their loafers and ties and slid into their boots and camouflage, not really giving a damn if they killed a deer or not, because there was plenty of time for that. This was just being able to run the woods like crazy without having to answer to anyone. Because, as the younger brother had said, "When a boy is fourteen, he's got to be turned a little loose. We ain't kids."

They found the clearing and tree stand where they'd been earlier, seeing those young does and a fawn, practicing that silence with their daddy, waiting for a buck to enter that clearing, step inside that ring and sacrifice himself. But instead, a doe had sniffed something, heard a creak of the wood in that slapped-together lookout, and darted off down the trail. The older brother knowing the deer would come back, bringing the buck with them.

They both plugged in some snuff and sat on their haunches, looking into the wind. The younger brother crashing together a pair of horns that they kept on the dusty floor. He crashed them together again and again, knowing that a buck couldn't resist the sound of a fight, and, goddamn, neither saying that word out loud but both of them thinking it, here walks up the prettiest twelve-pointer they ever saw, thick-necked and proud. The younger brother let the older get the shot, moving up the barrel and finding a line in the scope. But he could only pull that trigger with shaking hands, the bullet leaving with a mule kick, scaring that big boy away, knowing there wasn't no fight, only a couple kids up a tree house.

"He'll be back."

"No he won't."

"How do you know?"

"He hadn't gotten big by bein' no retard."

They dug into their sacks, a couple pieces of jerky washed down with the Mountain Dew, turning their bottles into spit cups and not talking at all, because there wasn't a hell of a lot that either boy could say that would surprise the other. They waited for the buck to return for a good couple hours, trying the horns again, crashing them together like bone cymbals and sitting back on their haunches, waiting for a tick of sound. By then the night had started to fall, maybe a good thirty minutes past when they'd said they'd head home. And so they packed up their gear, laying their hunting rifles back into their padded cases, and wandered back down to the four-wheelers with their heads lowered.

"You see that?"

"What?"

The other craned his neck and veered off to the right, just off the side of the wide, cleared field, making his way to an old dead pond that someone had tried to start way before they were born but gave up on, the water not having a source or a place to go. Cypress had taken root in the shallow water, and not a living thing thrived there except for some turtles and snakes. During the summer the whole thing would just dry up, and they'd find footprints of deer and raccoons that padded across the open space.

The twins both walked closer, both of them pulling their rifles from their cases and walking slow and steady to the big oak tree, circling it twice. With the canopy of dead branches laced above them and in the failing light, mud sucking at the soles of their new boots, they somehow didn't really grasp what they were seeing, stopping to look at it and then looking at each other as if they needed confirmation.

A body lay facedown at the edge of the dead pond, a girl, with bare legs and no shoes, the wind catching up under her skirt and showing off her panties. The boys more embarrassed than scared. One of them got close and toed at the girl's shoulder, her head covered in a bloody pillowcase, showing right clear where the bullet had gone.

Her skin as white and puckered as the belly of a fish.

"Why'd they put that sack on her head?"

" 'Cause they didn't want her to see what was coming. What do you think?"

13

"How many times had she been shot?" Quinn asked.

"Just once," Lillie said.

"Was she beat up?" he asked.

"I don't know," Lillie said. "Luke Stevens hasn't looked at the body yet."

"How long she been there?"

"Maybe a week," she said. "Hard to tell. Some animals got to her."

Quinn was in the back field of the farmhouse, the burn pile still smoldering. He'd thrown in some dry branches and fallen logs to get it all going again before he'd heard Lillie's Jeep. And now she stood over him as he sat on his haunches poking at the fire, getting some warmth in the early night. The sleet had stopped, but it had grown colder, the wind kicking up the flames and carrying off the smoke and sparks into the dark. Two big pecan trees near the house looked like old sentries.

"Not much we can do now," he said. "You call the preacher?"

"Wesley drove up there," she said. "He delivered the news personally."

"That's pretty stand-up."

"That's his job." Lillie shrugged. "Wesley said they had to put the preacher's wife on suicide watch."

"Had to be expecting this."

Quinn found a cut log and sat down, Lillie sitting beside him, placing her hands under her arms, leaning forward toward the fire. Quinn poked at its edge with a stick, stamped out some loose sparks that had caught on the dry grass. "You want a drink?" he asked. "Boom actually left a half bottle."

"I'm on duty," she said.

"So what?"

"Wouldn't sit too well with the public."

"It's good stuff."

"You drink on recon?"

Lillie felt warm next to him, her knee and leg bumping into his, reaching her hands out and warming them and then placing them back under her arms. Quinn straightened his knees, the soles of his old boots toward the heat. They didn't talk for a long while, Lillie walking up to the Cherokee, checking in with the dispatch, and then coming back to sit beside Quinn.

Lillie seemed smaller and younger with her curly hair pinned up and no makeup. She wore jeans and a county sheriff's jacket zipped to the neck, a holstered gun, mace, and a set of handcuffs at her slender waist.

"I feel sorry for her folks," she said. "I don't care what path that girl took. Delivering that kind of news is the very worst part of this job."

"Any good parts?" he asked.

"Sure," she said.

"Anything we can do tonight?"

"Both witnesses to that fire are dead."

"Plenty of folks left who might know something."

"I got some names," she said. "I'm going to kick over some logs tonight."

"You mind if I come along?"

"Nope."

"I'll be your muscle."

"I don't need muscle."

"What makes you so damn tough?" Quinn asked, smiling.

"It's not what you think."

"What do I think?"

"I hear people talk about me," she said. "People been talking about me forever. A girl tries to play with the boys, and they think there's something wrong with her."

She knocked his knees with her leg and

smiled back, looking down at her hands.

"You aren't the same, Quinn. Not like when I knew you."

Quinn watched as she put a hand to her lean face as it moved from shadow into the firelight.

"You sure used to be angry," she said.

"I'm not angry."

"See what I mean?"

Lena wandered down to Hell Creek at dusk, getting down on her knees and praying for a while, feeling the big weight behind her before she even heard his voice.

"You ain't hungry?" Gowrie asked.

She didn't answer. The brown water moved slow and sluggish over rocks and sand, thin slivers of ice collected by the muddy banks.

"We gonna get your boy out," he said.

"When?"

"I ain't payin' no bail. But we got him a lawyer from Memphis. The lawyer says they ain't got a case. The case on him is on account of me."

She turned and looked at Gowrie, standing on the banks of the creek, some light snow scattering all about him, him wearing no shirt, only a military jacket open over his big chest, showing the tats and rib bones.

His face shrunken and drawn, as if his features had been cut from stone.

"They think he'd turn, but that ain't how we do things. No, sir."

"Who are you?"

"I told you. We're a family."

She nodded, reaching for a tree branch and standing, feeling cold enough now that she'd go back with him, follow that muddy trail back to the ragged trailers in the gulch. Gowrie reached for her elbow, soft and gentle, and steered her back up the well-worn path, talking and talking, barely able to take a breath between his thoughts, saying that the law in this county was nothing but a dirty joke and that he'd bust old Charley Booth out of jail himself if they even tried to keep him tied in legal knots.

"They just want to fuck me."

"Where are you from?"

"What's that matter?"

"Just askin', is all."

"Ohio. Near West Virginia."

"Why are you down here?"

"Come on," Gowrie said, trudging up through the gulley, all the wash of gravel and trash and beer cans swept down into a fanned-out pattern of mud, steeped in boot prints and hooves, the earth smelling of sulfur. It was getting dark, and most of

Gowrie's people were in their trailers, yellow light coming from crooked windows lined with tinfoil and cardboard beer cases pressed flat against the glass. Somewhere, someone was playing a guitar and beating on some drums.

"I got you a bed," Gowrie said.

She looked into the open mouth of the old barn, searching for Ditto.

"I got you some candy bars, too. Can you drink beer?"

"I don't drink."

"And you don't fuck, neither."

He laughed while he led her up some crooked steps and opened the door to his beaten trailer, two women and an old man sitting together on an old sofa watching *Family Guy,* smoking weed and drinking. The old man stared at Lena, offering her a taste of his Jack Daniel's bottle, the girls too baked to turn from the cartoon. Gowrie tugged at his Army jacket and tossed it on a pile of dirty clothes, now only wearing a tight pair of blue jeans and combat boots, his back a road map of tattoos of dragons and ancient symbols. He cracked open a beer and pulled the joint from one girl's fingers.

"Daddy, don't you got somethin' to do?"

The old man stood up, stoop-shouldered,

and loped out of the room. The girls shifted, one wearing pink sweatpants and a tank top. She was skinny, and her face had small sores across it, as if she suffered some kind of pox.

Gowrie moved back through the kitchen, piled high with dirty paper plates and crushed beer cans, cigarette and roach butts in jelly jars. In the middle of all the junk, Lena spotted dozens of guns, pistols and shotguns and those guns with the big fat clips that could hold a million bullets. Boxes and boxes of shells and bullets.

Gowrie flipped on the lights in a room with a mattress on the floor, filled ankle-deep in clothes. "There's a blanket in that corner. If you get cold, let me know."

There didn't seem to be any heat in the trailer besides a little radiator by the television.

Gowrie smiled at Lena, her noticing the blackening edges of his teeth, the parched lines around his rheumy eyes. He just nodded and walked away, leaving the door wide open, the canned laughter and sound effects from the cartoons filling the trailer.

He was gone for a long while. And Lena was grateful for the food Ditto had found for her earlier, knowing she wouldn't have to leave the room till morning.

She found a bathroom, no toilet, only a

166

hole cut in the floor, where she squatted and peed, and returned back to the room, trying to lock the door but finding it didn't even have a knob. The window above the bed was covered in more tinfoil, and empty beer cans and cigarette butts littered the bed. She lay for a long time in the darkness, twice feeling the child kicking inside her as she stayed wide awake listening to the noise of the television, the pinging of sleet on the roof. Men were talking out by the window and then were gone.

She dozed off.

Jett Price's mother was a big woman, so big she could barely fit through the door of her small ranch house out toward Drivers Flat. She wore an enormous housecoat, and fuzzy pink slippers caked with mud, and didn't seem a bit impressed when Lillie introduced herself as a deputy sheriff and asked if she might come in to talk. Connie Price just turned, not shrugging or changing expression, but just headed back into the darkened house, switching on an overhead light that shined on a table filled with several framed photos of a boy and a girl mixed in with statues of angels and Jesus, the same children that Quinn had seen in the file on the fire.

The school pictures had been paper-clipped to details on their death.

Cakes and cookies and pies, neatly wrapped in cellophane, covered a dining-room table. Big Connie Price pulled out a cigarette from a little cove by the kitchen and lit up, taking a seat by her bounty of food, explaining — talking now for the first time — that she had an event at the church and was running late. "Will this take long?"

"No, ma'am," Lillie said.

She nodded.

"Very sorry to hear about your family."

"They were supposed to be with me. Their mother, that's the one who left 'em with Jett. Jett had no business taking on those children."

Quinn didn't know what to say, offering only another "Sorry."

"Everybody's sorry," Connie Price said. "I'd prefer not to discuss this, if it's all the same. Why are y'all here anyway?"

Lillie said, "There's some questions about the fire."

"You mean about how my son could have been so damn almighty stupid to leave a skillet on his cookstove?"

"No, ma'am," Lillie said. "We were wondering about the relationship your son had with Jill Bullard."

"He was seeing her."

"And Keith Shackelford?"

"He was from somewhere abouts in Memphis. They were in the Army together, drinkin' buddies. My son killed his own children 'cause he was drunk. That's what you want to know?"

"My uncle was Sheriff Beckett," Quinn said. "He'd taken a personal interest in what happened to your family."

"How's that?"

"Did you ever speak to my uncle?"

"He was at the service for the children," she said, nodding. "He came by twice after that. He was a fine man. I was sorry to hear of his passing."

"Did he ask you questions about the fire?" Quinn asked.

"No," Connie Price said, stubbing out her cigarette and checking her watch. "Why would he?"

"I don't think he was convinced it was an accident."

"They did an investigation," Connie Price said. "The fire marshal said things like this happen all the time and not to blame my son. But who else would you blame? He killed his own children."

"Ma'am," Lillie said. "Did you know anyone who'd want to do Jett harm?"

"Not like this. Who'd want to kill children?"

"Did my uncle ever give you reason to think he doubted what happened?"

She shook her head.

"Jill Bullard was found dead today," Lillie said. "She'd been shot."

Price put one hand to her mouth and placed the other on a chair to steady herself. She reached for the gold cross on her neck and kept her fingers there. She shook her head over and over.

"Could Jett have owed anyone money?" Quinn asked.

"Jett always owed people money. When you get yourself into drinking and drugs, that's what happens."

"You recall any names?"

"I really got to be going. I was supposed to be at church twenty minutes ago to help them set up."

"Yes, ma'am," Quinn said.

"Do you know anyone we might speak to?" Lillie asked. "Folks who knew Jett or Keith Shackelford or Jill?"

"You can talk to Jett's ex. She'd be glad to heap some blame on my son. Not that I disagree."

Quinn helped carry the pies and cookies to Connie Price's Chevrolet sedan in the drive. She closed them all up in her trunk, keys in hand.

"Where'd your son serve?" Quinn asked.

"He was in the invasion of Iraq," she said. "He carried a Rebel flag on his tank when it rolled into Baghdad. I have pictures."

"Was Shackelford part of his unit?"

"You'd have to ask him," Connie Price said. "I don't exactly know when they met in the service."

"I'm afraid he's dead, too," Lillie said.

"When?"

"Right after the fire."

"That's a lie," Connie Price said. "He may not be much to look at, with those burn marks across half his face. But I just saw him last week."

14

Lillie got an address on Shackelford from a previous arrest, and they found it strange that it was down in Sugar Ditch, the black district of the county. She called back to dispatch to verify, and apparently he'd been living with a black female who'd been arrested at the same time for possession of crack. The house wasn't more than a shed painted a putrid green with a failing roof and asbestos siding. A few hard knocks on the door brought out a scared old black woman who found the law on her poorly screened-in porch. The house smelled of clean laundry, and the floorboards hummed with an unbalanced load. The old woman said she didn't know the white man, had never met the white man, and didn't want to meet him in the middle of the night. Lillie asked about his girlfriend, and she shook her head more, saying she'd only rented the house six months ago. The arrests had taken place two years ago.

"You take the east side of the street and I'll take the west."

"For what?" Quinn asked.

"Ask them if they've seen Shackelford or his girlfriend."

Quinn nodded.

"And Quinn?"

He turned.

"Don't act like a sergeant."

"Roger that."

Quinn found people at only two of the six houses where he knocked. One of them remembered the girl — named Latecia — but couldn't recall ever seeing a white man in the neighborhood. Lillie pretty much found the same thing, only learning that Latecia left more than a year ago to move up to Chicago. One woman, she'd said, recalled a white man but never spoke to him.

They made their way back to the Jeep and climbed inside, Lillie calling back to night dispatch — dispatch being Mae, a portly country woman who'd worked for the county as long as Quinn could remember — to get her to run both names through the state system.

Lillie wheeled the truck around and saw a short black man carrying two armfuls of groceries under the streetlamps. She slowed to a stop but kept the engine running while she got out. Quinn stayed put, seeing her talking to the man but not hearing what she said. Lillie was smiling, and the man laughed, and then he said something to her and pointed back down the road and then again to the south.

Lillie climbed back behind the wheel.

Quinn waited.

"He said he'd seen Latecia last month at the Fast Stop."

Quinn nodded.

Lillie turned north again, picking up the county road and heading through the slum district of burned-out trailers and houses rotting along the dry gulley that gave the neighborhood its name. During the summer after the rains, the smell of the sewage and garbage became so foul that it gave the air a kind of rotting sweetness.

Lillie punched the cigarette lighter and let down the window an inch.

"You mind if I ask you something?"

"You're going to ask anyway."

"Why'd you and Anna Lee break up?"

"We never really did."

"Come back?"

"When I joined the Army, we made a promise we'd stick together," he said. "But about six months in, the letters stopped coming, and she wouldn't return my calls."

"You didn't want to know?"

"You can't make someone love you," Quinn said, watching the old houses and trailers converge at a corner grocery, with barred windows decorated with beer advertisements. They sold fried chicken and pizza, barbecue on Saturdays.

"I would've wanted an answer."

"Never got one."

"You want one now?"

"Not really."

Lillie killed the engine.

"What if I said you were lying?"

"I'd say that'd be your right."

He got out of the Jeep, Lillie trailing him as he opened the door to the old grocery store and held it for her. Lillie waved and addressed the cashier as Miss Williams, and Miss Williams told Lillie she was real sad to read about her momma in the newspaper.

"You know a woman around here named Latecia?"

"I know four."

"Last name is Young."

Miss Williams shook her head and took a seat on a metal stool behind a glass case filled with overcooked chicken and pizza drying out under the heat lamps.

"She's got a tattoo of a rose on her arm."

The old woman nodded. "Seen her last week."

"You know where she stays?"

"I cashed a check for her."

"Got an address?"

"Sent that check to the bank."

"You mind calling me if she comes back in?" Lillie asked.

"What'd she do?"

"Nothing. Trying to find her boyfriend, but I'd appreciate you not telling her that."

Lillie handed her a business card, Miss Williams nodding and placing it on the lip of the cash register. She turned and looked up at Quinn for the first time and smiled, her right front tooth made of gold. "You Jason Colson's boy."

He looked at her.

"Your daddy was just plain crazy."

"How'd you know?"

"You look just like him."

"And how'd you know him?"

Miss Williams laughed. "Boy, I used to change your diapers."

Just as they made it back to the Jericho city limits, Lillie had a call: a horse had escaped its fence and was running down the middle of Highway 9. She dropped Quinn off at

176

the farm and sped off, lights flashing, toward the town Square and away. And Quinn was left there, shaking his head and smiling, deciding to drive back into town to see his mother, maybe stay the night.

Ten minutes later he walked up the driveway on Ithaca Road and spotted two shapes moving by the windows of the little ranch, his mother and some man he'd never met. The thought never occurring to him that she may have been dating, that there could be someone else she'd spent her time with in between taking care of Jason and going to church.

Quinn checked the time. Twenty-one hundred hours.

The man was tall, with a wide, full stomach, and wearing a baseball cap. His mother brought him a plate of pie and he smiled up at her. She took her place across from him, and they sat and ate, not seeming to say a word to each other.

Twenty-one hundred.

Quinn wondered if the action had started to heat up at the Rebel Truck Stop.

Quinn grabbed a cup of coffee at the diner and sat behind the wheel of his truck for a while. The coffee was terrible and weak, and reminded him of the chow hall at Benning.

He'd learned to appreciate strong coffee out on maneuvers, grounds and all, and wished he had some now. But sometimes coffee is just warm company, especially when it's cold with the heater off in your truck, and he sat there in a dark corner out by the gas tanks, watching the rows and rows of trucks, parking lights on, but otherwise pretty still.

His cell rang.

"Where are you?" Lillie asked.

He told her.

"Your mother's worried."

"Didn't know I had a curfew."

"You want me to join you?"

"Nah," Quinn said. "I don't think this is worth your time."

"You looking for Kayla?"

"Yep."

"Think she knows some more?"

"I do."

"You want to call me if you get something?"

"You miss me?" Quinn asked.

Lillie hung up.

He spotted Kayla nearly an hour later, making her way between trucks, hopping up into cabs or craning her head up to windows, smiling and talking, and moving down the line with a few rejections. She had on tight white jeans and that same puffy pink coat and carried a child's backpack over her shoulder. Quinn followed her, turning down a row of trucks and then losing her, crossing behind an eighteen-wheeler, chugging exhaust in the dark, and then coming up on her.

She was talking to a skinny man in a flannel shirt and ski hat. She handed him some cash and then turned and noticed Quinn. Quinn stood maybe ten yards from her and nodded back. The man looked back to Kayla and then to him.

She started to walk, and the man held her arm, pulling her back, and came toward Quinn.

"Who are you?"

"I want to see Kayla."

"Why?"

"That's between me and Kayla."

"You know this fucker?" he yelled over his shoulder.

Kayla walked up, head down, hands in the pockets of the big pink coat, and said he was okay, that she knew him. The man didn't stop staring at Quinn, Quinn noting the man was just plain ugly, with a misshapen face and weak chin, acne across his forehead and on his neck.

"You got a problem?" he asked Quinn.

"Ugly doesn't make tough."

The man made a move for Quinn, and Quinn punched him in the stomach, knocking him flat on his ass, leaving him gasping for air. Quinn stood over the man, just observing, until he got to his feet and walked away.

"Who's he?" Quinn asked.

"My boyfriend."

Quinn didn't say anything.

"I don't want no trouble," she said. "I haven't even started to work."

"The girl is dead."

Kayla shrugged. Her face was white and chapped, dark hair catching a long streak dyed red. The diesel smell was strong, pumping and fuming around them.

"Thought you'd want to know."

"I didn't know her."

"Her real name was Jill Bullard."

Kayla shrugged again. "Nobody has real names out here. We're all just kind of passing through until we can get to Memphis or Jackson."

"Can I buy you something to eat?"

"I got to work."

"Sure like to know anything about her."

"I told you. What the fuck."

"You know where she lived?"

"The point is to be working all night," she

said. "Then you go home. You see?"

"You just carry everything in that back-pack?"

"Your girl Jill kept a locker," she said.

"You know where?"

"What, are you gonna break into it?"

"Sure."

"Are you going to arrest me?"

"I'm not the police."

"Then what the fuck do you care?"

"Can you show me the locker?"

"You really buy me something to eat?"

"What about your boyfriend?"

"He's a pussy."

Quinn grabbed a tire iron from the Ford and tucked it inside his coat, following Kayla inside the Rebel Truck Stop. The restaurant and shopping mart was still, late on a Sunday night. The cashier, watching a small television, peered up for a moment with his old hooded eyes and then went back to his show as Kayla took Quinn back to the bathrooms and showers, a long row of telephones and video games, pinging away, in the hall. She nodded him over to a bank of lockers and showed him one in the right corner, saying she remembered the locker because it was the same as her lucky number.

"Thirteen?"

"Been lucky for me."

Quinn listened for a moment and waited a beat as a fat trucker came out of the toilet, smelling like five-cent aftershave, a toothpick in the corner of his mouth.

When he was gone, Quinn slipped the edge of the tire iron near the lock and gave it a sharp tug. The lock busted right apart, denting the frame, but the locker opened.

He reached inside and found some folded clothes and a pack of condoms. She'd squirreled away some beef jerky and a bottle of Aristocrat vodka, a carton of cigarettes, and three pairs of panties.

"You ever heard of a man named Keith Shackelford?"

"No."

"You ever see Jill with a man?"

"I always saw her with a man."

"This guy may have burn marks on him."

She shook her head.

Quinn squatted down and reached deep in the locker, finding a thick leather-bound book, or what could pass for leather. It was a case for photographs, branded with Native American symbols and designs. He unbuttoned the cover and flipped through twenty or so pictures.

He closed the locker door and stood up,

flipping through more, reaching a side pocket and finding a thick pack of more photographs bound with a rubber band. In the weak fluorescent light he sorted through pictures of Jill Bullard. Jill playing with Beccalynn at some park. Jill and her parents. Jill with some man he did not recognize but would check against Shackelford's mug shot. Jill partying out on Beale Street. And then a shot that just kind of left him cold, paralyzed, before he flipped the image, front to back.

"You know this girl?"

"I got to pee," she said.

"Do you know her?"

Kayla looked at Quinn, her mouth open, backing away, looking as if she might cry.

Quinn turned back to the photo. Jill Bullard and another girl, clicking glasses at some club, both in short skirts and tight tops. Good times.

He didn't bother to go after Kayla.

He knew the girl.

Caddy.

15

Sometime in the early morning on Monday, just as light was coming on, something woke Lena in that old trailer. She turned and saw the door was open, nothing in the frame, the girls gone now. She rolled back over, eyes closed, and then opened them to find the old man — Daddy Gowrie — standing over her, his pants unhitched to his bony knees, and saying, "Shh. Shhh." Over and over.

Lena wanted to scream, but the sound caught down deep in her throat. She pressed herself against the mattress and dug her heels into the coils, trying to get free of the blankets. As she scooted back, she felt hard steel and reached down and found a pistol — guns seeming to grow like mushrooms around the trailer — and she pointed it right between the man's legs, down to his flaccid place, and told him, without any kind of thought, that she'd be happy to remove what was troubling him.

He kept saying, "Shh. Shhh," until another man rushed the door, and the old man nearly tripped over himself while he hitched up his pants and turned to run. Gowrie yelled, "Pa!," and then, seeing him fiddling with his pants, Gowrie coldcocked the old man across the jaw, sending him down to his knees. Gowrie kicked his ribs twice so hard that Lena screamed, getting her breath back, as she steadied the gun in her hand.

Gowrie turned to her and held out his hand, his head wrapped in a red bandanna, a cigarette hanging from his mouth, wearing a dirty T-shirt and jeans, no shoes, making her know that he'd run from somewhere to find the situation.

"He's a sick man," Gowrie said. "Git."

He kicked his father again, and the old man scrambled to his hands and feet and skittered out of the room and down through the open front door. Gowrie reached for a lighter on the kitchen counter, clicking flame to cigarette, and then looked back to Lena, studying her with more appreciation. The wind seemed to enter the room and pull out every breath, the whole space feeling more empty than anything she'd ever imagined.

"Next time, pull that trigger. That old man

has had so many weapons aimed at him, I think he's gotten used to it."

The front door battered against the trailer wall in the cold morning wind. Gowrie stood there, smoking, as she lowered the gun. And in walked Ditto, out of breath and red-faced, his eyes flitting from Lena back to Gowrie, standing there with some measure of toughness but still too damn afraid to ask questions.

Quinn and Lillie were back down in Sugar Ditch searching for Keith Shackelford's girlfriend, finding nothing new from Miss Williams but meeting a teenage boy in the Fast Stop who knew her. He said he'd seen her down at a yard sale a couple days back, and after getting a decent idea of where he was talking about, they piled back into the Jeep and headed deeper into the Ditch, finding an empty lot where a fat man was sitting in an easy chair. The fat man wore sunglasses in the weak winter sunshine, holding court by a camper behind an old pickup and two long tables filled with about anything you could imagine: old clothes, dishes, hats, CDs, microwave ovens, and a couple television sets. Lillie let Quinn do the talking this time, Quinn getting a feeling that Lillie was testing him to see if he

186

could handle not being a hard-ass. He greeted the fat man and introduced himself, asking about Latecia.

"She bought two pairs of shoes for her kids."

"You know where she lives or works?"

"Where she gonna work 'round here?"

"Who was she with?"

"Boy named Peanut."

"You know where I can find Peanut?"

"What you want with Peanut?"

"We just want to talk to Latecia. She's not in any trouble."

"I heard that shit before."

But the fat man told Quinn, with a grunt, not ever leaving the folding chair, and pointed them back the way they'd come, a block over from the Fast Stop, where they could find Peanut playing spades under an old pecan tree.

"Thanks," Quinn said, offering his hand.

The man looked at his hand and then up at Quinn. "I ain't seen a sheriff's car down here in two years."

The pecan tree looked like it had been sculpted, not grown, sitting there in the side lot of the liquor store, rooted in the air with most of the dirt eroded away, leaving only a tangled mass in the hard-packed ground.

Quinn and Lillie parked on the street and approached the game, the five players not glancing over once as they got close. Quinn watched their hands and movements more out of instinct than any real worry. He could only imagine these guys thought they were going to get tossed from their daily game. Lillie greeted them like old friends, and apparently knew a couple of them from some minor arrests. They lifted their eyes from their cards and said hello, none of them moving or asking what they were doing wrong. The men were all in their twenties and wore heavy coats and scarves, and crisp and bright new baseball caps.

"Which one of y'all is Peanut?" Lillie asked.

No one looked up.

"I'm not here to hassle any of you," she said. "I'm looking for Latecia Young. And Latecia isn't in trouble, either. We're trying to find a fella named Shackelford."

One of the men lifted his eyes from his cards, front chair legs settling down to the dirt. He was skinny and wore a St. Louis Cardinals cap. He had green eyes and an earring in each ear. He looked to Quinn and then Lillie, and nodded. "That guy is a piece of shit."

"So we heard," Quinn said.

"She don't have nothing to do with him no more."

"Where is she?"

"She at work."

"Where does she work?"

"She's a maid at the Indian casino."

"Which one?"

"I don't know," he said. "She gotta go back to Jericho with y'all?"

Lillie shook her head. "We just want to know where to find Shackelford."

"She stay in the Gray Stone with her momma," he said. "First one on the right when you drive in. Upstairs."

Lillie nodded and he nodded back.

"You won't find her till tonight." Peanut's eyes went back to the cards, carefully choosing a couple, as Quinn and Lillie turned to walk away from the old tree.

As they reached Lillie's Jeep, the phone rang in Quinn's pocket, and he answered.

"Quinn, can you meet for lunch?" Judge Blanton asked, taking a long breath. "Stagg made an offer."

"I can be there in ten minutes."

Quinn parked outside the El Dorado Mexican Restaurant a little before noon, saying hello to the owner, a portly little guy named Javier who'd owned the place since at least

Quinn's twelfth birthday party. It had been a good birthday party, with a piñata and too much candy, and Quinn vaguely recalled vomiting in a sombrero. But Javier didn't seem to hold a grudge, as he led him through the main restaurant past a buffet getting stocked with ground beef and cheeses and tons of chips and tortillas. Quinn hadn't eaten since his mother's church spread yesterday, and he felt like grabbing a plate right there, eating while listening to what Blanton had learned.

But he removed his hat and walked into the large, empty room, seeing food already laid out on a large table, steaming piles of chips and plates of enchiladas and tacos. Plenty of salsa, guacamole, and beans, and right near the end sat Johnny Stagg, in a buttoned-up hunting shirt, along with an older man in a suit and red tie.

Stagg stood up and offered his bony hand to Quinn.

Quinn just looked at it, and Johnny sat back down.

"Didn't know we had company," Quinn said.

"Figured we could make this a friendly meeting," Blanton said, keeping his seat and motioning to an open chair. "Does that work?"

190

"What's the offer?"

"Let's eat first," Blanton said, pulling out a chair. "Would you like a beer? We're no longer a dry county."

"I'd like to see the offer."

Blanton reached into an old leather satchel and pulled out a legal file, handing Quinn the top sheet. Quinn read it.

"The timber's worth more than this."

Blanton nodded that old buzz-cut head and met Quinn's look with hangdog eyes. "And he'll excuse all the debt."

"It's fair, Quinn," Stagg said, scratching his cheek. "But let's break some bread or some of them ole tortillas." Stagg snorted at that, wide-mouthed with big teeth, nodding to the man in the suit. The man in the suit nodded back.

"Who's he?" Quinn asked.

"Mr. Lamar, come down from Memphis. He's an attorney."

Mr. Lamar kept his chair and nodded to Quinn, smiling as if all this was polite as hell. The suit he wore wasn't the kind you saw men wearing at the Sunday service, heavy wool and pin-striped, a perfect cut. He estimated the man's watch cost about five grand.

"Just why do you want that old farm so much?" Quinn asked.

"I don't want you to take this personal," Stagg said. "I got to look after my accounts. I'm so very sorry about your uncle, but business don't stop."

"Is that why you sent those men over to our farm the other night?"

"I don't know what you're talking about, son."

"Of course."

"Let's just have lunch," Blanton said. "We can talk business over in my office later."

"There's nothing to discuss."

"Hold on, now," Stagg said.

"I see those shitbags on my property again and I'm in my legal right to shoot every one."

Stagg took a deep breath, smiling and shaking his head with a tired understanding of the world. "I know you're not a big fan of this town," Stagg said. "I figured that's why you never came back. This stuff only ties you down."

"You don't know a thing about me."

"I know'd you hadn't been home in six years."

"Been a little busy."

"To see your momma?"

"I've seen my mother plenty since I've been away."

"But you hadn't come home," Stagg said.

"You ain't a lot different from your daddy out in California, doin' anything you can to crawl free of this town. You got it written all over your face that you're too good for this place. Quinn Colson ain't nobody's redneck."

Quinn stood there over the table laden down with hot food as Javier brought out a round of frosty Mexican beers. "This is a waste of my time," Quinn said. "Thank you, Judge."

"Hold on," Stagg said, scrambling to his feet and reaching for the upper part of Quinn's arm to stop him from leaving. "I'm doing this as a favor to the judge and your momma. Mr. Lamar come all the way down here to file a lien, and I told him you were a reasonable man and that we could work this thing out over lunch. Sit down. We don't want this goin' in no court."

"I'm not hungry," Quinn said. "And you can remove your hand, Johnny."

"Come on," Stagg said, letting go and smiling a big jack-o'-lantern grin with his veneered teeth. "We don't have to talk business. Right? Just a friendly lunch. You check out that offer and you'll see it's on the level."

"Johnny, you're so crooked you probably pay this fella here to help you screw on your pants every morning."

Lamar shifted in his chair, straightened his red tie, and raised his eyebrows at Judge Blanton, giving a sly little smile about what he'd just witnessed at this civil meeting.

"See you, Judge," Quinn said, and walked out of the restaurant.

He was in the lot and opening the door to the old Ford when Blanton walked up on him and said: "It's a fair deal."

"Not even half the land value?"

"Quinn, why do you want that burden?" Blanton said. "I'm working for you and I'll do what you say. A little personal advice? Walk away with some money in your pocket."

"That land's been in my family since 1895."

"The offer may not be generous, but it's fair. If that fella Lamar in there pushes it, you won't have nothing. He's the kind that makes five hundred an hour. You might even owe some."

"I'd rather burn it down."

Blanton looked out on the downtown Square and reached into his coat pocket for an old gold timepiece. He fiddled with it in his left hand, winding it up, before turning back to Quinn and giving a generous smile. "Okay. I'll fight them."

"Good."

"But you need to understand the odds."

"I do."

"You could lose everything."

"At least make that son of a bitch work for it."

"Hamp dumped this on you."

"I'll finish it."

"Damn, you are Hamp Beckett's nephew to a T."

"I appreciate you saying that, Judge."

Quinn smiled. The old man smiled back and patted Quinn's shoulder, before walking back inside the El Dorado.

Quinn took a hot shower and shaved and dressed in an old flannel shirt, jeans, and cowboy boots, his mother warming up a plate lunch for him. She'd gathered leftovers from his homecoming party, ham and potato salad, some sweet-potato pie from Thanksgiving. He thanked her and sat at the kitchen table, Jason in a high chair across from him, working on small bits of ham and green beans, chugging down some apple juice, and then staring at Quinn until something about Quinn's face tickled him a great deal. Quinn winked at him. And that made the situation somehow even better.

His mother finished cleaning up a bit around the sink, a local radio station playing some old-time gospel, and she sat down by Jason, wiping his face with a damp rag. She smiled at Quinn. Quinn had seen that look before, the sadness before he'd leave.

"Do people say things about me? About how I've been gone so long?"

"People in Jericho have little to do but gossip."

"But they say things about me, about the way I feel about my family."

"I don't pay it a bit of mind."

"They're wrong, you know."

"Believe me, they know about every trip I've made over to Columbus, Georgia, to see you. They know everything you've been doing."

Not everything.

"I don't like it."

"Shush," Jean Colson said, leaning back in her chair, looking much older than the mother he'd seen in his mind for so long. Lines on her face, creases around her eyes. "Just wind."

"It's not because I don't care about you or Caddy."

Jean looked across at her son and reached for his hand. He met her halfway.

"A man does what you do and you got to put up some barriers, some walls. Your grandfather had to do the same thing. I know who you were protecting."

Quinn smiled at her. Jason tossed the plate of food down to the floor with a clatter, laughing.

"Guess he doesn't care for my cooking," she said.

"I'll be back," Quinn said. "Sooner this time."

"You take care of you. I got things here."

16

Latecia Young wasn't happy to see Quinn, and was even less excited when he mentioned Keith Shackelford's name. She just kind of hung there in the doorway of her project apartment, arm propped on the frame, looking Quinn up and down, and then walking back to her kitchen, not saying come in but not telling him to get lost, either. Quinn entered, removing his baseball cap as he did, and followed her, where she was heating up a cold plate of mac and cheese. She ate the mac and cheese standing up, twisting open a half-drunk bottle of Diet Coke while they talked, nodding and agreeing with what he said, like she really didn't have any choice in the matter. Quinn was pretty sure she thought he was with the sheriff's office, but he never said that, only said that his uncle had been the sheriff.

"And you haven't seen Keith all year?"

"Nope."

"You know where he's living?"

"Las' time we talked, he'd been staying with Jett. I don't know where he went after the fire."

"You seen him since?"

"Don't want to, neither," she said, shaking her head. "Heard it fucked him up real bad."

Latecia was muscular and thin, light-skinned, wearing a threadbare T-shirt and faded jeans without shoes. A light blue maid's uniform hung on the back of a bathroom door.

"He call you?"

"Sometimes."

"But you don't answer?"

She shook her head.

"Can you call him back now?"

"You want me to lie?" she asked, resting her arm on a refrigerator. She'd been inked with a blue tattoo on her bicep of praying hands. "Play games? Hadn't been for that fire, I don't think I would've ever gotten away from him. You ever had someone grabbing you so tight while you know they the one drownin'?"

"Why was he drowning?"

She shrugged.

"Just call and say you have something he

may want. Tell him you're gonna drop it off."

"Shit, no."

"Will you give me the number?"

She looked Quinn up and down again and then stared at him for a beat, thinking and trying to decide how this whole thing would shake out. "I got myself clean. I haven't had a drink in six months. I don't even smoke."

Quinn nodded.

"I keep my job for another three months and I get my kids back."

"How many kids?"

"I got a boy and a girl. The boy is six and the girl is eight."

"Who's got them now?"

"They with a foster family," she said. "They father was worse than Keith. Used to beat me if I even thought about leaving. How you get into these things? I can't think right for myself."

"Did you know Jill Bullard?"

She shook her head, looking down at her untouched dinner.

"What about Keith and Jett Price? They spend a lot of time together?"

"Sure."

"What'd they do?"

"Drank, smoked weed. Talked war and drank. Jett sold guns, I think. They used to

200

sit around all day in their underwear and play video games till they'd get a call and git gone."

"Where?"

She walked over to a chair where she'd hung her purse, reaching inside for a cell phone and scrolling through the numbers. She repeated the number to Quinn.

He memorized it.

"Don't you tell him where you got this."

"No, ma'am."

"What'd he do now?"

"I don't think that fire was an accident."

"Lots of folks wouldn't mind seein' Keith dead."

"Like who?"

"Are we finished? This may be shit, but it's my goddamn dinner."

Quinn called the number, and Keith Shackelford picked up on the first ring.

"Jett Price's family wanted to check on you," Quinn said. "Make sure you didn't need any money."

There was a long pause.

"Who the fuck is this?"

"I'm a friend of the family," Quinn said. "The church took up a collection. But, sorry to bother you."

"Hold up. Hold up. How much we talkin',

201

preacher man?"

Quinn picked up Lillie, and they drove northwest about thirty minutes into Webster County and the town of Eupora. There wasn't much to Eupora besides a big gas station coupled with a McDonald's, a run-down motel, a family fish buffet, and a pizza joint by the railroad tracks. The address Shackelford gave had them turning off Highway 9 onto a side street behind a state mental hospital.

Shackelford lived on one side of a tired old duplex, the other apartment looking abandoned, with a plywood-covered window and a screen door hanging loose from the frame. They passed the house once and then parked down the road, walking back, Lillie saying she wasn't happy with how Quinn had set this up.

From across the street they could see in the apartment's long shot of hallway, running from front door to back, a shadowed figure looking out from the frame.

"You see that?" Quinn asked.

"He see us?"

"I think he sees that uniform."

"Son of a bitch."

The shadow turned and darted full speed down the hallway, hitting that back door at a rush, and ran into a wide, open field chest-high with dead grass and junked cars. Quinn took off at a sprint, running around the house, spotting the figure, swallowed up by the field, moving in slow motion, feet weighed down.

Quinn caught him by the collar of his T-shirt and wrestled him down into the winter mud.

Keith Shackelford wasn't much to look at, but most people in the gas-station restaurant couldn't keep their eyes off him. Half his face had been ruined in the fire, with bright red skin and deep rubbery scars across his throat. Both his ears had burned to nubs, and he had no eyelashes or eyebrows to speak of. His hair had been burned away, although he kept a ball cap down over his eyes, black and red in honor of Dale Earnhardt. Quinn couldn't figure out for the life of him how Keith Shackelford could then pop a cigarette in his mouth and click open the lighter.

"I appreciate you coming with us," Lillie said.

"Didn't know not coming was an option," he said, turning his eyes toward Quinn.

"You had a choice," Quinn said.

"So I guess there ain't no donation plate."

"Sorry about that," Quinn said.

"And you ain't no preacher."

"Nope."

They drank coffee in the rear corner of the little McDonald's connected to the gas-station convenience store. Keith took a seat in the very back, eyes down, trying not to lift them off a paper cup that he didn't touch.

"How well did you know Jill?" Quinn asked.

"How'd you find me?"

"Does it matter?"

He shrugged. "She was around. With Jett a lot. I think he liked her a hell of a lot more 'an she liked him. She was only around when he had money. You could always count on Jill to be around then."

"You didn't care for her?"

"Did I say that? I'm sorry she's dead. You could tell she'd been a good-lookin' girl before she got all messed up. Had Daddy issues. I guess you know her daddy was a preacher. Those kids never turn out right."

"What were y'all into?" Lillie asked, Quinn noticing how relaxed she asked it, slipping back in her seat, reaching for a cigarette herself, making the whole thing nice and easy, conversational.

"You name it," Keith said, placing his

hands on the table, wearing thin gloves, a flannel shirt buttoned at the wrist and the throat. "I tried every drug known to man, and I'm still sitting here with y'all and drinkin' coffee."

"And you served with Jett?" Quinn asked.

"No," he said. "We was both in the Army but not together. He'd been out for a few years when I come back from my last tour. You military? 'Cause if you ain't, you need to get a refund on that haircut."

"I am."

"Still?"

"Yep."

"Reserves?"

"No," Quinn said, reaching for his coffee. "I'm in Third Batt of the Seventy-fifth."

"You a Ranger?" Keith asked. His thick scarred eyelids opened, making him look confused, his face naked and seeming like that of a man much older than twenty-five.

Quinn nodded.

"Goddamn," Keith said. "I saw two Rangers get in a bar fight one time in Memphis, and they done beat up the bouncer and two cops. Took about a dozen men to control them, and they was still fighting. Y'all are crazy as shit."

Quinn shrugged.

Lillie said, "We're thinking that Jett may

have owed some folks some money when he got killed."

"Sure. He owed me some goddamn money."

"Some people may have wanted to scare him a bit?" she asked.

Keith looked down at his coffee. He looked around the restaurant and caught the eye of a teenage boy eating a cheeseburger and staring at Keith's face. Keith looked at him and flipped him the bird. He shook his head. "What are y'all driving at?"

Quinn looked at him.

"I done my time," he said. "Okay. I got the hell out of Dodge and got free of that kind of life. When a man gets turned upon the spit, he starts to contemplate his soul. I can imagine hell feels a lot like waking up in the middle of the night with your clothes on fire and children screaming. I tried to find those kids. I tried. I see 'em every night. That little girl comes to me sometimes. Jett's daughter told me it was okay. I tried, man. But half that damn trailer was up and burning after the explosion."

Lillie exchanged looks with Quinn.

"What exploded?"

"Half that trailer."

Keith put a hand to his destroyed face, his fingers moving up to his temples and lost eyebrows. He shook his head. "You ever get to that point that you just don't give a god-damn?"

"What explosion?" Lillie asked.

She knew. Just like Quinn knew.

"They said they'd pour gasoline on me and finish the job if I said a word," he said, starting to laugh. "I guess that's what hap-pened to Jill. You know what? She was never too smart."

"What explosion?" Lillie asked.

"What'd you think it was?" Keith said. "A grease fire? Goddamn. When I come to, I looked for my britches and my gun, think-ing my ass was back in Fallujah. You know what I'm sayin', Lieutenant?"

"Sergeant," Quinn said. "I enlisted just like you."

Keith met his eyes for a second and then looked away. He nodded to himself, as if making up his mind.

"What the hell did y'all think Jett Price did for a living? He couldn't even finish the paperwork to get disability. That dumb son of a bitch was cooking meth all around Tibbehah County. He'd been doing it since he got back, and I was helping him. The lab exploded and burned that trailer down, not a goddamn skillet. Okay? We straight?"

Quinn leaned in and grabbed Keith by

the forearm, Keith's face softening in pain. "For who?"

"Come on, man."

Quinn didn't let go, and he felt Lillie touch his arm.

"Who?"

Quinn squeezed until he could feel the flesh become bone.

"You ever heard the name Gowrie?" Keith asked.

Quinn looked over to Lillie.

"He have a run-in with Sheriff Beckett?"

"Sheriff Beckett tried to run his ass outta the county when Gowrie started actin' up."

Lillie nodded, listening, not offering anything back.

"Gowrie said he was gonna kill him. Can you imagine having the balls to take out a lawman like that?"

17

"So how'd this whole deal work?" Quinn asked. "This shit Gowrie was running."

"I'd sure like to get home," Shackelford said, sitting in the backseat of Lillie's Cherokee. He stared out the window at 9 as they passed a sign that read 18 MILES TO JERICHO. "You got no cause to take me in. I got mud in my boots and up my ass when you tackled me like that."

"Deputy Virgil here is just giving us a ride to town."

"Gowrie sees me with y'all and he'll kill me."

"No he won't," Quinn said. "We'll use an unmarked car."

"You don't know Gowrie."

"He's of no concern."

"You gonna watch my ass for the next few years, Ranger? 'Cause I'd prefer not to end up like Jill Bullard's dead ass. Didn't you say the buzzards had got to her?"

"Just keep me on the right roads."

"I don't know what you want."

"He wants to know about your damn operation, shithead," Lillie said. "Jesus Christ."

"Goddamn, she's mean."

"I'll pay you for your time," Quinn said, turning around to look at the bony, hairless man. "Okay?"

"I ain't exactly welcome in Tibbehah County," Shackelford said, sort of talking to himself. "How'd y'all find me? 'Cause if you can find me, I'm thinking I better boogie on down the road."

"Let's meet back up at the sheriff's office at ten o'clock," Lillie said. "That'll give me some time to talk to Wesley."

Quinn nodded.

"I still don't know why y'all need me," Shackelford said. "You getting some kind of pleasure in watching me shit my pants?"

Quinn remained silent, driving a twelve-year-old green Buick Lillie had borrowed from impound, looking for the cutoff road that Shackelford had told him about. They passed the remnants of an old country store, a lone trailer filled with sharp light, and more leaning barns that would be swallowed in kudzu come spring. The sides of the road had been recently shaved away, leaving no shoulder, only a steep drop down into a gully filled with brush.

"You don't talk much, do you?" Shackelford said.

"Nope."

"Bet you was a good soldier. How long you been in?"

"Little more than ten years."

"You seen some shit?"

Quinn didn't answer him.

"Can't you talk about operations?" Shackelford asked.

"Where's the cutoff?"

"Just around this bend," he said, scrunching down into the passenger seat, making himself small, Dale Earnhardt cap covering half his scarred face. "Shit."

"No one can see you unless I turn on a light."

"I don't take chances."

"How many places cooked for Gowrie?"

"Many as thirteen and little as five or six."

"How much money?"

"Me and Jett got paid per batch," he said. "I don't know how much Gowrie sold it for."

"How much per batch?"

"Maybe five hundred. I didn't exactly keep a record."

"Where'd he sell it?"

"I don't know. Didn't ask."

"Who collected?"

"Him and his daddy. You ever met Daddy Gowrie? He's a mess. Dumber than dog shit. Once tried to rob a bank with a salad fork and did a ten-year stretch at Brushy Mountain."

Quinn looked at Shackelford, down in the floor of the car, hairless and pink, and then up to a bent-up road sign with an arrow pointing down another county road. They drove up through wide hills and down into valleys that used to be farms but now had mainly become rows of pine for timber. The land had been stripped and planted and then clear-cut down to nothing, making the whole landscape feel used.

"Look, these things move around some," Shackelford said. "This is where I know they used to cook. But Gowrie's gonna shake some things up every few weeks in case the law is on him."

"Is that it?"

Quinn motioned to a mailbox in the shape of a horse's ass, the head looking away from the mail slot.

"That's where it was."

Quinn killed the engine and grabbed the door handle.

"What if I run?"

"Are you under arrest?"

"I don't know."

"I'm not the law."

"You sure feel like the law."

"Shut up and sit tight."

Quinn walked the road a quarter mile down into a cleared circle with two mobile homes up on concrete blocks. He circled the property twice before he was sure no one was inside either trailer. He tried the doors, finding one unlocked; the other had to be busted open.

Both were empty.

Quinn jogged back to the Buick under a patch of moonlight and spotted Shackelford, standing by a ravine, taking a leak. "Can you please take me back to Eupora?"

"You've shown me two places."

"So?"

Quinn reached into the glove box and found the Tibbehah County map he'd bought, circling the sites they'd already visited.

"You said you knew of at least thirteen cook spots."

"I said I know where they used to be," he said, zipping up his fly and turning back to Quinn. "I didn't make you no promises."

Quinn scratched his neck. "What do you want?"

"I don't want nothin'."

"He killed my uncle."

"Probably," Keith said. "He sure killed Jill. But that don't mean nothin' to me."

"Where next?"

"You know, I used to be good-looking," Shackelford said. "You better believe it. I was king-shit stud in high school. Played football. Ran track. I got more tail than you could shake a stick at."

"Where's next?"

"You know your way up to Fate?"

Quinn circled the hamlet on the map, got into the car, and cranked the engine, which sputtered twice before turning over. He drove back down the hill and pulled onto the highway to town, where they'd hit 9 going north.

"Latecia said where to find me?" Shackelford said, righting himself up into the seat and cracking the window, the cold air feeling good in the cab, blowing away some of Shackelford's body odor. "Right?"

Quinn didn't answer.

"Man, if Gowrie had known I liked black women, he'd a shit a brick. 'Course, Latecia was light-skinned, hot as hell. Guess that don't make no difference."

"What do you know about him?"

"He's a crazy-ass, nigger-hating nut job," Shackelford said, coughing up a lugie and spitting out the window. "What else is there to know? He likes to shoot guns, shoot crank, and talk about the End Times like some kind of wandering preacher. I did business with him. I didn't say I followed him."

"Who'd he do business with?"

"I don't know."

"He didn't sell what y'all made in this county?"

"He sold some, I guess," Shackelford said. "But he said he wouldn't shit where he ate."

"I heard that before," Quinn said, taking a soft turn in the road, stealing a glance at Shackelford. "Taliban said they sold poppies only to the infidels. Their politicians made excuses for those shitbags, saying the farmers couldn't survive."

Shackelford took off his baseball cap and creased the bill. "I sleep in on Election Day, never figured a single politician to be worth a shit."

"You ever hear Gowrie talk about Johnny Stagg?" Quinn asked.

"The county supervisor?"

Quinn nodded.

"Not that I recall."

"Stagg sent over some of Gowrie's boys to steal some of my uncle's cattle."

"You know, most of those boys believe in Gowrie, like he's some kind of prophet. I went out there one night to some kind of barbecue, and he showed us an old movie about the mongrelization of the races. Said if we didn't come together to fight it, we'd be the new niggers. What the hell does that mean? But he did make some pretty good ice cream. Peach, I think."

They drove north, turning on the Square to the northwest part of the county on the other side of the Big Black River, a full moon shining out onto the flooded land like a mirror. They crossed over an old metal bridge that had always reminded Quinn of an Erector set.

"You headed back?" Shackelford asked.

"You got more places to show me."

"I mean, headed back to the AFG."

"I'm headed back to Benning."

"You know your next deployment?"

"Ranger instructor."

"No more stormin' the castle, huh?"

"Why don't you shut the hell up?"

Quinn studied the broken line on Highway 9, not being able to see an inch beyond those headlights. He turned on the radio, George Jones singing he had stopped loving her today.

A little before midnight, Quinn spotted a cherry red El Camino bumping out from a dirt road that Shackelford said led to Gowrie's compound. The headlight high beams washed up over Quinn's face before the car headed on down south. He cranked his car and followed, Shackelford stirring to life next to him, having been asleep for the last hour after spending a long while bragging about what a high school hero he'd once been. Before the meth had parched him out into something he didn't even recognize.

"Where are we?"

"That truck ahead just came out."

"You see who it was?"

"Nope."

"What is it?"

"Red El Camino."

"Shit, that's Daddy Gowrie, unless someone took his truck. You see how many people are with him?"

"Another man in the passenger seat."

Shackelford scrunched down and reached into his thin leather jacket for a pack of cigarettes, cracking the window and lighting up. "Man, I'd sure love to have a beer right about now. There's nothing like getting a warm six on a cold day. You know?"

"I do."

"How far do we follow them?"

"Far as they go."

Shackelford smoked down the cigarette, tossing the butt into the night. The shadows would fall across his scarred face sometimes, and Quinn could kind of piece together what he must've looked like, but when they got close to the truck stop, streets lit up and shining through the window, he transformed back again, wrecked and old. His face looking like melted wax.

"There you go," Shackelford said, pointing to the El Camino parked at the front entrance to the truck stop.

Quinn idled at the low row of pumps, watching an old man in a worn blue jeans jacket and ski hat walk inside and come back out, thumping a pack of cigarettes and carrying a Coke bottle. The El Camino's brake lights clicked on, and it backed up, exposing the man in the passenger seat while they circled out and headed back for the road south.

Quinn shook his head when he saw the face, and he slipped the old Buick into gear and followed, slowing for the Highway 45 ramp.

"He's headed to Memphis," Shackelford said.

"You got somewhere else to be?"

"You recognize the other fella with him?"

"Yep," Quinn said.

"Brother Davis," Shackelford said. "Got that church in the old movie house."

"Met him with Stagg."

"Well, there you go."

"Why's he buddies with Daddy Gowrie?" Quinn asked. "He get a cut?"

"A church sure is an easy place to drop off some cash, 'specially durin' a real good sermon."

"Are you shittin' me?"

"I wouldn't shit no Ranger," Shackelford said.

"Like a bank?"

"That's where they count up the money."

"You said you only dealt with Gowrie and Daddy."

"That was me. Other folks made donations. Not a bad way to do business, all truth be told."

The cherry red El Camino cut over on Highway 78 and hit Union County, and got off at the New Albany exit, heading the opposite way from town, down one narrow country road and then another, finally disappearing onto a private dirt road.

"They see us?"

Quinn had turned off onto the shoulder

219

of the road, car still idling. "We'll find out."

The El Camino spurted out from the dirt road twenty minutes later and drove back toward the highway, taking the turn north for Memphis, Quinn keeping a good hundred yards behind it.

"Wish we had one of them tracking devices like you see on those CSI shows," Shackelford said. "We could stop off at a beer joint and find 'em later."

"You sure want a beer."

"Shit, you cut right into my drinking session, calling me up and saying you were a preacher and then coming to get me with that woman deputy. I hadn't run like that in a while."

Shackelford laughed. Quinn smiled.

"I'll get you a six if we stop."

"You said something about money, too."

"How much would you need to blow town?"

"You mean out of Mississippi?"

"Yep."

"Few hundred."

"Okay."

"Just like that?"

"What did I say?" Quinn said, keeping Daddy Gowrie's taillights in view, watching them disappear between eighteen-wheelers

and cars, till they hit the Tennessee line and
the outskirts of Memphis.

18

That little boy Ditto looked out for Lena. She couldn't walk two feet outside the trailer they'd given her without him falling into stride, making sure she got down to the old barn where she'd stock up on some peanut-butter-and-jelly sandwiches, a couple of Hershey bars, and maybe a bottle of Mountain Dew. He was trying not to talk so much, but it seemed the restraint just wasn't in him, as he'd hold her plate or carry some freshly cleaned laundry some of the women had washed and hung in the freezing daylight. At first Ditto was kind of a pain in her ass, and she got tired of all the stupid questions he was asking her. And maybe it wasn't appropriate to be seen with him on account of her waiting there for Charley Booth.

But that nervous little pig-faced boy knew how to run interference, and it had been maybe eight times that one of those jail-hard creeps — not Gowrie himself but that skinny guy Jessup who sucked Gowrie's asshole for free or that big fat pig everyone called Tim, or Hogzilla — smiled at her like she was walking around naked. She guessed they figured since Charley had been with her, they sure had a chance.

"Don't you need some vitamins or s-something?" Ditto asked, kind of stuttering, trying to figure how to pull out some kind of conversation. "I can run down to the Dollar Store for you. I saw they was selling a dang pint bottle of chewables for five dollars."

"I'm fine."

"My sister got herself pregnant, and she was always taking vitamins her doctor give her," Ditto said, smiling and then looking a bit confused. "You got a doctor?"

She shook her head.

"How long you got?"

"I don't know," she said. "Maybe a couple weeks. That baby's been in me since March. I feel like I'm about to bust."

"I'll take you to a doctor."

"I don't need no doctor."

"It ain't gonna just pop out like no calf," Ditto said. "A calf lands on its feet."

"I know how a calf lands."

"I knew you were a farm girl."

"Some guy gave me this," Lena said, reaching into her old coat pocket for a business card. "If something happens to me, would you call him? In case I go batshit crazy, with all that pain I hear about."

He nodded.

"Ditto?"

"Yep."

"What in the world are y'all doing here?" Lena asked, taking a seat on the stoop of the old trailer. The shame of it was that the shithole felt as much like home as anywhere she'd ever been. She'd never lived in the same place longer than six months.

"Training," Ditto said.

"For what?"

"Gowrie says a war's coming," Ditto said. "I don't know about that, but he pays us regular to run errands for him, drill and all that. He's got a zip line put on top of that hill over yonder where we slide down and shoot guns."

"What's that prove?"

"It's all about getting ready."

"For the war."

"I guess," Ditto said. "Oh, hell. I don't know. I didn't drink all the Kool-Aid."

"I'm glad," Lena said, leaning into him, thinking that she liked the smell of his cigarette around her. He didn't move, like he might spook her away, stock-still, and not able to speak.

"I've been wishing that Charley Booth would leave you alone," Ditto said. "He isn't right in the head. You understand that about him, don't you?"

"What'd you mean?" Lena asked, feeling something funny and sharp and getting to her feet, reaching for the railing. A sharp pain, and the splat of something big and wet across the wooden planks.

"You just piss yourself?" Ditto asked.

"This baby's comin'."

The highway into south Memphis was pretty much industrial, with gas stations and trucking companies, cheap roadside motels, and some Mexican markets and Tejano bars. Quinn knew the city pretty well, Memphis being the city of choice for North Mississippi kids who wanted to cut loose but needed something bigger than Tupelo. There were signs to Graceland and signs to the airport, the sky overhead dotted with blinking lights. Not far from Winchester Road, the El Camino slowed and got into the turn lane. Quinn tried not to make a show of slowing himself but thought that if he'd been spotted it was too late anyway, so he just fell in line with the turning car.

"He's headed to the airport."

"I doubt Daddy Gowrie has ever been on an airplane," Shackelford said. "He seemed confused about indoor plumbing."

About a mile down the road, you could see the lights and neon of a club. DIXIE BELLES advertised hundreds of the SOUTH'S FINEST WOMEN, AMATEUR CONTESTS, and HALF-PRICE LAP DANCES. Daddy Gowrie turned into a busted-up parking lot, and Quinn drove right on past, getting a glimpse of the grizzled little man as he crawled out of the cab and started to comb his thin, greasy hair with a pocket comb in the flickering light.

Brother Davis followed, grinning up at the neon sign with his gold teeth. He borrowed Daddy Gowrie's comb and went to work on his ducktail.

"Daddy know you?"

"Is this a face you'd forget?" Shackelford lit another cigarette and nodded. "You bet. Even before I became so unforgettable. I whipped his ass one night after he stole a pint of whiskey from me."

Quinn nodded back.

"I know," Shackelford said, waving the smoke from his face. "Stay here. Will you at least describe to me all them titties?"

Quinn waited five minutes before following the men inside, paying the five-dollar cover and paying ten for his first drink out of a two-drink minimum. The girls were cute but hard at the cash register, commenting on his buzzed hair, and they told him he could get a free lap dance with a military ID.

Quinn grabbed a Budweiser and walked into the club, scanning the big open space for Daddy Gowrie and the preacher.

Most strip clubs were the same, but he could tell right away this one beat the crap out of the ones lining Victory Drive in Columbus, Georgia. He'd dropped so much money in those places when he'd been a young man, maybe eight, nine years ago, he couldn't even imagine. There was always a Ranger who'd get stupid and drunk, falling in love with one of those girls. Quinn actually knew two that married girls they'd called dancers, and when Quinn met one of the dancer wives, he had already seen her naked a half-dozen times.

All the same shit, stage lights, bad music, and some goofball DJ trying to be funny, making sure all the fellas knew to tip their waitresses.

He hadn't been inside five minutes and had been hustled twice and asked to buy another drink three times.

Daddy Gowrie and Brother Davis had found a table close to the stage, where a girl worked a pole to some electronic shit music. At Daddy Gowrie's feet sat a small bag, maybe a little larger than a grocery sack, that he'd touch every few minutes, feeling for it and then returning his hands to the table.

Brother Davis moved up to the stage and put a dollar bill in his gold teeth. A woman pressed her titties together and snatched it from him. Ole Daddy Gowrie watched and clapped, smiling a big shit-eating grin and slapping his knee while he reached for a couple shots from the waitress and handed her back some cash.

He threw back both of 'em, motioning to her that he wanted a couple more.

The room was dark. They couldn't see him. If they'd turned the houselights on, they wouldn't have noticed anyway, as the girl threw her bikini top down on the stage and hugged the pole.

Two more girls followed.

Daddy drank four more shots. Brother Davis drank three beers within five minutes.

A few songs later, Daddy Gowrie reached into his pocket for a cell phone and nodded to what he heard. He got to his feet, grabbed the bag, and walked back behind the bar, where he knocked on a metal door.

The door opened, and he was gone.

Quinn ordered another Budweiser but didn't drink it.

It was oh-one-hundred.

He wondered if Shackelford had bailed.

Quinn didn't care. He'd gotten what he needed, now had to figure out what to do with the information.

The music changed, and a tall blonde in boots made of fur high-stepped it down the center of the runway to Led Zeppelin. Quinn watched for a bit till his eye caught another couple girls, sitting down at a table with a couple college boys. One of the girls reached out and grabbed one of the boys by the hand and led him back to a VIP room, where he'd get a lap dance for forty bucks. The other girl, dressed as a Dallas Cowboys cheerleader, made small talk with the kid left at the table. Quinn's eye shifted to her from Brother Davis, who was getting dead drunk and moving with the music.

Quinn tilted his head, the strobes and lights of the stage making weird patterns on the walls and across faces. He could only see the girl's neck and a tattoo on her shoulder blade.

She turned in profile, and Quinn just shook his head.

He drank the beer in two sips and stood, a girl in black panties and bra grabbing his belt from behind and asking if he wanted a dance. He dodged her and walked over to the table, looking down at the cheerleader.

She craned her neck up at him, eyes glassy. "Boy, you look just like my brother."

Caddy agreed to follow him out to the parking lot, where she lit up a cigarette and leaned up against a brand-new red Mustang that she bragged belonged to her boyfriend. She wore a long fake-fur coat over her cheerleader getup and tried to keep balanced in her white boots, pretending that she was sober and goddamn well in charge.

"I wondered how long it would take till you came up here."

"I wasn't looking for you."

"You know military gets free lap dances," she said. "You taking advantage of that?"

"You should call Mom."

"That's it? No speeches?"

"What the hell, Caddy. You really need a person to warn you off working a pole?"

"You know how much money I make?"

"I met Jason."

She took a drag of the cigarette and let out a long exhale, kneading her fist into her eye. She met Quinn's gaze and then craned her neck back at a big jet taking off and buzzing over the concrete-block club and the Dixie Belles' neon sign.

"How is he?"

"Why don't you go home and find out?"

"You want me to support my son by checking folks out at the Piggly Wiggly?"

"I don't think you send a dime home."

"Momma tell you that? 'Cause that's a damn lie."

"I didn't come to find you."

"Liar."

"You should have come to the funeral."

She reached into her pocket for another cigarette, finding an empty pack, squashing it in her hand and tossing it to the ground. Her glassy eyes focused on Quinn's face, and then she muttered something that he didn't understand.

"What?"

"Forget it."

"I just followed an old man up here from Tibbehah County," Quinn said. "He brought a sackful of meth or money and dropped it off behind a metal door behind that bar. You know anything about that?"

She laughed at him.

"What's funny?"

"What the hell you into now?"

Quinn reached out and grabbed her arm.

He looked down at his sister's face, not really seeing his sister now but seeing that kid she used to be at Halloween, when she'd put on makeup and pretend to be a princess or a witch.

"He's a good boy, Quinn."

Quinn nodded. "You saddled Mom with him. Don't try and get noble now."

"Fuck you."

"Who's on the other side of that door?"

"Big money."

"Big money got a name?"

She placed her small thin hands into her coat, covering everything but her knee-high white leather boots. "Let me give you some advice, dear big brother. You got no idea what kind of people run the show."

"I'd like to know."

"Why do you give a shit?"

"They killed Uncle Hamp."

"Bullshit."

"Who runs this place?"

"Good-bye, Quinn."

Caddy turned, shoulders hunched, and walked back toward the music and lights. Quinn stayed there and watched her go, wanting to grab her, throw her in the car, and force her to go back to Jericho and be a good daughter. Now a good mother.

"See you at Christmas?" he said to her back.

She kept walking, flipping him the bird.

You can't make a person be what you wanted. Caddy had been broken since she was twelve. He had some ideas why, but they weren't discussed. You don't talk about such horrible things in a place as bright as Tibbehah County.

"You find what you were lookin' for?"
Shackelford asked Quinn right before they
hit downtown Memphis, Quinn not saying
a word since he'd cranked that old Buick at
the strip club and headed into the city. He
slowed at the Greyhound bus station on
Union, still lit up in the early morning with
a few street people shuffling about. Quinn
braked under a streetlight and knocked the
car into park, reaching into his wallet.

"I got my shit back in Eupora," Shackelford said.

"Anything that can't be replaced?"

Shackelford shook his head.

"I'd get out of town for a few weeks."

"You planning on a shit storm?"

Quinn didn't answer, handing him four
hundred dollars, and only asked if he had a
place to go.

"I got an Army buddy in Atlanta," Shackelford said. "I guess he wouldn't mind seein'

my pretty face."

Quinn nodded. Shackelford absently shuffled the money in his hand and then tucked it into his T-shirt pocket under his leather jacket.

"You gonna kill Gowrie?"

"I appreciate the help," Quinn said. "You're stand-up."

Shackelford looked at him and nodded, offering his hand. Quinn reached out and shook the man's hand, skinny and feeling almost hollow.

"Hell, I didn't do nothin'."

"Gowrie forced you out and you came back anyway. I'd call that stand-up."

Shackelford waited a beat, breathing, and then nodded before he opened the door and headed on into the bus station.

Quinn stayed a moment after the door slammed shut, smelling the diesel fumes of the Greyhounds, and watched Shackelford disappear before he headed back south.

Quinn's cell rang about halfway back to Jericho. It was Anna Lee.

"You asleep?"

"I'm headed back from Memphis."

"Quinn, did you give some girl Luke's number?"

"She was pregnant and needed a doctor."

"That girl called us at supper, and Luke drove off to find her. He hasn't answered his phone in nine hours."

"Sounds like the girl's in labor."

"He's not at the hospital."

"Call Wesley."

"I called him," she said. "He wasn't worried."

"I'm sure Luke's fine."

"He went out to that compound up in the hills."

"You want me to call Wesley for you?"

"Why in the hell would you put Luke in with those people?"

"I'm sorry, I thought Luke was a doctor."

"Those people out there. Holy Christ. Why'd you set him up like that?"

Gowrie left after the screaming got too bad, after her water broke on the steps with Ditto and ran through her panties and down her legs and she was left in that dirty little room with four women stoned out of their minds. Not a one of them had five years on Lena, and they kept on telling her everything was going to be all right. The hell it was. She kept on punching that number on the cell phone, the one she'd been given at the truck stop, feeling like this was the only way the goddamn pain would stop. But the girls tried to soothe her, bringing her some pills, which she spit on the floor, and a hit of whiskey, which she did drink. Just about twilight is when time kind of stopped, and she threw that phone to the floor and began to walk the creaky floor of that trailer, women on each side of her, telling her to be cool. Be cool? She walked and couldn't breathe, those damn girls not giving her the space. She held on to her big belly and thought of Jody. Jody Charley Booth, and what he'd done by planting his seed in her, after lying on his back and looking up at the stars and telling her how good it felt when he didn't have to wear one of them things. And she'd asked if he'd finished within her, and he swore on his momma's life that he hadn't. And she believed him.

Not 'cause she trusted him, but 'cause it was what she wanted to believe, and if Charley Booth was going to be beholden to her and they'd live together, and he'd go out and make sure they was taken care of, she'd never, ever, have to step foot in Alabama again.

"You want some more whiskey?"

"Hell no, I don't want no whiskey."

She doubled over, the pain something fierce, her busting apart at the seams, muscles and organs coming undone, that baby on the move and wantin' out of there. And as she got on all fours on the bed, a woman bringing a cool cloth for her neck, she had the scariest thought of all. What if she was too small? What if the baby couldn't get out? She'd hide it. She'd hide it. 'Cause she saw, in her mind, Gowrie walkin' in and splitting her in two with a hunting knife and having no more worries about it than gutting a fish. She'd be a fish to Gowrie. And that's all she'd be.

Men were in the room now. She could smell them. She could smell and feel better than she ever had before, and she wished at this moment that she wasn't feeling a goddamn thing. They craned their necks and looked at her bare legs, the women trying to push those grinning bastards out.

"She don't look right," Gowrie said.

A hand reached for her, and she turned and grabbed it and bit down with all she had, tasting fur and blood and bone. The man yelled and backed away. And she rolled over to her back, scooting far against the wall, feeling the cold tin against her back and telling the man to get the hell away from her. "Don't you cut me. I ain't no fish. Goddamn you, don't you."

He held his arm where she'd bit him and dropped to a knee by her bed, reaching for the hair that had gone wild over her eyes. His glasses caught light all funny in the weak glow of the lamp. He held his hand over her forehead and told her to just hold on, the pain letting go, like the busting wasn't gonna happen at all. Everything gone still as a lump in her.

I can't feel nothing. I can't feel nothing.

His hand held hers. He was nice-looking, with green eyes and brown hair, reminding her of that fine doctor on *Days of Our Lives*.

"Call 911."

"Shit, no," Gowrie said. "Brought you here, didn't we?"

"She can't have this baby here in this filthy room."

"She called a doctor. I don't need the law."

That's when the pain came on so strong that her spine bucked from the bed, and she dug her nails into his arms and said, "Goddamn you, Jody. Goddamn. You killed me."

The doctor just said, "Hold on."

20

Wesley Ruth met Quinn at the Tibbehah County line, his sheriff's truck pointing north on a muddy shoulder and chugging exhaust in the cold night. Quinn pulled opposite him, headed toward Jericho, and Wesley let down his window, Styrofoam spit cup in hand, and said, "You sure like waking me up at night. Is this going to become something regular?"

"Anna Lee's worried."

"You think maybe she just wanted a reason to call?" Wesley said. "I'd really prefer not getting in the dead center of this shit."

"You mind riding out there and checking up on him?"

"Say, where'd you get that ole junker?" Wesley asked. "Where's your truck?"

"I borrowed it."

"We got an old car just like that in impound last week."

"No kidding."

Wesley eyed him for a long moment and spit some snuff out in the coffee cup. He nodded and said, "Fine, I'll ride out there. But I think Anna Lee is twisting your pecker."

"You talk to Lillie tonight about the fire?"

"Yes, sir."

"That's a hell of a revelation."

Wesley nodded at him and played with the bill of his baseball cap, spitting again. "Quinn, you know anything about Keith Shackelford?"

"I know he was Fourth Infantry."

"You know he's a meth head and a professional fuckup?"

"Said he was clean."

"He's a freak show," Wesley said. "His life has been spiraling down the shitter since he got out of the Army. I thought he was dead, and I really don't appreciate you all dumping his ass back on my doorstep."

"Doesn't it bother you that the arson investigation of that fire was fixed?"

"Keith Shackelford makes his living as a federal snitch," Wesley said. "He works both sides. He got in with some blacks up in Memphis and sold them out to the DEA, and then he come down here and tried to do the same thing to Gowrie's bunch."

"Whose side are you on?"

"You pay him?"

Quinn didn't say anything.

"He'll tell you what you want to hear, conspiracies and lies about your uncle," Wesley said, rubbing his temples from fatigue. "But sometimes people are such fuckups they leave grease on the cookstove, and sometimes old men get so damn depressed they stick a gun in their mouth."

"Keith Shackelford was cooking meth for Gowrie."

"I don't doubt it," Wesley said. "But I wouldn't believe any stories that turd tells me without checking them out."

"Will you check it out?"

"Goddamn, Colson. I said I would."

"You mind if I ride with you to check on Luke?"

"Let me stick my boot in that anthill, partner."

"I can play nice."

"I love you, brother. But don't treat me like a moron."

Anna Lee drove over to the farm at four a.m.

Quinn hadn't been able to sleep, thinking about Caddy, standing there pissed off in a Dallas Cowboy cheerleader's outfit and a

242

fake-fur coat, bragging about her new convertible and what a good mother she'd been. He sat outside on a rocking chair in the cold silence, covered in horse blankets and smoking a cigar. Hondo had wandered on in from the back field and now stood barking at Anna Lee's car, hair raised, the night brisk and clear, with a moon so huge that it lit up the pasture and glowed off the tin roof of the barn.

Quinn's aunt's old laundry line stood bent and crooked on the hill like some kind of crazy Calvary.

Anna Lee stepped out in jeans and a sweatshirt, a knit hat and gloves, and made her way up to the screen door, spotting him sitting there in the dark, giving her a little start, before she stepped inside and sat down in a chair opposite him.

"You hear from Luke?"

She let out a breath and shook her head. Quinn could tell she'd been crying. Hondo sniffed her and sat back down.

"I called Wesley."

"Wesley said he drove over to that compound, or whatever in the hell it is, and he wasn't there. Said the girl wasn't there, either."

"You ask folks at the hospital?"

She used the back of her hand to wipe her

eyes. "No, Quinn. I didn't think of that. Hell, I've been calling every thirty minutes."

"Sorry," Quinn said. "The girl needed to see a doctor. I didn't see any harm in that."

"I didn't mean to jump your ass."

"Old habits." Quinn smiled at her.

She took off her hat and leaned forward in her chair. "If she'd gone into labor, Luke would've called an ambulance."

"Maybe there wasn't time."

"If the delivery was rough, he'd need help."

"You know, I got holed up in this Afghan village one time with two pregnant women, both going into labor from stress, thinking soldiers were there to kill everyone. I've never heard more screaming and pain in my life. We were blowing up a mess of ammo the Taliban had stashed and we could still hear those women."

"Luke would've called."

Quinn nodded. "Shit. Okay."

She wiped her face and nose with the hat and blurted out a nervous laugh, nodding. Pulling her hair away from those wide brown eyes, she said, "You will?"

Quinn put his hand on her knee and smiled at her. "I'll find him."

Quinn found the back door to his mother's

house unlocked and slipped in again, just like he had as a teenager. She was asleep on the couch, same as she'd always been back then, an empty wineglass by the remote, the television showing the menu from a DVD of *Hooper*. His dad had worked on that film, jumping the car over that gorge, playing stunt driver for Burt Reynolds, several years before Quinn was even born. He remembered watching that movie and *Billy Jack* and a mess of Southern-chase drive-in movies, where his dad had stunted as moonshiners and hell-raisers, maybe the best time in Jason Colson's whole sordid history.

Quinn left the television on and slipped back into his old bedroom, finding the old footlocker he'd kept as a boy, his grandfather's old WWII issue, the key hidden behind an old photo of Anna Lee.

He turned the key and found everything as he'd left it six years ago: washed and dried hunting camos, so worn they felt soft to the touch, and an old pair of Merrell boots. He pulled out the gear, along with two double-edged knives, and then felt the sides for the loose board he'd fitted as a false bottom. Underneath, he found his dad's Browning .308 hunting rifle, with a sling and four packs of a dozen bullets. He slipped all of them from the Styrofoam cases and into the pockets of his hunting jacket after he'd dressed.

He moved back out the way he'd come in and walked down Ithaca Road to his F-150 and cranked the ignition. It was nearly five a.m.

He called Anna Lee again.

She hadn't heard from Luke.

Boom lived in an old shotgun shack at the edge of hundreds of acres of cotton farmed by his family for the last two generations. He didn't come out for several minutes after Quinn began to bang on the sagging screen door, finally emerging in old-fashioned long underwear and scratching his ass.

"Son of a bitch."

"Come on."

"Where are we going?"

"I said come on."

"I'm sleeping."

"You can sleep on the way."

Quinn was already halfway back to his truck. That big moon hung way out there over the fields, the dead cotton plants brushing against one another in the wind. Boom's New Holland tractor sat parked under a crooked barn roof.

"Where we headed?" Boom called out from his doorway.

"Hunting," Quinn said.

"Bullshit."

"I need some help."

"You mind me putting on my pants first?"

"I'd prefer it."

They drove north through the heart of Carthage, nothing more than a defunct general store, a rotting building that had been a post office, and a corrugated-tin building that housed a volunteer fire department. Boom fed bullets into Quinn's big-ass Colt Anaconda with incredible dexterity in that one hand and then loaded another deer rifle Quinn had brought from his uncle's stash.

"How many guns?"

"I got my old .308. And my .45. Can you balance your rifle on a limb?"

"Yeah. But you got a plan?"

"Just want to look around is all," Quinn said. "I promised."

"Why'd Anna Lee come to you?"

"She blames me."

"This would work better at night," Boom said. "Sun will be rising soon."

"Let me worry about that."

"Then how come you need me?"

"I need you to watch my six."

"Sure," Boom said, reaching into a red-and-black-checked coat with his hand for a cigarette, popping it in his mouth and then going for the lighter. "I can watch your ass. This big .44 is pretty sweet. I think I can handle that kick."

"These folks are living on Mr. Daniels's land," Quinn said, hanging a left on County Road 29.

"Mr. Daniels's been dead a long time," Boom said, face lighting up in the glow of the cigarette. "His kids divided the land, logged it out."

"Gowrie bought it?"

"I don't know who owns what. Down that fire road, his people brought in a mess of trailers. They got signs up and all kind of shit. You got to walk to get down there."

"How far?"

"I don't know. Figure a mile. I don't make a regular visit."

"How come?"

"They got a sign that says they don't appreciate people of color. You see?"

"Yeah, I saw the sign." Quinn had half a cigar down in the tray. He reached for it, punching the lighter. "Nice."

"How you know Luke's down there?"

"I saw the girl with Gowrie at the truck stop. She's broke, and I think she took up with his people."

"Maybe you lookin' for an excuse?"

"Maybe."

"Good excuse."

Quinn, having hung a left onto County Road 29, killed his lights, shut off his engine about two miles down and coasted to the bottom of the hill. He found a little patch of cleared land, where he parked behind a thick mess of privet bush and tangles of dead kudzu.

"Luke could still be deliverin' that baby."

"Sure."

"But you want to call on 'em anyway."

"I just want to look around," Quinn said. "You don't have to go."

"You callin' me a pussy?"

"I just said you didn't have to go."

"Goddamn. Are we friends or what?"

21

Rangers have always prided themselves on their skills in the woods. Although Quinn had never been on a single mission that wasn't in the desert or up a mountain, he'd been trained for years at Fort Benning to move through the deep woods at night, up, down, and around those red clay hills of the Cole Range, being smoked to shit by his instructors until they damn near killed him. He'd marched the range so many times by himself or with his platoon that he could move blindfolded, feeling each twig and branch, moving from tree to tree, always forward, always toward the objective, the SLLS still resonating in his brain. *STOP. LOOK. LISTEN. SMELL.* You do this a thousand times, a million times, as a Ranger, it becomes so commonplace that you stalk men and encampments as well as you breathe.

Behind him, Boom sounded like an elephant, hitting branches and tangles, but Quinn never thought for a moment they'd be heard. When they got close, he'd search for a decent vantage point, never asking Boom once if his shooting had suffered without the arm.

If there were trouble, Quinn knew Boom — one-armed or not — could drop half those bastards with that big .44.

They followed the fire road, walking a good hundred meters along a deer trail through brush and thickets. Most of the trees were newly planted pines, the blanket of rusted needles as soft and quiet under their feet as carpet. Quinn slowed as they spotted the beaten trailers and motioned Boom forward, Quinn pointing over to a low-hanging branch where Boom would balance his rifle and pick off any targets he saw fit.

Quinn, the .308 slung on his back, .45 in his belt, would make his way down the eroded slope and into the ravine running into old Hell Creek.

Boom winked at him and took position.

He was having a ball.

It was coming up on 0530.

"Just a look?" Boom said, whispering.

"Trust me," Quinn said with a grin.

A soft dawn shone from the east across

the still trailers, no lights or activity. He could hear the gentle hum of generators in a sorry old barn, leaning hard to the hills, the tin roof crudely painted with a Rebel flag. Quinn edged through the woods the way a deer would, keeping just out of reach of the clearing, watching everything.

A trailer door opened, and an old man stumbled out, took a leak, and then moved down toward another trailer, slamming the door. A girl, maybe fourteen, in a yellow oversized sweatshirt and panties, emerged from the crooked barn holding a laptop computer under her arm.

She smoked a cigarette in the cold and finished it off before heading up a long trail to another trailer and a crude parking lot filled with an old black Camaro, a blue GTO, and Daddy Gowrie's cherry red El Camino. Assorted busted-up trucks and sleek muscle cars.

Quinn checked the time again, not needing it but reacting as he'd been trained.

Size, Activity, Location, Uniforms, Terrain, Equipment.

Four men headed out from another trailer. All of them had shaved heads. Two wore camo jackets, one wore a woolly pully, and the last was in a sleeveless T-shirt. The same boys who'd tried to steal his uncle's cattle for Johnny Stagg. They weren't armed, but Quinn knew there would be guns in the trailers or down in the barn.

The men headed down to a smoking trash barrel and added in some stray branches and scrap wood. One of the boys, the skinny shitbag who'd confronted Quinn at the farm, held a joint in his hand, smoking it down before passing it along. His eyes looked black and cheeks hollow.

Quinn stayed there a good hour until the sun came up, turning everything a slate gray and then a bright purple, more men and women coming out of trailers, most headed down to the barn to fetch food on paper plates and then returning to their heated shitholes.

He figured on about eighteen folks. Eleven men. Seven women.

Quinn sighted the men down the rifle's scope, a clear, clean shot of each of their heads, big as dinner plates. He missed his M4 carbine, maybe some flash bangs and grenades, but the hunting rifle would do just fine. The problem was on the reload, but if things got tight, he had four clips for the .45.

He shifted the scope from man to man, watching as Gowrie walked out from the trailer farthest up the hill and joined the men, Quinn taking aim like he'd just found the big prize buck.

Gowrie snatched the joint out of one boy's fingers and headed off to a drainage ditch, where he unhitched his pants and started to piss, standing ankle-deep in rubber muck boots. He had thick black hair on his shoulders and a map of jailhouse tattoos on his bare back.

Gowrie was a massive target in Quinn's scope. His shaved head, balding at the crown, was dead center for the .308, which could blow a hole the size of a baseball through his skull. Quinn could drop him before his boys even knew what happened, pick up the girl and Luke, and boogie on down the road, no one the wiser.

How many people would even miss the son of a bitch?

Quinn listened, looking for any sign of the girl or Luke, noting all the action and folks in the camp, the comings and goings, who carried a weapon, what kind. He kept the sight in on the same place, Gowrie moving back and forth in the crosshairs, the bridge of his nose dead center.

Quinn took a deep breath, feeling the trigger under his finger, thinking about Uncle Hamp cutting down bamboo to make cane poles, teaching him how to drive a truck when he was twelve. He saw his uncle walking down a fire road at sunset into the heart of that never-ending forest after ten-year-old Quinn had started to believe he was the only man left on the planet. Uncle Hamp welcomed him with a smile and took him down to the Fillin' Station for four cheeseburgers and a scoop of ice cream.

He'd never stopped looking for Quinn.

Gowrie looked feral, with those broad tattoos across his back and shoulders, lording over these shitbags. He was animated and wild, sucking the smoke deep into his lungs, not feeling the cold on his bare chest.

Quinn felt that trigger so perfect on his fingertip. He breathed soft and easy.

Quinn lowered the gun. *And waited.* The only guilt Quinn felt was for the damn ease of the shot.

About that time, Quinn heard a girl scream.

Pain was a son of a bitch, and every time Lena wanted to get up the doctor kept on pushing her down and telling her it was better for the baby, and she couldn't get up and move on out of this filthy room in this damn dim light and walk out into the cold darkness. The pain kept on coming along and then it would stop, and then start again,

Lena wishing it would just hit her hard and constant and not make her feel like things were going to get any better. One of Gowrie's women, a girl not much older than her with big tits and streaked hair, held one of her arms, and the doctor motioned for another young girl to hold the other, both of them loopy and giggling but strong, when she'd buck up and tell 'em, baby or no, she was getting the hell out of there.

"Come on," the girl with big tits and silly hair said. "Just take it easy."

"You done this before?" she asked.

"Hell no."

"Then why don't you shut the hell up," Lena said.

She wanted to be cold. Lie on a cold stone somewhere.

The doctor had her legs spread open, her underwear cut off and tossed away, a big tent of sheet over her legs. She couldn't see what was going on there and didn't really care, just fought with those girls and gave one big huge massive push that felt like she was trying to take the biggest damn dump ever. She forced herself to her elbows, legs spread apart, vision dimming, the words and sounds and screams going dull in her ears, as she yelled and pushed and felt her whole body just arch and ache with pain, the pain no longer coming in waves but just a steady kind of hurt, a tensing of everything in her, as she pushed and pushed, the doctor telling her that she wasn't pushing and her calling him a goddamn dirty liar and him saying if she didn't start pushing the baby wasn't coming out. And Lena said, "I don't care if it ever comes out."

"Yes, you do," the doc said.

"You lousy bastard."

"Grab my hand and squeeze till you think you're gonna break me," the doctor said. "Call me Luke."

"I'll crack your bones like a pecan, Luke."

The pain hit her again, and her elbows gave way, those pimply-faced girls holding her down, acting like they knew something, like they had some kind of strength or knowledge that made them right for this. But them girls would be on their backs right now, legs spread so wide they was going to split, if Gowrie didn't have sense. That man had more sense than Charley Booth, Jody Charley Booth. In jail. In prison. A big smile on his face. *Yeah, I didn't finish.*

Hell he didn't.

"Don't cut me. I ain't no fish. Goddamn, don't you cut me."

And she pushed hard and long, and breathed and breathed and breathed, 'cause that was something that people all around her were saying: Breathe, breathe, breathe. "Hell yeah, I'm breathin', and hurtin', too."

And then the hurt stopped, Lena thinking that her heart and insides had done exploded. No breathing, no pushing, no pain. Maybe she was dead?

"One more time," Luke said. "About there."

"I'm done."

"Push."

Goddamn, she hurt, but then she started to notice the soft light around the doc's face, such a soap-opera hero, with nice clothes and smelling clean, not like those rats who hung out at the barn down the hill. Not like Jody. Two of them dumb girls were cooing and carrying on about something in one of them's arms, and she couldn't see it but it seemed to be bringing them a mess of pleasure. Goddamn, she hurt.

Lena tried to right herself in the bed, her legs feeling slick, body just filled with nothing but air. "I'm dying. I got things blowing up in me."

She was alone and standing on a hill and looking down into a valley covered in nothing but corn and sunflowers in the wind. The hills had snow, and a man with no eyes held her hand. Blood rushed through her ears, sounding like a heartbeat. Her body felt hollow as she opened her eyes, the world coming back into focus.

"You want to hold her?" the doctor asked.

"What? Hold what?"

"Your daughter," he said, his profile coming into view as he turned to her and handed her that little baby wrapped in a towel decorated with beer bottles and Mex hats. "That's your baby."

"I hate you, Charley Booth," she said, her eyes closing again and then opening. "I hate you."

"We need to get you out of here," the doctor said, whispering into her ear where those tramps couldn't hear.

Quinn saw Luke come outside a trailer, wiping blood off his hands with a dish towel and having some words with Gowrie in the cold. Gowrie smoked down a cigarette as he listened and then tossed it, growing wild-eyed and ranting. He snatched up Luke by the arm and screamed at him.

Luke pulled his arm away and reached for a cell phone in his pant pocket, yelling back at Gowrie before Gowrie took the phone and threw it as far as he could out into the woods.

Luke started to yell some more.

Gowrie pushed him flat on his ass and pulled a Glock from his branded belt, tapping the barrel into Luke's forehead.

Luke calmed down.

He sat there, white dress shirt covered in blood, propped up on his elbows, and nodded. Gowrie grabbed him by the front of his shirt, yanked him to his feet, and opened the door, throwing Luke back inside the trailer.

Quinn readied himself, lowering the rifle and throwing it back over his shoulder with the sling, taking the .45 from his belt. He could hear the blood flush with excitement in his ears, feel a smile on his face. He'd seen all he needed.

He'd be an easy target running from the concealment of the woods to the trailer, about twenty meters, to get the girl and Luke and bring them all the way back to the county road where he'd parked the truck.

He looked across the way to Boom and nodded. Boom had his six.

The generators hummed up the ravine from the leaning mouth of that old barn, where two pit bulls were staked to chains. If they let the dogs loose on him, he'd have to kill them, but he hated to do that. He could take out an enemy with little remorse, but he figured a dog was a pawn in the situation.

Quinn reached into his pocket for an old nickel-plated Zippo and took the long way around to the barn, finding an easy trail, the dirt of it smooth and silent under his old Merrells. He moved up and over a grouping of trailers, hearing a television going, some men playing cards — spotting them through an open window that was letting out the stink of dope. All the men soft and lazy. Trash had been dumped down into a gulley, and it smelled like this is where they'd been dumping their shit, too.

The sky through the leafless trees turned a soft gray and blue. Quinn moved to the back of the barn in that first light, finding a soft, easy way, so quiet that the pit bulls didn't even lift their heads. Two large Honda generators sat, thumping and shaking, among piles of gas canisters. In a mess of junk he spotted a cord of hemp rope and he cut off a solid two feet of it with his buck knife, opened the tank, dipped one end in like a wick, and slid the other end into the tank.

He lit the end and moved back out to the woods, taking the same path he'd walked before, listening to the men laughing, playing spades, the television blaring loud from another trailer, a man and a woman passed out in a bed that looked like a rat's nest.

Smoke curled and snaked from the barn.

And a few minutes later the barn exploded, emptying the trailers as men ran down to the fire. A couple of them shooting into the flames, as if bullets would stop it.

Quinn watched as Gowrie, shirtless and sweating, worked to fill buckets from the creek.

"I think you got a celebration goin' on," the doctor said, not looking at all excited about the prospect. All that shooting and yelling.

"They always shoot guns and blow shit up," Lena said, the baby suckling at her breast, the doctor telling her how all that worked. "It's not on account of me."

The doctor leaned forward on the bloody bed, head in hands.

"What's the matter?" Lena asked.

"Your boyfriend won't let us leave," Luke said. He had soft green eyes and nice teeth.

"He ain't my boyfriend."

"Where's the child's father?"

"County jail."

"Of course." The doctor nodded and stood, peering outside a dirty window, shaking his head more and pacing. "We got to get you to a hospital."

"I feel fine. Let me sleep. Jesus."

"You're losing a ton of blood, and that son of a bitch out there said I was to attend to you here," the doctor said, sitting down on the mattress and bloodied sheets, feeling for her free wrist and pulse and then holding her hand. "He said he doesn't want the police. I didn't say anything about the police."

"Gowrie hates government."

"No kidding," the doctor said. "He said he'd like nothing more than to blow my fucking brains out."

"You married?" Lena asked, feeling lightheaded, stroking that little pink baby, wanting like hell to leave with this doctor. "You have a nice face. Such a nice face."

"How do you feel?"

"Fine, fine, fine."

"You look white as a sheet."

"I just dropped a child," Lena said, speaking so low she wasn't sure she had spoken at all. "Takes some out of you."

"You have a phone?" the doctor asked. "Gowrie pitched mine in the woods."

She shook her head, smiling at the doc some more and then smiling down at the baby's face, touching its nose and little ears, feeling such a strange damn connection. Lena closed her eyes. "Ain't she pretty?"

"Do you have a phone? Listen to me. Wake up."

"Won't do you no good," Lena said, eyes closed and feeling at peace, smiling big. "Phones don't work in the hills. You can't get no signal. It's like being on the moon. I said that you have a nice face. You heard that?"

Quinn sprinted from the concealment of the woods to the trailer, holding the rifle in his right hand. He made it to the steps, not a shot fired, no one even spotting him. He looked up into the woods to where Boom waited.

He nodded, not seeing his friend but knowing he was there.

Quinn tossed the rifle over his shoulder and grabbed the .45 before he kicked in the front door and checked all corners for movement. A ragged couch and chairs, trash bags and stuffed animals.

No one.

He made his way down the narrow hallway, kicking in another door to find Luke Stevens in a dress shirt spotted in blood. Luke looked up and smiled.

"You hurt?"

Luke shook his head.

"Anna Lee called."

Luke nodded. Quinn didn't expect a thank-you as he opened the door wide to see the girl lying in the bed, more blood around the sheets. She looked to be about twelve, with her hair matted around her white face, holding a child that could be her sister.

Her face and throat had been drained of all color. Her eyes were glass.

Luke cleaned his hands on a towel. "Can you get us out? I got a gun in my face. A goddamn gun."

"Can she be moved?"

"We don't have a choice."

"Come on. Boom's watching our back."

"Quinn?" Luke asked, touching his arm.

Quinn looked at him.

"They won't let us go."

"They got more troubles."

"Where's y'all's truck?"

"A mile down the road," Quinn said. "You hold the baby. I'll carry the girl."

22

"You carried her the whole way?" Lillie asked.

"That girl didn't weigh a hundred pounds without that baby in her," he said. "When you carry a grown-ass man a few klicks, that'll get to you."

"You've done that?"

"Sure."

"With bullets flying?"

"Something like that."

"I had to carry my ex-husband from the barstool to the car many a night."

"I didn't know you were married."

"You never asked."

"Someone I know?"

"Lord, I hope not."

They sat across from each other in the back booth of the Fillin' Station diner. Quinn drank black coffee and smoked a cigar, a nice perk of being in a town where smoking wasn't outlawed. He'd eaten breakfast, still feeling like you should eat when you get a chance, still wearing his hunting camos from a few hours before. Of course everyone else sitting in the Fillin' Station at nine a.m. on a Monday morning was dressed for hunting. An entire family, mother, daddy, and a little boy, dressed in identical camo getups, sat at a table by the front door. You got your hunting in before work or school.

"Why didn't you kill him?" she asked.

"Gowrie's not worth it."

"When we got the call, about what had happened, I figured we'd be cleaning up bodies."

"The situation definitely presented itself."

"I went down with two other deputies this morning. We arrested Gowrie for pulling that gun on Luke."

"He still in jail?"

"He'll be out by noon," she said. "His lawyer got all charges dropped."

"Come again?"

"Luke Stevens seems to have seen things different than you."

Mary, the waitress, came over and filled their cups, asking them if they had had a fine weekend. And both Lillie and Quinn looked up at her and smiled, saying it was pleasant, all things considered. She touched

267

Quinn's shoulder with her weathered hand and squeezed, saying, "We appreciate you."

"Don't you need to sleep?" Lillie asked when Mary walked away.

"I'm not tired."

"You stayed up all night."

Quinn shrugged. "What exactly did Luke say?"

"He didn't remember a gun being pulled on him."

"I saw him," Quinn said. "Gowrie hammered the barrel of a Glock between Luke's eyes to make him pay attention."

"Lawyer got a signed statement from Luke."

"How does a man like Gowrie get a damn lawyer?"

"Anyone with money can get a lawyer. And this guy is high-dollar. Came down from Memphis."

"Johnny Stagg has a high-dollar attorney from Memphis," Quinn said. "What's his name?"

"I think his name is Lamar," Lillie said. "His suit probably cost more than I make in a month."

"Yep."

"He and Stagg have the same lawyer?"

Quinn nodded. He drank some coffee, smoked the cigar, and watched the camo family get up from the table, the father peeling off a few bucks for Mary, and heading back out to the deer stand.

"I'd like to talk to the girl," Quinn said. "She'll have a different story."

"Her name is Lena," she said. "Found out the father of that baby is a boy we have staying at the county bed-and-breakfast. His name's Charley Booth."

"You ask him about Gowrie?"

"He wouldn't say shit if his mouth was full of it."

"What did he do?"

"Possession of meth. Intent to sell."

"You think Lena will go back to their camp?"

Lillie nodded slow, leaning back and resting her arm across the edge of the seat. "I guess that depends on where Booth winds up."

"What's he like?"

"A real prize. Cracker Jack material."

Across the town Square, through the gazebo and around the veterans' memorial, Quinn spotted a group of five men loitering around an old pickup truck with its fat dual exhausts thundering. It was the truck with the back window painted with the face of an evil clown, green hair and bloodshot eyes, death metal screaming on the stereo.

Lillie walked next to Quinn, headed back to her Cherokee, as he watched Gowrie slide around the truck and grab hold of the neck of a skinny boy with jug ears like a brother. He wore a pair of calf-length blue jeans, a chain hanging from his waist, and a baseball cap cocked on his head.

"Charley Booth," Lillie said.

Gowrie hugged the kid and patted his back.

Lillie got into her Cherokee and pulled the seat belt across her and cranked the engine, Quinn tossing his cigar and climbing in before she backed out. She reached over and flipped on the heater, the morning feeling gray and cold, while they slowly made their way around the Square, pulling past Gowrie, sitting on the tailgate of the truck.

"Pride of the South," Lillie said.

"You bet."

"The clown's a nice touch."

Gowrie smiled a rotten black smile at Quinn and waved like they were old buddies. His face was red and wind-chapped, his shaved head covered with a do-rag of the ole Stars and Bars.

"You want to flush the toilet on these turds?" Quinn asked.

"I'll grab the rope."

"You would, wouldn't you?"

"I loved your uncle. I just don't much give a shit anymore."

"About what?"

"The law."

"Justice moves slow, partner," Quinn said.

"How's it move for a Ranger?"

"Like a scalded cat."

"I bet your blood is boiling."

"I want Stagg."

"You talk to Wesley?"

Quinn nodded, Lillie's Jeep trailing off to the north on Main, past the old general store, the Odd Fellows Hall, the Ace Hardware, and a Baptist church. Every other business had been boarded up, FOR SALE signs in their windows or nailed to the plywood over the doors. The gates to the old feed store had been padlocked for some time.

"He chewed my ass out this morning for interviewing Shackelford," Lillie said. "Said Shackelford was a professional snitch and a liar, and I told him that sometimes liars hit a truth every once in a while. He may not be the man to put on the stand, but you got to listen to what he's telling us. Shit."

"We sure could have used Wesley last night."

"He drove over to the compound but didn't see Luke's car," Lillie said. "Without a warrant, there wasn't jack he could do."

"You on duty?"

"Sure," Lillie said, turning the wheel gently, chewing gum, tapping her fingers on the center console. "I stay on duty. Why?"

"Let's go see the girl."

Lena was resting when the men walked in, three men she'd never seen before in her life. One was scrawny and craggy-faced, wearing a blue suit and a bright yellow tie. He looked like a farmer playing dress-up. The other was tanned with graying hair, in a pin-striped suit and red tie. He wore a silver watch bigger than a fist and smelled like money.

The third man nodded to her, showing the glint of a pair of gold teeth. Not dressed up, just wearing shiny khaki pants and a gold shirt with a cross on its breast. The logo read WINNERS FOR JESUS.

"Ma'am," the craggy-faced man said. "I'm Johnny Stagg. This is Mr. Lamar, an officer of the court. And I brought along Brother Davis. Brother Davis is the pastor of the Living Waters Church here in town."

She continued to lie on her side. The man Stagg sat without being asked, the slick lawyer and the pastor standing by the window, looking out into a small garden where she'd been watching cardinals and finches fight over a birdbath all morning. The room smelled fresh and sharp, the linoleum floors scrubbed with piney cleaners.

She noticed all the men breathed very loud but let the silences fill the room.

"What do you want?" she asked.

Lena was spent. She did not try to move from her resting spot. The nurses had brought her a hamburger and some cherry pie, and she'd devoured them.

"We heard y'all had a rough night," Stagg said, smiling, grinning, like an old friend of the family. His teeth were plastic-looking and big as tombstones. "Thank God, you and this fine-looking baby pulled through."

Lena just stared at him.

"We just wanted to make sure you don't hold Mr. Gowrie responsible for your health issues," the slick lawyer said.

"He tried to make me stay," Lena said. "If I hadn't gotten help, I might've died."

"He was doing what was best," Stagg said.

Lena felt a shadow over her and looked up at the face of the slick attorney. He gave her a reassuring smile and said, "Have you spoken to the police?"

"No."

"Do you intend to?" the attorney asked. The crystal on his big watch cast the light in her eyes and made her squint for a moment.

"What do y'all want from me?"

"Are you going to call the police on Mr. Gowrie?"

"No. I mean, shit. I don't know," Lena said. "My baby is coming back soon. I have to feed her."

"This is a morning of miracles," Brother Davis said, folding his hands together. "Can we all pray for a moment?"

"The doctor said I would've died if I'd stayed."

"Dr. Stevens said everyone was feeling great stress during the birth," Lamar said. "Is that correct?"

Lena just stared at him, the lawyer standing over her, rocking up on his shoes and smiling down at her.

"Mr. Lamar has prepared a statement," Stagg said. "We'd like you to look it over and sign it. It makes sure you don't hold anything against Mr. Gowrie."

"What's in it for me?"

Lamar looked over to Stagg and grinned. Stagg nodded to Brother Davis.

The preacher with the gold teeth sat down

at the end of Lena's bed and smiled at her, looking content and confused at the same time. He reached over to her finished plate and ran a finger through the last bit of whipped cream and licked it. "We got a special fund for women in your sit-ation. Money and such that can buy clothes, get a baby the right kind of nutrition."

Lena rolled to her back and tried to find the controls to raise the bed.

"That's all you got?" Lena asked.

"She sure is a pretty thing," Brother Davis said. "I just been watchin' her down in the nursery. Got to hold her. So little, and cute as a bug."

Lena tried to get out of the bed, but as she tried to stand her feet disappeared from under her. She fell right onto Stagg's lap, and his bony hands helped her get some balance and sit back down. He held her hand and rubbed it. "You're not in the right mind. Givin' birth is hard on a woman."

Lena pulled back her foot and kicked as hard as she could, knocking Brother Davis to the floor. "Y'all get the fuck out of here. And if you step back into this room or go near my baby again, I swear to God I'll kill you."

"Now, that's a pretty picture," Quinn said,

watching the exit to the hospital from the passenger seat of Lillie's Jeep.

"I never doubted Johnny was a shitbag," Lillie said, "but to show up at the hospital."

"They're leaning on the girl," Quinn said, remaining quiet for a long while. "Why would Stagg be such a friend to Gowrie? What's in it for him?"

"Money."

"He doesn't need money."

"You want to bet?"

"I thought Johnny was moving up in the world."

"He was."

"And?"

"He got into some development project that screwed him."

"How'd that go?"

"I don't know much about it," Lillie said. "I know he got the whole town fired up that all this business was headed our way."

"What happened?"

"Stagg says it's still in the works. All I know is, the site's still empty, and no big companies are knocking on the door of Tibbehah County."

"Who'd know more about it?"

"The old woman," Lillie said. "You remember Miz Mize?"

23

For as long as Quinn could recall, Betty Jo Mize had been the owner, publisher, managing editor, and lead reporter for the *Tibbehah County Monitor.* The thin paper was published twice a week, her standard column taking up most of the front page, and, when she was truly moved, the text flowed inside, next to the advertisements for specials at the Piggly Wiggly, church notes, and legal announcements. She was the master of the prayer chain, the potluck supper menu, the special Christmas memory, and endless tales of when Jericho had been a prosperous town. Quinn had made her column dozens of times, Betty Jo still calling him Jason and Jean Colson's boy, although his parents had been divorced for more than fifteen years.

She was small and frail and white-haired, standing a few inches over five feet, and had been rumored to have been on death's door since 1986. She often credited her faith in Jesus and the prayers of the community for her good fortune. She was a regular at the First Baptist Church, a member of every women's club in Tibbehah and its two adjoining counties, a great-grandmother, an avid gardener, and a vicious gossip with a taste for Jack Daniel's, cigarettes, and filthy jokes.

Quinn liked her a lot.

"I'm glad you didn't go and get yourself killed, Quinn."

"I appreciate that, Miz Mize."

"Have you seen your daddy lately?"

"No, ma'am. It's been years."

"That's right," she said. "He was a good-looking man."

"Yes, ma'am."

Quinn nodded. Out through the painted window advertising THE MONITOR, he saw two boarded-up storefronts side by side, the old sporting goods store, now a check-cashing business advertising EARLY PAYDAY LOANS.

"Quinn, you do realize there are three kinds of sex?"

"No, ma'am."

"A man your age needs to understand that. First there is house sex."

"Sure."

"See, when you first take a wife, you have sex all over the house."

"I bet."

"And then comes the bedroom sex. You and your wife only have sex with the lights off and under the covers."

"Yes, ma'am."

"And then comes hall sex."

He nodded, waiting.

"That's when you pass each other in the hall and say, 'Fuck you.' "

Quinn smiled. Betty Jo leaned back into her desk chair, surrounded by all kinds of Mississippi newspaper awards, framed columns, pictures of kids, grandkids, and great-grandkids. There was an entire collection of ceramic figurines of children praying, lots of dead plants and coffee mugs, two proclaiming her THE WORLD'S GREATEST.

She grabbed both of them and walked behind her desk, pouring coffee. "Your mother has a new man."

"I know."

"You want to know about him?"

"Not really."

"He's okay, Quinn. Really. He's been married twice, isn't too bright, but what the hell."

"I'm sure he's a good man."

Betty Jo sat back down and passed a coffee mug to Quinn, lighting a cigarette with a small gold lighter. "I heard you've been spotted around on leave with Lillie Virgil."

"Yes, ma'am."

"I like her."

Quinn was quiet. Betty Jo smoked and winked at him.

"You hear about the Italian couple on honeymoon?"

"Is this the one where the bride's name is Virginia?"

"Shit," Betty Jo said.

Quinn smiled and leaned forward in his seat, noticing the old paneled walls and hard fluorescent light, lots of dust and old knickknacks, stacks and stacks of newspapers. The room smelled of coffee and nicotine. "I want to know about Johnny Stagg."

"Good Lord, Quinn. I just ate lunch."

"You know anything about him doing business with a man named Gowrie?"

"I know who you're talking about. That trash got himself arrested this morning for pulling a gun on Dr. Stevens."

Quinn nodded.

"You know much about Gowrie?"

"He showed up a couple years ago. Inherited some land or bought some land, I'm not really sure. But he's not from here, and if it was inherited, it was from some kind of distant relation."

"You know about the drugs?"

"Of course. Everyone in town knows that."

"You write about it?"

"He hasn't been arrested until this morning. I can't print rumors."

"And now he's out."

"You're kidding me."

"Luke wouldn't press charges."

"Why's that?"

"I hope to find out."

"That doesn't make a damn bit of sense."

"Are they friends?"

"Stagg's on the hospital board."

"Why would anyone allow that?"

"He's promised to build something bigger and a lot better." Betty Jo looked at Quinn like he was a little slow. "He already got a certificate to build from the state. You can't have a new hospital without that. Quinn, you never heard of the Tibbehah Miracle?"

"Lillie told me some."

"He put together an industrial-complex deal that supposedly would've saved this county. Part of the deal was a school and a regional hospital."

"What happened?"

"They cleared the McKibben land, put

up the signs, and nothing is coming up but weeds."

"Bankrupt?"

"Johnny says everything is still going to plan. Just spoke in front of the county supervisors last week."

"Who's backing him?"

"You figure that out and let me know."

Charley Booth came to Lena at the hospital with a bouquet of daisies and dressed in a fresh white T-shirt and black jeans. His hair had been slicked back, and he walked up to her, Lena holding the baby, and gave that same semisweet smile he'd given her when they'd first met. "May I hold him?"

"Her."

"May I hold the baby?"

And Lena didn't see no harm in it. After all, the baby — she had not decided on a name yet — was half Charley Booth's. He'd gone to full-time Charley Booth now, and that was good since there would be paperwork and things to fill out, that big black nurse already pestering her. Lena was thinking of something that would bestow some kind of dignity on the tiny girl. She was a tiny girl but needed a big name.

"What you gonna call her?"

"I hadn't set on anything," she said.

"How about Wanda?"

"That's a terrible name."

"That's my momma's name."

He stroked the little girl's face and looked up into Lena's eyes and said, "We gonna be a family."

"You told me to go to hell when you was in jail."

"I ain't in jail now."

"I don't see how that changes anything."

"We're getting out of here."

Lena didn't say anything, her damn breath had caught in her throat, and she turned to look out the window, searching for the birds in that dirty water. She didn't want Charley Booth seeing she was about to cry. But son of a bitch, it was comin' on.

"How long till they turn you loose?" Booth asked. She saw where he'd nicked his slim, slight chin while shaving off that peach fuzz.

"This isn't jail. It's a hospital."

"When are you gonna get well?"

"I'm not sick."

"This isn't how I thought things would be," Charley said. "You got to believe in that."

"Let's take a walk," Lena said, propping herself up from the pillows, finding her feet on the floor. "My ass hurts something terrible."

They found the hallways bare and open and wandered down one end to another, this hospital nothing like the places she'd seen on soap operas. She looked the big black nurse in the eye, this time nodding a hello because she had the father with her and wasn't just a no-account girl with no damn sense or plan on bringing a child into this world. Charley nodded, too.

He carried the baby, and they all made their way down to the vending machines. He punched up a couple Coca-Colas and some Little Debbie snack cakes. "Can she have one of these?"

"Do you have a lick of sense?"

They sat down in that small, silent room with no windows, just a narrow door. It smelled like burnt coffee and sugar. Someone had left a Bible and a Danielle Steel novel on the table, and Lena thumbed through both of them, searching for a name for the baby, thinking maybe the books had been there for a reason. Her whole life felt like it was coming together.

"How about Raphaella?" she asked.

"A what?"

"For her name?"

"That doesn't sound like a Christian

name," Charley said.

"Says here that it's a name of Mediterranean aristocracy."

"I don't like it."

"Or we could call her Ruth. That's right here in the Bible."

He opened the snack cakes and pulled out one for himself and pushed the package toward her, biting off half and chewing while he rocked the little baby, touching her little nose with the edge of his finger.

"I want to take you down to Florida with me."

"You got money?"

"I will have money," he said, dropping his head into his hand. "Reason I treated you like that was to push you away. I know you could do better."

"We're already in this thing."

"I got money coming," he said. "Can you hold tight for a couple days?"

"I don't have no money," she said. "I don't have no insurance. I get one more day here."

"You stay with me."

"Back at Gowrie's?"

"I got my own trailer," he said. "I can't leave without my money. Then we go to Florida. I already got it all planned out in my mind."

"What's in Florida?"

Charley Booth smiled, sticking the rest of the snack cake in his mouth and chewing in deep thought. "I've always wanted to open up an ice-cream stand."

Lillie drove Quinn out to the old McKibben place, a thousand-acre parcel that had been the envy of everyone in the county. Original hardwoods and big thick pine trees, three creeks that had sprung off the Big Black River and ran through the land adjoining a National Forest. The McKibbens had kept it in their family since after the Civil War, the southern edge of the property the site of a cemetery where hundreds of soldiers who had died after coming to the hospital in Jericho were buried. Quinn had hunted the land many times with Judge Blanton and his uncle, even his father on occasion. An invitation out to the land was an entry into the old times of deer camps and the wild woods where Mississippi ran thick with panthers and black bears. Before Quinn had shipped out, he'd walked the northern edge of the property and found an arrowhead, maybe a thousand years old, and had carried it with him as a good-luck talisman from one warrior to another.

The old creek bed where he'd found it

was strong and slow, moving over the pebbled bottom in a place that remained cool even in the hottest month, deep patches of moss on rocks.

And now he and Lillie stood maybe a half mile from that place, and it seemed as if Quinn had entered a moonscape. Most of the thousand acres had been cleared down to the earth, gravel roads had been laid down and foundations poured for the Tibbehah Miracle that had never arrived. Johnny Stagg's dream of a sprawling development to bring industry and commerce to back-woods Mississippi. All through the open gashes in the earth were scorched burn piles, logs as big as trucks that had refused to burn, charred and left to rot.

"They stopped work about this time last year," Lillie said, the cold wind whipping her hair into her mouth. "Stagg keeps on saying this is going to happen, but no one has heard of one company coming here."

"Now he's hooked in with some bad folks in Memphis."

"How bad?"

"I followed Gowrie's daddy up to Memphis last night to a strip club. He was making some kind of deal."

"Maybe Gowrie's daddy just likes to check out naked girls."

"And gets invited into a back room with a fat satchel?"

"Was it that obvious?"

"I don't think Daddy Gowrie can spell subtle," Quinn said. "Did I mention Stagg's personal preacher, Brother Davis, was with Daddy Gowrie?"

The wind shot like a bullet across the cleared land and stung his ears and face. Quinn placed his hands into his pockets and turned all around him, a stranger in a place that had once been so damn familiar.

"We had a run-in with Gowrie and his daddy back in April," Lillie said. "Gowrie'd beaten a man at the Southern Star pretty bad. He bit a damn plug out of the man's throat. He claimed self-defense."

"Why didn't my uncle run him out?"

"We're not the DEA, Quinn," she said. "Your uncle wanted us to do the best we could. But he was hoping to get some state people in here soon. He knew what was going on and knew Gowrie ran most of the labs."

"And then came that fire."

"Wesley brought back two graduation photos of Jill Bullard," Lillie said. "Somebody used that girl all up."

"She and Caddy were friends."

"How?"

He told her about Memphis, and they didn't speak for a long while, Quinn hearing his boots on the turned soil. Some battered earthmovers sat still up by a massive footprint of concrete.

Quinn headed back to the Jeep, Lillie in tow.

"Do you remember that time that you and Wesley threw that keg party out here? You must've had two hundred folks."

"Charged five dollars per head."

"That was a good party. We had a bonfire, and that old black man played the guitar. Who was he again? That was fun."

"Till those deputies like you showed up and ruined it."

"How long did they chase you?"

"A couple hours."

"But you lost 'em?"

"Didn't take much."

"Your uncle knew."

"Oh, hell yes. He knew it was me. But couldn't prove shit."

"Did that bother you?"

"Should it have?"

24

"He's hunting, Quinn, I don't know when he's coming home," Anna Lee said, standing on her porch with her arms folded across her chest. Her door was open, and a big-screen television hung on the wall playing Fox News, a woman making inane conversation about several more servicemen killed in Kandahar. The room was furnished with a big brown leather couch and heavy wood furniture and gold lamps. "I'll have Luke call you when he gets in."

She tried to close the door. Quinn wedged his boot in the jamb.

She wore a thin T-shirt and jeans, no makeup. She smelled of soap and shampoo.

"He say why he dropped charges on those men?"

She shook her head, and looked down at his boot and then up at Quinn. She stared at him for a long time, chewing on her lip. "I don't know."

"I'd be a little pissed if someone hammered a gun into my forehead."

"Wesley said it's resolved. Okay? Do you mind?"

She pushed at the door.

"Okay. This is where it's getting a little confusing to me," Quinn said, pulling his foot back and smiling. "You show up at my uncle's farm last night, worried out of your mind. You basically beg me to go over to that peckerwood compound, blaming me if anything happened to Luke. Does this picture ring true?"

She held her arms around her waist, thin T-shirt blowing in the cold, her skin looking pale in the fading light. He could hear the buzzer going off on the stove. "I got to go," she said. "Shit's burning."

"You tell Luke that if he's a stand-up guy, he'll file those charges. Those shitbags might have killed us all last night."

"He'll do what's best."

"I bet."

"Luke is the most stand-up man I've ever met," she said, jaw clenching. "I don't have time for this. It's cold and I'm not wearing shoes."

He touched her shoulder. "Since when does Luke work with Johnny Stagg?"

"You've lost your mind."

"Stagg serves on his board."

"Stagg serves on the board for the electric company, too. He's a county supervisor. That's just what he does. Damn it. Let me go."

"Stagg just called in a big favor for getting that hospital certificate."

"You'll have to talk to Luke about that instead of bullying me."

"People wonder why I left this place."

"I sure as hell don't," Anna Lee said, slamming the front door.

The glass rattled, and a pine wreath fell to the ground. There was a lot of garland on the porch, strung in with Christmas lights and magnolia leaves, plastic shaped like flowers. Quinn recalled the old Victorian as being a ghost house when he was a kid, a big vacant shell where you'd step up and throw rocks at the window or sneak girls inside to slip a little to drink or smoke dope and make out.

Quinn stepped up to the glass door to knock.

But he dropped his hand, changing his mind.

There was a small playground across from the Baptist church where Quinn sat with his mother, watching Jason navigate a small fort, a couple slides, and a climbing wall. Up and down, back and forth, jumping and scrambling. Falling and rolling. He always got back up on his feet and cried only once, and only then because one of the swings had been wrapped high above him and he couldn't reach it. Quinn got to his feet and unraveled it for him, Jason jumping into the seat and holding on to the chains.

"You eat lunch?" his mother asked.

Quinn shook his head.

"We could drop by the Sonic. How about a burger and a milk shake?"

Quinn felt for the cell phone in his pocket, checked the number, and saw it was Anna Lee. He turned off the ringer.

"They could call you back anytime," she said. "Right?"

He nodded.

"Did you go over this year?"

"Just for a couple weeks."

"It's not the time. It's what y'all were up to."

"It was boring, just some recon stuff."

His mother nodded, not believing him, and walked over to the fort, waiting for Jason to navigate the steep edge. Jason found a way out from the bar, teetered around the top, held on to the handrail, and then for some reason — Quinn hoped it was that Jason knew that his grandmother was under him — he just let go with a high-pitched laugh and fell into her arms. She let him go, and he ran over to a metal elephant that had been set on a heavy-duty spring, about breaking it as he rocked back and forth.

"Thursday?"

"They gave me a week," Quinn said. "That was generous."

"The U.S. Army can stand to do without you for a week."

"Just how long has Anna Lee been coming over, helping with Jason and all that?"

"I can get someone else. There's a little girl at church who's sweet and pretty reasonable."

"So you're full-time now. With Jason."

"It's temporary."

"You sure?"

"Caddy is looking for work in Memphis, staying with a friend, trying to get into a stable situation. She said she's looking for good schools right now. She's made a real change, Quinn."

Quinn took a breath. He folded his hands in his lap, rubbing them together, placing them back into his jacket pockets. "Shit, it's cold."

"Does it bother you?" she asked.

"Caddy can do what she likes."

"I mean, about Anna Lee?"

"I won't lie," Quinn said. "Ever since I got back, Anna Lee has acted like I've wronged her. I guess we remember events in different ways."

His mother didn't say anything.

"And I don't want to hear a word about how she was trying not to get hurt," he said. "You know how many boys in my unit get the same shitty letters? All that broken-hearted BS looks like it's written by the same person. I just wish one girl would own up that she was tired of her boyfriend being away and wanted to screw around."

"You believe that?"

"Are we gonna go to Sonic or what?"

"We can go to the Sonic."

"You mind if I ask you something?"

His mother waited.

"All those times Dad left, headed out to wherever he went, did you get mad?"

"He had to make money."

"Even though he wasn't always on a job."

"Quinn, I love you," she said. "But don't try and rope me into your dilemma."

"Can you do me a favor before I leave?" Quinn asked.

"Anything."

"All right." Quinn smiled, put his hand on her back. "How 'bout we take Jason to say good-bye to his great-uncle."

Jean Colson just shook her head.

So they stood there, looking down at the ground. Jason had wandered off one row over to pet a stone bunny that had been placed over a grave. The cemetery was big and flat and treeless, reminding Quinn of something that a farmer would design, not landscaped, only long, even rows of headstones waiting for the final reaping. The stone for his uncle had his name and birth and death, underscoring he was a Christian. Nothing about his military service, or that he'd been sheriff. On the mound of dirt, dead and dying flowers lay in the cold. A big wreath shaped like a gun had been sent by the Mississippi Law Enforcement Association.

"That's not in good taste," Quinn said.

"What happened wasn't for public knowledge."

"So, you want to say a few words?" Quinn asked.

She shook her head.

"It would mean a lot."

"I don't know."

"Might make you feel better."

She nodded and closed her eyes. She inhaled for a moment before she began.

"Okay . . . You were a good brother when you acted right," she said. "You could be fair but not always. Some folks might have said you were pigheaded and stupid, and I think that did play a role in this final stupid act you've left us with. But who am I to judge? I don't judge you, Hamp. I'm your sister. I guess you can't hold a dead man accountable to things that have been said. But he's here with me and part of this family, and even to this day I want to kick over this headstone for you ever calling that boy a" — she was whispering now — "a damn mistake. Only mistake I know is self-pity."

His mother kept her mouth open, breathing, like she was about to add a little more, but then she took a step back and simply said, "Amen."

"Amen," Quinn said.

The wind across the treeless graves seemed even colder, light fading down even at four p.m., Quinn recalling how damn desolate this county could be during the wintertime and then how green and alive it could be during planting season. He reached for a yellowed rose from the flower gun and set it at the base of the headstone.

"Is that it?" his mother asked.

He nodded.

Quinn's cell phone continued to buzz in

his coat pocket. He reached to switch it back off but saw it was Lillie. He answered it as his mother went to scoop up Jason, both of them still at the grave site.

"Where are you?" Lillie asked.

"A little family time."

"Can you get over to your uncle's place?"

"Sure. Can it wait?"

"There's been some trouble. You need to get out here right now."

25

Quinn drove over the Sarter Creek bridge and stopped his truck with a skid on the gravel drive, running for the burning barn caught up in flames and smoke. A big shed had gone up, too, but the fire had already ripped through it, and all that was left was a heap of crackling and snapping wood. Lillie met him on the hill and said she'd called the fire department, volunteers arriving in spurts, spilling from pickup trucks and old cars. The red engine was the last vehicle to arrive, and got stuck twice in the mud before getting close enough to get a decent shot at the barn that now was pretty much ruined and leaning because of the destroyed beams.

He called for Hondo but couldn't find the dog.

A young boy, maybe twelve, ran up to Quinn. He was barefoot, even in the cold, and as soon as he began to speak it was easy to tell he was somewhat mentally deficient. He asked Quinn about all those dead cows.

"There weren't any animals in that barn," Quinn said. The heat was tremendous across his face, and ash blew over them in a steady wave of wind.

The boy shook his head and pointed to the muddy pasture, where a half-dozen cows lay on their sides, the blood clearly visible across their flanks.

Quinn walked toward the animals, the barn behind him, the cars and trucks and commotion, men smoking cigarettes and calling home on cell phones. A hell of a banner day for Tibbehah Station No. 8. One of the firemen joked to another: "Anyone want to grill up some T-bones?"

The cattle had been raked with automatic weapons, looked to him like small caliber, probably .223 assault rifles. There were more dead animals down in the creek, two calves dead in shallow water running with blood, and a momma cow that lay on her back in a sandy creek bed, probably toppling over while trying to get away, mouthing for air like a beached fish. He heard more cries from cattle along the edge of the creek.

Quinn walked back toward the house through the heavy black smoke in the air, wondering why they'd spared the house, but then he spotted the long black charred marks across the east side. A fire had been started but didn't take. They'd only been able to bust out a couple windows.

He found the Browning .308 in the back of his truck and loaded it with bullets, followed the broken path and skittered down the muddy bank to the dying cow. He took a breath, and the rifle recoiled in his hands.

He walked to another, reloading, and did the same.

A third, and then there was an electric silence in his ears.

Again he yelled and whistled for Hondo.

As he crossed the road and entered the drive, a blue sedan pulled up behind Quinn's truck and killed its engine. County fire marshal Chuck Tuttle stood up out of the car, a leather jacket over his shirt and tie, a toothpick hanging out of his mouth, picking the last bits of a leisurely meal before getting down to work.

He shook his head sadly when he saw Quinn and offered his hand.

Quinn just stared at him, his right hand hanging at his side.

"Everybody all right?" Tuttle said, again shaking a hangdog head.

"I must've left the skillet on too long,"

Quinn said.

"Come back?" Tuttle said, a confused smile on his lips.

"Looks like a grease fire to me."

"You trying to burn down them old barns?"

Quinn didn't say anything.

"All right," Tuttle said. "Let me take a look. Some teenagers probably thought this place was abandoned."

"How much?" Quinn asked. Tuttle turned to walk down to the barn.

Chuck Tuttle pulled the toothpick from his mouth and spat.

"I sure as shit hope Johnny Stagg made it worth your while," Quinn said. "I wonder how those kids felt as they were being burned alive."

Quinn felt a gentle hand on his shoulder and found Wesley looking down and smiling at him.

Tuttle kept walking down the hill. Wesley blew out a long breath and took in the whole scene, slipping off his baseball cap in some kind of reverence. "Holy shit."

"Tuttle said it was some kids."

"I saw the cows. This wasn't no kids."

"You believe Shackelford now?"

"I never argued there weren't some evil people living among us," Wesley said, placing his cap back on his head, hands on his hips. "I just didn't see any conspiracy in what happened. Look at Gowrie, look at what he did here. You see that shit from a mile away."

"You see Hondo?"

"Shit."

"He's not down with the cattle."

"I'll drive up the road into the hills," Wesley said, nodding. "You want to ride with me?"

"Nope."

"Quinn, I know what's on your mind."

"I'll wait."

"Come on with me. Let's go find that dog. You can't do nothin' here."

"I want to stay."

Wesley nodded and patted his arm again, crawling into the sheriff's truck and driving slow up the gravel road into the hills, looking for that lost dog.

Quinn walked back to his truck, slammed the door, and accelerated in a slew of gravel and dirt in the opposite direction toward the main road back to town. The smell of charred wood and smoke bringing back thoughts of a firefight on top of a snow-capped mountain a few years back. A seventeen-hour gun battle over rocks and in caves, five soldiers dead.

The Army lost track of enemy dead after three hundred.

Charley insisted on it. *Absolutely insisted on it.*

The baby, still with no name, had to come, too, he said. He wouldn't have a child that wasn't raised in a proper church. And Lena made the point that any church that made its home in an old movie theater wasn't a real church at all. Charley got all solemn about it, thinking — as if the dummy could think — and told her that churches were built with lives and souls. How in the hell can you argue with a load of crap like that? The marquee was still advertising BIG MOMMA'S HOUSE 2.

Of course Lena had been raised in the church, knew the liars and the creeps, the fools who fell out on Sunday, rolling in the aisles, while the big-toothed preacher passed around the collection plate. She knew the old men who carried weathered Bibles and hugged you a little too close when you turned thirteen and wore a little bra. But Charley had said something about them all getting fed, and since they'd left the hospital that morning, having to sneak out a back door on account of Charley saying he couldn't deal with the government, she hadn't had much besides a hamburger and a cold Coke from the Shell station.

She'd slept thirty minutes in the back of a broke-down van.

For the last hour she hadn't been paying much attention to the sermon, maybe on account of the preacher being Brother Davis and her having used profanity with him and all earlier, but then he started repeating and repeating that he was a worthless soul and a nobody and a fool, and that got her attention — Lena thinking he'd learned something — until she realized he was speaking as Moses.

Brother Davis wore a suit that looked as if it had come off a corpse — the kind you see your grandpa renting before they plant him. It was dark brown, and he'd matched it with a stiff brown tie with a deer head painted on it.

"Moses said to God, 'Do you know my name? I ain't nobody,'" Brother Davis said, seeming upset by it, shaking his head, making you know that he often felt like nobody, too. Everyone did. "You see, dear friends, Moses didn't think he was special. He wasn't no household name among the Israelites. He was even a wanted man in the pharaoh's country."

Lena turned to study Charley's profile,

the dummy nodding with great understanding as the preacher continued. "He had wanted posters throughout Egypt. 'Wanted Dead or Alive!' And Moses said to God again: 'I know you ain't talkin' about me.' And then God says to Moses . . . Say it with me, folks: 'I am that I am!' "

The forty or so creatures in the movie theater repeated it back, their words echoing off the walls and down the long sloping floor, where you could still see the candy and bubble-gum stains. Lena rocked her baby, watching its pale blue eyes wander blindly across her face. Lena thought maybe she could pray for some kind of miracle to get out of this world and back home. She said a little prayer.

"God said, 'I send you,' " Brother Davis said. "You thought when you faced that ole Pharaoh and them Israelites that you are alone. But I'm asking you to use the name that is above all things. Y'all know what I mean."

Brother Davis prowled back and forth from his Hollywood pulpit.

"How do I face financial struggle, the physical struggle, the demons in my body? You are strong in His name. In His name. Because everything is His name. His name is above cancer. Above struggle. Poverty. Affliction. His name is above everything. His name! PRAISE HIM!"

Two rows back a man started to scream: *"Shana-meana. Honi-aname. Shana-meana Homa-aname."*

"Jesus Christ," Lena leaned over to Charley and whispered. "They gonna start that business? We won't be out of here till midnight."

"Shush. Hadn't you ever heard an unbridled soul speak?"

Lena whispered again to Charley, this time saying she had to pee pee, and he looked real aggravated as he stood to let her and the baby out, not even offering to help her a little bit, everyone too concentrated on Brother Davis, lost and wandering, picking manna from the air, proud as hell of that cordless microphone, where he could leap off the stage and touch folks' hands like he was a damn Kenny Chesney. Gowrie and his daddy sat in the last row, not even bothering to dress for the night service. Gowrie had on an old Army coat, the hair on his face about the same stubbled length as that on his head. His daddy wore a ragged T-shirt that read HAULIN' ASS, with a girl wearing a thong riding a motorcycle.

Gowrie winked at her and reached out to touch the baby — some kind of gesture of forgiveness — as she turned and gave him her backside, shouldering the door and heading into the lobby.

A card table had been set up with free Bibles with plastic covers and tons of pamphlets on the End Times, and those comic books you see in gas-station bathrooms about men humping each other or drinking bottles marked with xxx, as if liquor came like that anymore.

She sat in a hard plastic seat and leafed through them as she pulled up her sweater and set the baby to her breast, the baby finding her nipple as easy as you please. Lena saw one comic where Jesus appeared at a bar and the man was too drunk to even realize there was a man with long hair and a beard — wearing a robe and sandals, no less — trying to chat him up.

"How old is she?" asked the woman behind the card table, knowing the baby was a girl on account of the pink blanket.

"One day."

"She sure is hungry."

Lena rocked her in that hard school seat.

"Y'all should be alone," the woman said.

Lena heard someone strumming an electric guitar, and the drum machine kicked in, an off-key voice singing some Christian rock.

"I would like that."

She led Lena down a long hallway and back behind what would've been the screen of the old theater. The noise was muffled by a big concrete wall, and she could sit there without men coming in and craning their heads to look at her young titties. She closed her eyes, falling asleep for a long while, not dreaming but dead asleep, then breaking awake and back, feeling the baby suckle on her, her body feeling hollow and bled out and spent. Hands shaky and hungry, wishing that son of a bitch onstage would get done with what he had to say so they could get to that food she'd been promised. Brother Davis's words sounded as if they were coming from the bottom of the sea or an old worn-out videotape:

"They will see the bloodstained path that was in my death in my resurrection.

"When you say you can't or shouldn't, know that I have gone before you. I have prepared the way. And know I am working through you. Hallelujah!"

"Hallelujah," Lena said, very small, snuggling her baby. "Get done, you asshole preacher."

She rocked the child among the stage props that had been made by children, castles and dragons and sheep and robes.

She fell asleep again to the pounding of words and a wave of nonsensical stuttering going over the people like water. She stood and walked in the dim light, running her hands over the piles of plastic swords and fake trees, looking for a way out.

Against the back wall was another card table, two of them pushed together, lined with piles of guns and fat bundles of cash.

Holy shit. Cash.

For a moment Lena felt like a spell had come over her, and she stepped toward the table, reaching for the pile of money, smiling, feeling like it might actually be a real thing — a holy prayer answered! — when the door slammed open and two of Gowrie's boys rolled through it, full of piss and beer, pushing at her and asking her what in God's name did she think she was doing by breaking in back here?

"I had to feed my baby, you morons."

"You can't be back here," one of them said, indistinguishable from the other, with their tattoos and bald heads and black T-shirts. "No way. Come on."

They led her back to the sanctuary and sat her down, her legs feeling like they'd given out. The baby began to cry, and Lena moved her onto a soft shoulder to pat. The movie theater seemed like a bus station or purgatory, and if this whole thing didn't end soon she'd just walk clean out the door, Charley Booth in tow or not.

"God said, 'Moses, they may not like you, never like you, talk about you, gossip about you. But they will never be able to deny I am not with you.' And guess what they did? They lied about Moses, talked behind his back, even wanted to put him to death. But them ole Israelites could never deny he had been led by God's hand. They could not deny it."

There was a strong hand on Lena's shoulder, and she craned her neck to see Gowrie standing over her, a fat shadow, saying, *Amen. Amen. Amen.* He smelled like sulfur and smoke. His hands had been stained as black as tar.

Brother Davis moved on down the center aisle, people touching him, his stupid grin showing his golden teeth. "Moses says, 'God, I *ssss*-stutter. How can I *s*-speak through the Majestic One — how can You use one that cain't talk plain?' My friends, I am not an eloquent man, either. Hell, I don't even really know the word . . . I wasn't eloquent then and do not know, even if I'd had an encounter with the bush, if I'd be any different. We all have to deal with them issues. The Lord God doesn't want a perfect life. But y'all can relate to someone who has walked through the valley of the shadow of death and come out smelling like a rose.

"God says that's okay," Brother Davis said. "I need a leader."

Davis was on them now, laying his hand upon Gowrie. Gowrie closed his eyes.

"You may see a rod turned to a snake and a snake turned to a rod," Brother Davis said. "But who among us is not afraid to reach out and touch it? Do not have fear, my friends."

The people said, "Amen."

"Who in the hell goes to church on a Tuesday night?" Quinn asked.

"These folks have had church about every night since they took over the movie house," Boom said. "It's what they do."

"I wish it was still a movie house."

"You okay?"

"I'm fine."

"You look worn out."

Quinn shrugged.

They sat in Quinn's truck across the town Square, watching the men and women file out of the theater and climb into their cars and trucks, heading back to their compound. He saw Gowrie and Brother Davis. Lena walked with her child and a skinny boy with jug ears that Quinn believed to be the child's father.

"So what's up?" Boom asked.

"I got a little tour of the county the other night with a guy who used to work for Gowrie."

"The same one that was blown up?"

"Yep."

"And what'd we learn?"

"I got a pretty solid feel for Gowrie's whole operation here," Quinn said. "He cooks at a half-dozen trailers spread throughout the county."

"And you're thinking that we might want to shut 'em down."

"You think I should leave it alone?"

"Did I say that?"

"You don't need to be a part of this."

"You're forgetting one thing, man."

"What's that?"

"What you got in mind sounds like a hell of a lot of fun."

"You think?"

"Oh, hell yes," Boom said, smiling, half-light shadowing his face. "Let's kick that hatin' bastard square in the nuts."

Quinn smiled, cranked the old Ford, and knocked it into gear.

26

Five of the six went a little something like this:

Quinn would kick in the front door of the trailer. Boom would enter with that big-ass Colt .44 Anaconda and blast a hole in the wall if a man faced him. Another man might run from a back room, and Quinn would shoot at him with his .45, force him to drop his weapon, knowing if anyone came out with a gun pointed at him he'd have to neutralize him. Quinn was prepared to do it, had hoped that someone would come for him like that, wanting it. But instead they found most of these men and women napping, watching television, and one couple was having sex when they snuck up on their trailer.

The most they found at one trailer was three people. The third had been a child, not even eight. They didn't bind those folks. Quinn just held the man and woman, as

Boom holstered the .44 in his thick belt and dragged out their cook pots and boxes of Sudafed, fertilizer, and assorted crap.

The little girl watched the whole thing half asleep, and cocked her head at one point, looking at Boom, and said, "Where's your arm?"

He bent down and smiled at her. "I guess I forgot to put it on."

The little girl, dressed in pink pajamas, grinned at him. "You shouldn't do that."

At the other trailers, folks were kicked to the floor and bound at the wrists with thick plastic binders Quinn had brought. There had been a scuffle with one skinny man, but Quinn had twisted his arm behind his back until a joint cracked and kicked him in the head. The man got real still after that and rolled over like a good dog, holding up his wrists, guessing they were cops.

Quinn and Boom never said any different. They didn't cover their faces. Quinn wanted them to see him. What would they report? Two men had broken into their trailers, robbed them of their meth stash, and took their cook pots and chemicals, guns and knives?

Rangers trained every day they weren't on a mission. At Fort Benning, Quinn would send his platoon into the shoot houses —

often with other soldiers sitting in chairs and tables — and they'd have to shoot all around any friendlies, dropping bad-guy targets, live ammo flying around them. You kicked in doors, you broke windows. You hit them hard and fast, and often no one could react in time. It was all the element of surprise, that damn fist knocking you in the gut before you could find your pants.

He missed the flash bangs and his Remington pump. But, what the hell. He could've cleared these rooms with a butter knife.

It was only at the last house that someone fired a gun at Boom, a fat kid with a shaved head sitting in a La-Z-Boy, smoking dope and holding a .38 straight at the one-armed black giant before him.

Quinn shot the hand with the weapon, the fat, bare-chested baby falling to the floor, searching for a lost thumb, blood across the white leather of his couch.

"Oh, shit," Boom said, laughing.

They threw the boy a towel. The last time he'd seen the fat man, he'd been in the back of an empty cattle trailer, cocky and proud, as Quinn had just tossed them from his land.

"You tell Gowrie something?" Quinn said.

The boy's face had turned gray. But he

looked at Quinn and nodded, the dish towel soaked in blood, as he rocked back and forth, trying to find some kind of end to the pain and shock. He was crying and calling Boom a "no-'count nigger."

"Tell him I'm waiting for him."

"Shit," the boy said, almost screaming. "You think he's goin' for that? Y'all are dead men."

Boom patted the boy's bald head like you would a dog and said, "Shut up, Porky, while my buddy puts these cuffs on you."

Ditto shifted awake when he heard the cars sometime early in the morning. It was cold, and he slid into his mud boots and grabbed an old jacket and his gun — Gowrie telling the boys to always carry a weapon or he'd whip their ass — and scrambled down the wood porch of the trailer to the burning oil drum, where the boys always met. Gowrie was wild-eyed and mad as hell, not wearing a shirt, only jeans and boots, and screaming, wanting to know what the hell happened, people were supposed to be watching out instead of fiddling with their dicks.

Ditto knew they'd been hit.

All the screaming woke Lena, too, and Ditto saw her emerge from the trailer she'd been sharing with Charley and another couple boys. She stood on the railing in a puffy blue coat and watched them, listening to Gowrie scream and rant, until she rolled her eyes and went back inside and Charley took her place, wiping sleep from his eyes and stumbling down the long, endless hill, sliding down into Hell Creek. You could warm yourself by the fire and have a drink, while Gowrie said everyone needed to load up and prepare because this shit would not stand.

They'd had some kind of fun getting revenge for all that lost meat and ice cream and guns that had bent and twisted in the flames of their barn. But what this man had gone and done to Gowrie was a whole 'nother deal. This wouldn't just be some torched barns and dead cows. It was fixin' to get bloody.

Gowrie grabbed Ditto by the shirt and pulled him in, with that stink breath and hot words, and said, "Go get my daddy. Go. Now!"

And Ditto scrambled off, figuring maybe he could slip off as everyone assembled, maybe no one would notice him being gone, and he could make a couple phone calls, because back here in the booger woods ain't no kind of cell phone worked.

He found a path and then a trailer, and

318

knocked. He tried it again and then just walked in, spotting the old man and Brother Davis passed out on the floor, the television looping some kind of porno movie with two black women on a beach. He kicked at Daddy Gowrie, an empty bottle within fingers' reach, and he didn't move, and for a moment Ditto thought that the old guy might be dead.

He kicked at him again, and then kicked at Brother Davis.

But the old men were dead drunk, and he figured that's just what he'd tell Gowrie, to take some heat off him.

Back at the camp, trucks and cars had started up, blowing hot exhaust into the freezing air. Gowrie was squatted in the dirt, smoking a cigarette, in the headlight glow of his old black Camaro. He drew out some plans with a stick for a few of the fellas, and they smiled and grinned like some kind of dirty joke had been told.

And Gowrie looked at him and tilted his head.

"Him and the preacher are passed out."

"You try and wake 'em?"

"I kicked at 'em."

"Shit," Gowrie said. "Brother Davis backslides when he preaches like that. I can't fault him. Come on."

"Who's watching the women, the camp, if all of us leave?"

"How 'bout you?"

"I want to kill those bastards, too."

Gowrie spent the smoke, flicked it into the dirt. Ditto spotted tattoos on his biceps reading GOD, LOVE, MURDER, each word with a symbol: an angel, a heart, a gun. The older man took a swig of Jack Daniel's and passed him the bottle.

"You hold tight, little brother," Gowrie said, smiling with blackened teeth. "You sit tight with your guns on that road and you hit anything you see move. I don't care what you see."

Ditto nodded.

The boys were off in a plume of dust and exhaust, red taillights headed in a line up the hill and down the highway. It was cold and silent and still as they disappeared. He stood there, thinking of a way to walk to a phone. They hadn't left a single vehicle.

Lena returned to the porch, watching him. He smiled at her and moved to the base of the crooked wood steps.

"Don't you want to go shoot some people?" she asked.

"I'm watching the camp."

"Let me have a cigarette," she said.

"What about your baby?"

"She's asleep."

He reached into his old coat for the pack and a lighter. He sat down on the stoop with her on the most ragged piece of property he could imagine, half the land's pine trees not quite right for the cutting and the other half logged to shit. The charred rafters of the barn leaning into a weird heap in the moonlight.

"What happened?" she asked, taking a seat next to him, making his heart do a backflip.

"Somebody robbed our people. Tim got his hand shot up."

"Who did it?"

"That soldier," Ditto said. "Gowrie says he hates everything we stand for."

"What do we stand for?" Lena asked.

"Maybe you should ask Charley Booth about that," he said, smiling. "He seemed to be excited about all this mess."

"Why are you here?" she asked. "You sure don't seem to give two shits."

"You hungry?"

"I'm good," she said. "Why are you here?"

"I ask myself that every day."

"Hard when you got nowhere else to be."

"You need to get some sleep," Ditto said, taking the rifle and slinging it back on his shoulder. "We don't know what's gonna happen with these boys. Might be good if you found another place to stay."

"Soon as my limousine arrives, I'll let you know."

"But you'd leave if you could?"

She nodded.

"Without Charley Booth?"

She shrugged. "I don't even know who that son of a bitch is."

Ditto smiled so big he felt like his face might break apart, slipping his frozen hands into his pockets and stamping his feet onto the frozen, eroded ground. "Anyone ever tell you that you look like Taylor Swift?"

They came for Quinn at dawn.

He'd been waiting for the last four hours at the tree line near the old farmhouse and found the time sort of peaceful, seeing that first light bleeding across his frosted land and up through the base of the forest at the roots and then spilling up onto his worn boots. He'd brought nothing but his compound bow, a nice Mathews HyperLite that could send an arrow at 350 feet per second, and had dressed head to toe in camo, shielding part of his face with a camo ski mask. He was thankful for the morning light. Despite the thick clothes, he'd grown cold in the woods, and he'd hoped for some action just to move for a bit.

He breathed slow and even, heartbeat steadied, just like it had always been.

He'd heard their cars and trucks from a mile away. But they'd taken it in their minds to hike over from the main highway, maybe a half mile over some creeks, and then cut into the land, checking the farmhouse, finding it empty, and then heading across the break in the trees by the burned-out barn and up into the woods and the old oaks where Quinn waited. His bow drawn and ready as they walked right past him, following a deer trail up into the hills. Quinn counted fourteen of them.

He and Boom had decided to split the men, keeping most in a nice choke point of empty ground bordered by thick trees and briars and backed by a steep incline into the hills. The small clearing would've been a perfect place to put a deer stand, the men walking right into it, standing there talking and pointing, far from any cover.

Quinn smiled when he heard that motor start and saw his uncle's old four-wheeler come zipping and spinning wild down the hill trail, riderless, but scaring the hell out of Gowrie's boys, who let into it with shotguns and AKs they'd probably bought at backdoor gun shows.

They huddled over the toppled four-wheeler, lying on its side, motor high-pitched, oil spurting and wheels spinning, and Gowrie scouted the trees. He looked right at Quinn but didn't see him, instead just squinting into the light and spitting, pointing up the hill for some of his men to follow. Perfect.

Two cracking shots. A man yelled.

Quinn smiled. Boom was having a time, having found the right spot for the deer rifle, loaded, balanced, and sighted right down that path. Gowrie sent more men up the hill, keeping most of his boys in that open space that would become Quinn's kill zone.

Quinn took a breath and steadied himself, letting the string go and zipping an arrow right into Gowrie's shoulder blade, knocking him forward and then backward to his knees, the AK chattering away up into the laced branches overhead.

Quinn smiled again and reached for another arrow. Gowrie's men looked to the shitbag for some direction. He was just squirming and screaming.

The men had turned, feet planted on the hill, unsteady and off base and pointing. Some of them had dropped to the ground and covered their heads. The big fat guy had the bloody dish towel still wrapped around his missing thumb, and wore a shirt so tight it exposed a large hairy belly. He started marching toward Quinn and pointing.

"There he is. Git 'im."

Zip.

Quinn got him two inches away from the groin. The man screamed his dick had been shot.

Up the hill, Boom shot three more times. Gowrie's men let loose on him, but Boom had some solid concealment, enough to play with them until Quinn was ready.

Ten or so boys started to walk away and scatter from the kill zone but then turned back to where the fat man had pointed. Gowrie was on his feet, finding cover behind a fat oak, touching his bleeding shoulder and aiming the barrel of his AK toward the grouping of old oaks. He raked the ground, Quinn seeing he was just shooting, not aiming, not knowing from where the arrow had struck.

Quinn stayed concealed, still invisible and silent.

Half the group yelled and charged up the hill. A half-dozen more loud cracks from Boom's Browning .308. That was a hell of a gun.

"You chickenshit motherfucker," Gowrie

said, screaming. "You shot me in the back."

Three of his men had started to crawl through the dead leaves and muck toward him, the air cold and silent. He could see the hot breath of the men coming from the ground, each of them so damn easy to pick off that it wasn't even worth it, served up on a platter in that kill zone. Two more shots from one of Gowrie's boys, and a big fat plug of oak splintered by Quinn's ear, sending him flat to the ground in a roll. More shots. Gowrie laughing and yelling for them to kill that son of a bitch.

"Come on out," Gowrie said, yelling.

Quinn crawled on knees and elbows back behind a row of privet and dead kudzu and moved up and around the men. The bow didn't weigh much more than three pounds, and he could crawl as he entered the tree line again, swallowed up into the cold and mottled darkness and light, seeing the back of Gowrie's shaved head as the man screamed at his boys to keep going into the hills, keep shooting, kill the bastard.

The light flickered through the dead branches and onto the cold ground.

Quinn kept his breathing light, moving soft over branches and leaves, Gowrie making it so damn easy with all the noise, until Quinn was maybe twenty meters from him, watching the man aim his AK up the hill and yell for his boys, who'd gone over the crest and met Boom's gun.

One yelled back that they couldn't see the shooter.

"Who's dead?" Gowrie said.

"Jessup's shot. He's bleeding bad."

Down the hill, three of the men found the big old oak where Quinn had watched them, and they circled the ground with weapons raised, spotting his tracks in the mud. They kept moving past the old oaks and into the cleared ground toward the old house. Gowrie walked into the open ground, feeling Quinn had been flushed. When Gowrie turned, Quinn was on him, putting him onto the earth, facedown in the mud, his hand over Gowrie's mouth, with a knee into the base of his neck, and whispering:

"Why'd you kill my uncle?"

"Fuck you."

Quinn increased pressure on Gowrie's neck, feeling the vertebrae stretch and crack. High on Gowrie's shoulder, almost at the pit of his arm, the arrow had entered and stuck, the shaft still sticking out of him like a pin, Gowrie not being able to pull the hunting tip from his flesh.

Quinn grabbed it and turned, Gowrie screaming. Quinn kept his hand over his mouth, muffling the shouts.

He again asked him the question.

Gowrie's face was hot and red, and pain tears streaked his filthy face. "I didn't kill him."

"You work for Stagg?"

"I work for myself."

"You do business with Stagg."

Gowrie tried to buck Quinn off, but Quinn had a tight hold of his throat, knee still in his back, holding that arrow like a handle, while Gowrie's boys scattered and crept over woods that he and Boom had been hunting since they were boys, knowing every stone, every tree, every break in the land.

He heard feet behind him but without even turning said: "You kill him?"

"He's not dead," Boom said. "Shot him in the leg."

"We don't want to kill you pieces of shit," Quinn said. "We want you gone. You leave here, and I won't follow. You stick around town, and I'll start blowing shit up. It doesn't really matter to me."

Gowrie was gasping with pain, and Quinn worried that he might pass out. He twisted the arrow a slight turn just to make sure he had his complete attention.

"I think Stagg lets you work here for a

cut," Quinn said. "You boys come down with an invitation from some folks in Memphis. Isn't that right? You can do what you want in Tibbehah County and it doesn't mean shit. That's why y'all killed my uncle and Jill Bullard."

"Get off me," Gowrie said. "The sheriff killed the Bullard girl."

Quinn looked back at Boom. Boom to Quinn.

"Say that again?"

"He shot her 'cause she wouldn't shut the fuck up."

"You're a liar."

"Kill me, then," Gowrie said. "You the same as him."

"You got two minutes to collect your men and get gone," Quinn said, standing, catching his breath and watching Gowrie waver to his feet and spit, jacket hanging ragged and loose off him. He whistled for his boys.

"Stagg made a deal with the devil himself," Gowrie said. "Hell awaits."

Boom took a solid bead on Gowrie's head with the chrome .44.

"You go ahead and get smart," Boom said.

Gowrie looked at Boom and said: "All you got is a dyke woman and a one-armed nigger? Sleep tight."

Gowrie gathered his boys in a big sunny

field and headed out, marching down the gravel road.

Boom raised his eyebrows and lowered his gun as they crossed the creek bridge. "Who's he calling a dyke?"

27

Quinn was at the courthouse when it opened at nine, heading down into the basement to the chancery clerk, the keeper of land records going back to when the county had been purchased from Choctaw chief Issatibbehah back in 1823. Since the last time he'd walked down those steps, it looked like they'd bought two computers, trying to get on into the twenty-first century. But they still kept those endless shelves of fat, aged leather-bound volumes, hand-inked transactions of deeds, liens, bankruptcy records, divorces, and delinquent taxes. The basement was always filled with a mildew stench and spindles of dust in the little bit of light from narrow windows at ground level.

The job was elected, but unless you ran away with half the county's budget or performed an intimate act in public you could pretty much keep the job as long as you wanted it. For the last thirty years, Sam

Bishop had run the office due to Sam's interest in few things, outside church, bass fishing, and being a troop leader to the Boy Scouts. He'd been the man who'd kicked Quinn out of the Scouts at twelve for running a whiskey-fueled poker game one rainy night on the Natchez Trace.

"This is it," Sam said, passing two printed-out sheets across the desk. "Lists people or companies owning adjoining land. I sure am sorry about your uncle."

"I know these folks," Quinn said. "I recognize all the borders except the one to the west."

Sam reached for the sheet and looked at it through half-glasses, nodding. "Timber company, out of Bruce. That help any?"

"I don't know," Quinn said. "You mind if I ask you a personal question?"

"You aren't still mad about the Scouts."

Sam had grown a lot grayer since the last time he'd seen him. He seemed smaller, bonier, and Quinn noticed he'd developed a limp. He remembered him being strong and vigorous, and leading hikes that seemed to go on forever. But Sam had grown old, and the thought of it was strange to Quinn. The man had always seemed ageless.

"No, sir."

"Go ahead."

"What do you think about Johnny Stagg?"

Sam Bishop took off his glasses, keeping his eyes on Quinn while he slipped them into his checkered dress shirt. Quinn pretty sure he was wearing a clip-on tie. He nodded and said, "Well, as he's the head of the board of supervisors, I guess I'd say he's my boss."

"Y'all friends?"

Bishop walked back to a far wall and closed a door with a light click. He returned and lowered his voice, leaning over his desk: "Why?"

"I'd like to know just why Johnny Stagg is so interested in getting my uncle's land."

"Quinn, I could get in a hell of a lot of trouble speculating on land deals."

"He said he's going to file a lien."

"He hasn't yet," Sam said, whispering. "If that means anything."

"I just can't figure how the land would be much use to him," Quinn said.

Bishop reached for the two pieces of paper, slipping the glasses back on and running through each line with the eraser tip of a pencil, nodding. "You see this?" Bishop said. "That's the land you asked about. Your uncle's first tract. Would you like to see any additional parcels he might have owned?"

"How many?"

"Offhand, I recall three," Bishop said. "If you'd like, I'd be glad to pull up those records for you. If Mr. Stagg were to file a lien, it would be for all of Hamp's assets and land. You understand that."

"I'm afraid to ask," Quinn said. "But I bet you know."

"I really can't say," Bishop said, limping back to his office. "I can only comply with any requests from taxpayers here in Tibbehah County. This little jigsaw puzzle is up for you to decide."

Quinn hadn't gone two steps out of the courthouse when a sheriff's cruiser pulled in front of him and Wesley Ruth climbed out and whistled.

"How 'bout a ride?" he asked.

"No, thanks," Quinn said. "I have my truck."

"Not a request."

Quinn stopped and nodded. He walked around to the passenger seat and climbed in, and said, "Where to?"

"Let's ride and talk."

"You mind stopping for coffee?"

"No, Quinn," Wesley said. "I don't mind a bit."

"So this is when you tell me to lay off," Quinn said.

"Pretty much."

"What have I done?"

"There was some serious shooting going on last night on your uncle's land," Wesley said. "Wildlife and Fisheries got a complaint that someone was hunting deer with automatic weapons. They came out to see you and you weren't there, so they put in a call to me. You want to tell me what went on last night?"

Quinn shrugged. "Is my hunting license expired?"

"We also got five different reports of shooting goin' on all around this county," Wesley said. "Someone saw a one-armed black male and a white male accomplice. Guess who I just pulled in?"

"I have no idea."

"He won't talk," Wesley said. "Pretends he's never heard the name Quinn Colson. Seems like all the victims here are shitbag drug dealers, three of 'em with out-of-state driver's licenses, all part of Gowrie's crew. None of them will report a thing. Listen, man, I'm sorry about your barn and cattle. We'll get that son of a bitch for what he did. You got to believe there is no one that wants that turd flushed more than me. But you could've killed someone. I spoke to one fella this morning who said life was great while his missing thumb was in the freezer."

"You want to search my house?"

"How long you got till you report back for duty?"

"Tomorrow."

"Would you take offense if I asked you to leave early?" Wesley said.

"I might."

Wesley shook his head, taking off his ball cap and blowing out a breath, before finding a drive where he could stop and turn back around to town. "You sure know how to push a friendship."

"You said you were going to stop for coffee," Quinn said.

"I suppose I'm wasting my breath to ask what you and Sam Bishop were talking about?"

"I figure you'll ask him when you drop me off."

"I guess you're dead set on making me a bad guy," Wesley said with a slight smile. "You ever think that I'm just trying to look out for a friend and do my job at the same time? You put me in a hell of a situation."

Most of the lunch crowd at Varner's store had cleared by the time Quinn showed up. Old Mr. Varner was working the register, selling cigarettes, Coca-Cola, and gas, while

Judge Blanton finished off his plate of barbecue and beans and read the *Tibbehah Monitor.* He looked up and told Quinn to take a seat, and Quinn removed his cap and stood across the red-and-white oilcloth from him. "Figured you'd be packing up by now. Sit down."

"I was at Sam Bishop's office," Quinn said. "You want to tell me more about my uncle's other property?"

"I don't know what Johnny's gonna file on the lien," Blanton said, scraping up a mouthful of beans. "I'll let you know when I hear something."

"How 'bout you? You gonna sell your piece?"

"I've got a lot of land, Quinn."

"But only one parcel next to Highway 45," Quinn said. "Without those pieces, Stagg would be landlocked."

"Doesn't mean anything now," Blanton said. "Stagg's project is dead. Those leases would've only happened if they started construction."

"Would've guaranteed y'all a seat at the table. Full partners with Stagg."

"He needed our parcels. We would have been fools not to want in."

"I can't believe you'd throw in with that piece of shit."

Blanton pushed away his plate and leaned back in his chair. He took a deep breath as if to calm himself and nodded before he spoke. "You think because we invested in this project that makes me and your uncle corrupt? I don't know anyone in this county who wouldn't have wanted in. We saw an opportunity to make some money and for this whole county to come alive. That doesn't mean I'm in his pocket, or anyone's pocket."

"You should've said something."

"Stagg wanted it all," Blanton said. "The house. The farm. I was looking after your best interest."

"You should've told me about my uncle and Stagg doing business."

"I never lied to you."

"What would you call it?"

"Stagg would've been in his legal right to take it all," Blanton said. "Hamp owed Stagg a lot of money for a hell of a long time. Your uncle had his vices."

"Stagg lied about him owing on all that equipment," Quinn said. "Why didn't he just tell me he funded all those trips to Tunica?"

"Sit down, Quinn, and quiet down," Blanton said, looking over his shoulder to Varner, standing at the register. Varner was

338

listening and closed the cash drawer with a hard snick, meeting Quinn's eye and staring at Judge Blanton.

"Johnny didn't want to make your uncle look bad. If folks knew he'd had a gambling problem, owed money, half his cases would be called into doubt. That's a hell of an epitaph."

"You and Stagg should've worked out a plan before I came back," Quinn said. "You're tryin' to good-ole-boy me while Stagg's trying to cornhole me. How 'bout a handshake first?"

"No one's trying to screw you," Blanton said. "Take the money. Your mother and that little colored boy she's raising sure could use it."

"You can go to hell," Quinn said.

"Excuse me, boy?"

"You're fired," Quinn said. "I think my family can find some better representation."

28

Johnny Stagg didn't like those telephone calls when people asked you why the shit was flying when you were damn well trying to dodge it yourself. But the Memphis folks had called three times now, and on the last call asked him to drive nearly two damn hours up to the city and tell them about just what was going on with Gowrie. Johnny tried to pleasantly remind them that Gowrie was his own damn man, and if they had some kind of trouble with Gowrie, they needed to ask him. But that just wouldn't do, and so Johnny had to skip a fish fry with the Rotarians and an early Bible study led by Brother Davis to meet Bobby Campo up at CK's Coffee Shop off Union at eight a.m.

"We get the state people in and we're fucked, Johnny," Campo said, drinking a cup of coffee in a back booth and working on a Denver omelet. "You see that? Right?"

Campo was a Memphis boy but had gone

to Ole Miss with several folks that Johnny knew down in Jackson. That's how they'd become buddies. When Johnny wanted to get into the skin trade a few years back, Campo was the man who showed him the ropes and got a decent cut of the old Booby Trap, sending dancers down from Memphis and up from New Orleans. And when Stagg needed some support for a development no one had faith in, Campo produced miracles.

Bobby Campo was old Memphis, came from money, had it his whole life, and had made a lot more of it in the eighties with swingers clubs and later in the nineties with 900 numbers. Campo always dressed like a rich boy, pleated slacks and wild-colored dress shirts without ties. Today, he wore black suede loafers with gold buckles.

He'd been in and out of federal prison since Stagg had known him, most recently after pleading guilty to having live sex acts onstage at one of his clubs. He called it the price of doing business. But you'd still see him in the company of politicians and CEOs on fall Saturdays down in the Grove at Ole Miss, eating fried chicken off a china plate and drinking bourbon from a silver flask. Campo sent a lot of money to Jackson. He made a lot of important friends. If the development took off, Stagg already had a certificate for a regional hospital. Those things only happen with handshakes and winks with sharp men. Campo had handed him that gold key.

"So, what the hell?" Campo asked.

"Gowrie got robbed," Johnny said. "Five of them labs got busted up."

"New sheriff?"

Stagg shook his head. "Got into some kind of pissing contest with a local boy."

"Can you stop it?"

"Nope," Johnny Stagg said, pointing to a waitress and asking her for some ice water. "I seen Gowrie this morning, and that local boy done stuck an arrow through him."

"An arrow?" Campo asked. "You shitting me?"

"I think we all need to step back and reevaluate this partnership."

"You got a dead sheriff, and a dead whore found by a couple kids," Campo said, fingering his ear. "Now you got people playing cowboy and Indian up all around your county and you aren't at all worried about another couple murders? How long until you got troopers and DEA types crawling all over you?"

"I'm walking away."

"You made a deal with us," Campo said,

shaking his head. "You don't just up and quit."

"Since when does Gowrie work for me? I never made a nickel off that circus freak."

"He didn't show up at Dixie Belles last night," Campo said. "You know how much money that is?"

"That's between y'all," Stagg said, leaning in to whisper.

"Figured maybe you two wanted to cut us out."

"That's a damn lie," Stagg said.

"You gonna eat?"

"I don't know."

"Coffee?"

"Why'd you make me drive all this way? I got a family. Obligations."

"Last time Gowrie got out of line, you had the sheriff make some threats."

"The sheriff ain't around no more."

Traffic on Union skipped along outside the little diner, its big windows crammed with folks with heavy coats and whiskey breath. A homeless man sat in a chair by the bathroom and asked people who passed for a quarter. He shifted some change in his hands and punched up an old Al Green song on the jukebox.

"Where'd you find Gowrie anyway?" Johnny asked.

"Some boys in prison connected me to some folks."

"You always do business with the AB?"

"Gowrie came recommended. He's got friends."

"I don't care for them folks," Stagg said. "They've been wiping their asses with our county, treating it like a toilet."

Campo shrugged, and played with a gold ring with diamonds arranged in the shape of a horseshoe. "Johnny, I know you got ambition, and that means you sometimes have to work with people you don't like."

"Gowrie's the problem," Johnny Stagg said. "You said it yourself."

"He's your problem," Campo said. "You shut him down and find the money he owes me."

"Why am I left holding a bag of flaming shit?" Stagg said, still whispering as he stood up from the booth. "What you done for me was in exchange for protection in my county, letting things get done that you needed. I never wanted a piece of all this mess."

"Are you gonna eat or what?"

Johnny Stagg took a breath, feeling like he'd been sucker punched, all the wind gone from his lungs. "Naw," he said. "I guess I'm not hungry."

"Get Gowrie," Campo said. "Find my goddamn money."

Johnny Stagg sat in his Cadillac for a long time, thinking about all that cash he'd seen in Brother Davis's church, wondering just what Gowrie had planned for it, and why in the hell he'd ever joined up with Bobby Campo and this goddamn invisible confederacy of crooks.

"You always clean your guns before supper?" Lillie asked.

"Sure."

"Old habits."

"Yep."

"Your momma was looking for you."

"She didn't call."

"Yes, she did," Lillie said, handing him his cell. "This was in your truck."

Quinn had set up his iPod and mini-speaker on the old kitchen table, Loretta Lynn singing "Van Lear Rose." He'd carried that iPod from Fallujah to Kabul, and parts in between, providing company over the drone of that C-130, beaten and scarred but still holding a nice little jukebox. A little piece of home in foreign lands while he cleaned guns and waited. There was always the damn waiting.

"Any sign of Hondo?" Lillie asked.

345

Quinn shook his head. "Mr. Varner came out with a bulldozer and buried the cows. Said he hadn't seen him, either. If a dog's been shot, it'd crawl as far as it could get and die."

"He's okay."

"He guarded the house."

"I think that dog has taken a shine to you," Lillie said.

"If he comes back, you want him?"

"You don't mean that."

"I can't exactly bring him back to base with me."

Quinn sprayed some oil onto a rag and worked over the stock of the .308, and opened the breech with a hard snick. He reloaded and snapped shut the lever.

"They'll make another run at you," Lillie said. "You can bet on that. Wesley called in some troopers for help."

"I don't hear sirens."

"Your uncle made a lot of enemies in Jackson," she said. "Wasn't any secret they weren't welcome here."

"Just why is that?"

"He was stubborn," Lillie said. "You ever remember troopers hangin' out in Tibbehah besides on 45?"

"Something happened this morning," Quinn said, laying down the gun and reaching for the .45, popping out the slide. "I had a little chat with Gowrie."

"I know," Lillie said. "Wesley about shit a brick."

"I bet."

"How'd that chat go?"

"Gowrie was pretty open to the idea," Quinn said. "Of course he denied killing my uncle."

"What'd you expect?"

Quinn shook his head, the iPod shuffled onto Johnny Cash, playing "Daddy Sang Bass," low, while he fed bullets into the magazine of his .45 and tucked it into his Western belt. "He did admit to working with Stagg, but he said Hamp did, too."

"That's a nasty lie, coming from a shitbag like that."

"I don't know what to think," Quinn said. "But I'm not leaving till this is sorted out."

"You gonna go AWOL."

"If I have to."

"Is this worth screwing up your whole career?"

"Yep."

Lillie walked in close and slow and grabbed his arm, making him look at her. "I'm not leaving tonight," she said. "Wesley said that was fine by him. Boom's outside, standing watch by those trees. He said he'd stay out there all night if you'd bring him some whiskey."

Quinn didn't say anything, George Jones now sliding onto his digital mix, George telling them to step on up and take the Grand Tour of his empty house. He blinked, and Lillie moved in close and hugged him tight, rubbing his back. Quinn finding it awkward to hold her with the .45 and setting it on the table.

"Judge Blanton and my uncle were in that development project with Stagg," Quinn said, letting out a long breath. "Stagg wanted to run me out so he'd control a parcel of land he needed to connect it to the highway. Blanton lied to me about it. He's no different from all of 'em."

Quinn could feel Lillie breathing next to him as he wrapped his arm around her small waist. "You know you got friends, right?"

"Sure wish I knew where that old dog went."

They brought the boy back, bloody and busted up, and tossed him into the headlights of Gowrie's Camaro at the base of the ravine. Daddy Gowrie and two of the boys had fetched Shackelford up somewhere in Tennessee and drove him back to camp, knowing that Gowrie had figured him for the snitch. Lena had heard that it didn't take but a few phone calls to place him with Quinn Colson and some deputy up in Eupora. She'd even heard it might've been his own brother that sold him out for fifty dollars. A fifty-dollar bill looked as big as a bedspread right now to Lena, but she didn't think she could sell out any of her kin for a paycheck.

She was feeding her baby girl when she heard the ruckus and didn't have any choice but to stay in the trailer, with the heat and light, away from the screaming and yelling and all those fists and feet coming down on that poor boy's body. She had a piece of curtain cocked off the window, nothing but an old towel, but she could watch without fear of Gowrie seeing her, making her witness to that evil he was doing. But maybe he didn't care. He didn't seem to have any room for remorse in that shit-stained soul.

Ditto and Charley Booth completed the ring, but she could tell it was only Charley that found some enjoyment in the beating, all them acting like a bunch of wild dogs on a runt. Charley getting his kicks in and then stepping back like he was afraid he might get bit. But this was all in the game, the way that she'd learned Gowrie would bring a wayward boy back into the group. You beat him and humiliated him and then they'd be drinking beer and listening to their heavy metal by midnight.

Or that's what Charley Booth had said over supper.

She dropped the curtain and turned her head.

They was gonna kill him. Ditto knew it just as soon as he'd heard they were bringing back Keith Shackelford from somewhere over the state line. The dumbass had headed over to see an old girlfriend — that same girlfriend being an ex of Gowrie's — and it didn't take a half day to roust him up and drop him in a heap down by Hell Creek. And that's when the beating started, Ditto trying to disagree with all that, it being contrary to his nature, but his voice was so brittle and young that no one even turned their head when he spoke, just elbowed his ass out of the way as everyone wanted to get a piece of the man who'd fucked up the whole operation.

He figured he could get a gun, maybe fire some shots in the air like they do in old movies, but then he could see them guns turning back on him and him lying down in the same ditch as this unfortunate soul. He kept thinking that maybe they'd take it easier on Shackelford if the boy looked halfway human, but he had a face made of poured rubber and no hair and looked something like a creature that would live down in the center of the earth, coming up at night to catch some air and maybe howl at the moon. A man could beat on someone pretty severe who didn't seem real.

Ditto 'bout lost his lunch when he heard them bones breaking and caught a splatter of blood in his eye.

"Let's go."

Lena let out a cry when she saw Ditto standing over her, his face all flecked with blood and flesh.

"You cain't stay around here," he said. "Get the baby and y'all's things."

Lena considered Ditto's upturned nose and pudgy face, thick waist and short legs. But she saw something else in him, a real conviction of what he was saying, *Get on out before Gowrie does the same to you.* And, hell, he didn't need to say it. Lena had felt it since the first time she'd laid eyes on Gowrie.

"Where will we go?" she asked.

"Somewheres else."

"He'll find us."

"I ain't as stupid as Keith Shackelford."

She shook her head and walked the trailer, the thin floor creaking up under her, not having much faith in Ditto but picking up the baby's things anyway — not much besides what they gave her in a care pack at the hospital and some ragtag used clothes gathered up for them both by Gowrie's women. She stopped, holding some plastic grocery bags, and just looked at Ditto. "Where are my shoes?"

He got down to his knees and started patting around, reaching up under the blanket and covers, just as the baby started to cry. Lena picked up the little girl, soothing her head, the baby smelling clean and warm and good, while asking her to please be quiet, please be quiet. "Did Gowrie see me?"

Ditto looked confused.

"In the window? I didn't see nothin'. I swear on it."

He shook his head.

"Is he dead?"

"He's in the car. Messed up to shit. Gowrie took things out on him with a whipping chain and a baseball bat. Everyone thinks he's dead, they were good and drunk when I told them I'd get rid of what they done."

"You ain't got no car. We can't leave. Why did you say that? You gonna get us all killed."

"Hell yes, I got a car, girl." He pulled back the towel from the window, revealing the image of the black Camaro surrounded by burning oil drums. Ditto flipped the keys around his fingers. "Figured if he's gonna be pissed, might as well go all the way."

"I'm ready."

"Didn't figure on you sayin' good-bye to Charley. He's with all them down in Daddy's trailer."

Lena held the baby against her shoulder, the cries becoming softer, breaking into slow breaths, small whimpers, until they soothed her. Ditto carried the grocery bags in one hand and held Lena's hand with the other.

He started the car, those dual pipes on that black Camaro purring and throttling. "Ain't she a wet dream."

"Don't forget to put her in gear."

Holding the baby in the passenger seat, Lena turned to find the mass of Shackelford under a blanket, a bloody hand falling loose against the floor, but she saw him take an easy, soft breath and heard a ragged cough. When he turned to her, uncovering his face from the blanket, Lena nearly shit her drawers. "Where's that damn Ranger?" he asked in a cracked voice. "Goddamn. Y'all better find his ass."

29

Gowrie was there the next morning as promised, meeting Johnny Stagg in the back room of the Rebel Truck Stop with a lazy little smirk, a bad kid done wrong. And Johnny decided not to take him to task, this was going to be a straight business proposition, serving up a solid offer to make sure Gowrie knew it was time to shut down things for a while, roll on out of town, and head back up north to Ohio or Michigan or wherever the boy was raised. But there was blood all over him. Jesus, Johnny didn't figure on seeing that.

Gowrie noticed him looking. "I was painting."

"Didn't expect you before sunrise," Stagg said.

"I was up."

"What's happened?"

"Just some shit. What do you want?"

The room was filled with all kinds of

busted-up video games. Johnny made a fortune out of them before kids started hookin' up to their TVs and carrying games around in their back pockets. Most of them were broken, but sometimes he'd pull out a Ms. PacMan or an old shoot-'em-up and let the girls over at the Booby Trap have a go when things got slow. You never saw a competition in your life like a contest between women who were on the skids. He'd seen pretty hair pulled and death threats issued.

"Why don't you throw all this shit away?" Gowrie asked.

"Campo's been trying to find you. He thinks you're duckin' him and we've cut him out."

Gowrie didn't say anything, sliding out of his leather jacket real gingerly, favoring a bad shoulder, and slunk down into an old Turbo driving game. He played with the shifter, the screen just as black and dead as you please, and thumped at the wheel.

"You owe him some money."

"He'll get his money," Gowrie said, spinning the wheel to the right and then hard to the left, downshifting and back up. "This thing work?"

"We're gonna have to shut down for a while," Stagg said. "And you're gonna have to pay him what's owed."

"That's what you said," Gowrie said. "You ever think about my shit?"

Gowrie got up, favoring his left arm, and passed within an inch of Stagg's nose, looking at him hard, jail dog kind of stuff, and reached for the cord, searching for a place to plug in the game, juice her up. Gowrie's scent reminded Stagg of a feral animal. "Ah, hell."

"It ain't forever."

"You scared of that little Italian?"

"Do you know what kind of people Bobby Campo works for? They're blaming me."

"And how come this shit storm is flying 'round my head?" Gowrie asked, smiling. He found an outlet, plugged her up, and the game started to hum and chatter, loading. "That man wears shoes like you'd buy for a woman. Talks about his momma like she was the Mother Mary herself."

"I said Campo blames me," Stagg said. "How come he's got that idea? He's thinkin' I get a cut."

"You act like we've been buds for a while," Gowrie said, staring straight ahead, watching the colored cars and roads and checkered flag come to life. There was a city way off in the distance, and he watched it as if the whole window was real. He thumped

356

the steering wheel some more, shifted up and down, and mashed the accelerator. "*Let's go. Hell.* Shit, you started this mess, wanting my boys to steal that man's cattle."

"Boy, you're flying a million miles an hour on those eleven herbs and spices."

"That son of a bitch shot me in the back with an arrow," Gowrie said. "Missed my heart by an inch. So why don't you get Campo's dick out of your mouth before blaming me?"

"That don't sound Christian," Stagg said, smiling. "I don't care for that kind of talk."

Gowrie grinned back. "Only religion I found gets counted at the church."

"I'm headed to see Brother Davis right now," Stagg said. "I wanted to tell you face-to-face."

"You touch that money stash and I'll kill your ass."

"If that money don't get to where it's owed, they're comin' for me."

"I'm sick and tired of people using me up," Gowrie said. "You keep clean, don't you, Brother Stagg? You don't have to keep your money in some movie-house church."

Stagg didn't say anything.

"Hell no. You got clean money in a regular bank. Ain't no filth on those pressed good-ole-boy slacks."

The checkered flag flew, and Gowrie was off, shifting up and down, wrecking the car twice, spinning and getting the hang of it, in and out of all those race cars, moving on fast to that electric city on the horizon. After the third wreck he plugged a cigarette in his cracked lips and popped open a Zippo etched with a skull over a Rebel flag. There was more dried blood on the back of his neck, a dark stain spreading across his shoulder.

"Don't go near that church," Stagg said, resting his hand on top of the video booth. "You get gone."

"Just how you gonna make me do that, Johnny Stagg?"

"You figure that out."

Gowrie nodded. "What happens to my boys when we break camp? How we supposed to train? How are we supposed to live?"

"I'll get you some money."

"How much? You gonna compensate me for all I've lost?"

Stagg told him, and Gowrie crashed the car, rear-ending a tractor trailer and sending them both up into a big plume of smoke and fire. He crawled out of the booth, smoked down the cigarette, and tossed it to the concrete. "Like I said, none of this shit

358

would've happened if you hadn't sent my boys to steal them cows."

"They were mine."

"I don't give a good goddamn," Gowrie said, yelling and then smiling, breaking into a little laugh. "You kicked up a shit storm, and if you think I'm shagging ass without breaking it all apart, you are crazy as hell. What do you think we all stand for? You were to give us a base camp where we could run maneuvers and train. Now you treatin' me like I'm some kind of criminal. I'm the only thing you got between you and that crazy soldier."

"Acting sheriff called the state troopers two hours ago. They're coming for you."

Stagg stared at the dried blood across Gowrie's T-shirt. The blood had hair in it and torn bits of flesh, some of the blood had dried on his hands and up under his fingernails. Gowrie noticed him staring and smirked, and licked his cracked ole lips.

"You mind me asking you a question?" Stagg said.

"Shoot," Gowrie said.

"Just what do y'all train for?"

Gowrie popped a fresh cigarette in his mouth and reached on top of the video game for his leather jacket. He fired up the Vantage and blew smoke as he spoke. "I don't mind you asking at all, Mr. Stagg."

The smoke drifted up into the ceiling, and Gowrie slipped back into the jacket as Stagg took a step back and looked up at the two surveillance cameras over Gowrie's shoulder. He pulled any shit and he had four boys with guns ready to kick in doors and drop this piece of shit where he stood.

Gowrie watched his eyes and craned his head and looked to each corner, the cameras, and then back at Stagg.

He grinned.

"When you and your family are having bacon and eggs and sitting pretty as you please in that great big old house you got," Gowrie said, "you might start noticing things on the television. The battle for the Holy Land has begun, and the Beast walks among us. When airplanes begin to disappear and people you known your whole life start to vanish as they stand before you, don't come down to Hell Creek and be asking me for any help. No, sir."

"We have a deal?" Stagg asked.

"We're in a war. Don't you see it?"

Gowrie grinned a rotten smile and walked away, popping his middle finger over his shoulder as he slammed open the exit door and moved back into the purple night.

■ ■ ■ ■

Not much past four in the morning, Quinn and Lillie headed south on Highway 45 about twenty miles into Lowndes County. Some kid had called Quinn's cell phone, telling him that Keith Shackelford was in trouble, and Quinn was pretty sure it was a trap till Lena came on the line. And even now as they drove into the BP filling station, lit up like a beacon in the middle of acres and acres of dead cotton fields, he chambered a round in his .45, and Lillie stepped out with a shotgun, hanging down cool and loose by her leg. He scanned the parking lot, seeing a clerk counting out cigarettes by the register and a trucker taking in some diesel. Down by the air and water pumps, out back by the Dumpsters, he saw a pudgy kid with freckles and Lena sitting on a curb.

The kid got to his feet, giving Lillie cause to hold the weapon in both hands and turn in a full circle. Quinn walked easy and slow, gun in hand, till he reached the boy and asked him just what in the hell he wanted this early.

"Keith Shackelford called for you."

"Where is he?"

"Dead."

"What happened?"

The kid told him. Quinn looked to Lena, seeing she'd been crying. She just sat on her ass in the cold, keeping the baby tight to her chest and inside her coat, her breath fogging up around her.

"You need to get that baby somewhere," Lillie said. "It's thirty degrees."

"We ran out of gas," the kid said.

"Where were you headed?" Quinn asked.

The kid shrugged.

"Where's his body?"

"In the shitter."

"Excuse me?" Quinn asked.

"I tried to get him cleaned up and he died on me in there," the kid said. "I just propped him up on the commode, didn't figure on staying till the car died on us. I kept it running so the baby would get some heat."

"You get that baby inside."

"That man in there told us we couldn't hang about. He thought we might steal something while he was watching television. He figured right 'cause we needed some cheese crackers and milk."

"Get that baby inside," Quinn said, some force in it. "We'll get the police down here."

"Oh, hell no," the kid said. "Those police in Tibbehah are crooked as hell."

"Who are you anyway?" Lillie asked.

"People call me Ditto."

"What's your real name?"

The boy told her, and Lillie grabbed his arm and pulled him aside, telling him his short list of options. He nodded along with her till she let his arm go and he wandered back to Quinn. "You want to see him?"

"You see all this or he tell you?"

"I seen it."

"You beat on him, too?"

"Oh, no, sir," Ditto said. "No, sir. I tried and get him out. He wouldn't go to a hospital, said he was fine."

Quinn followed the boy back around the gas station, beyond the stacks of plastic crates and piles of bagged garbage waiting for pickup. The boy toed open the door and flicked on the lights, and they found Keith Shackelford seated on the toilet, shirt and pants bloody. His mouth was open and his eyes had been swollen shut. In a gesture of respect, the boy had placed that Dale Earnhardt cap atop Shackelford's head.

"He don't even look human."

Quinn regarded the dead man in the filthy stall, floor coated in grime and piss, and lightly shut the stall door. "You don't let anyone in here till I come back. You hear me?"

"You want me to stay here in the shitter with a dead man?"

"You stay here till I come back."

Quinn ran outside, Lillie walked back out from inside the station, shaking her head, calling the attendant a certified moron. "She's holding a child, for God's sake."

"You call Wesley?"

She nodded. "I'm sorry, Quinn. Jesus."

"If Gowrie had been in jail, this wouldn't have happened."

"You thought Shackelford had left the state."

"That kid said he'd gone to visit an ex-girlfriend who was a pump for Gowrie. What a dumb shit."

"Thirty degrees, and outside with a baby," Lillie said. "Kids this dumb shouldn't procreate."

Quinn nodded. "I brought him back into this."

"We both did."

"They worked the shit out of him," Quinn said. "Kid said Shackelford was beaten on until Gowrie got tired and winded. His face looks like hamburger. Man makes it through hell and back and gets into this."

"You think they'll testify?"

"Both of 'em are scared shitless."

About that time, Quinn's beaten truck

cranked and worked into a wide U-turn, heading past the pumps and hitting Highway 45 south, driving hell-bound for nowhere. Lillie was already on the phone to the local sheriff as Quinn jogged to the road's edge, seeing the silhouettes of Ditto and Lena, watching the red taillights of his truck disappear into the early morning.

30

Quinn had a hell of a breakfast a few hours later at the Fillin' Station with his mother, country ham with eggs and grits, black coffee and orange juice on the side, although Jean Colson didn't touch her plate. She drank coffee and picked at her eggs, passing a biscuit to Jason and leaning in every once in a while and asking, "How can you eat right now? After finding a dead man on a commode?"

"You eat when you can."

"I'd be sick to my stomach," she said, whispering.

"I've seen worse," Quinn said. "You done with that?"

Quinn sliced the biscuits, adding his ham, and drank some coffee, signaling to the waitress for a fill-up. He hadn't slept in a while, but the lack of sleep really didn't bother him. He went nearly a week without regular sleep when they took Haditha Dam back in '03. Those mortars kept pounding for nearly four days, driving his whole company nuts, while they called in air strikes and waited for reinforcements.

"How 'bout y'all get out of town for a little bit," Quinn said. "Just a couple days."

"You better worry about yourself," his mom said.

"Those deputies still watching the house?"

"It's just George and Leonard," she said. "Last night Leonard came in and watched the television with us. He's a nice fella. He's getting married next year. Really nice girl from Columbus, owns her own hair salon."

"So he watched television with you?"

"They show *General Hospital* repeats late at night."

The bell above the diner door jingled, and Wesley Ruth walked in, looking about ten years older, unshaved, but dressed in his official sheriff's uniform and an official ball cap reading TCSO. He sat his big frame down at the table without being asked and before Mary even got close said, "Coffee."

"How'd it go?"

"Hell of a thing when a crime scene is moved about forty miles."

"But he died at the gas station."

"I think I'll take Jason outside," Jean said, lifting Jason from the high chair and putting him over her shoulder, looking away from the men, strolling around and showing him all those great photos of Quinn as a boy and his grandfather as a semifamous stunt-man.

"Did your dad really work on *Billy Jack*?" Wesley asked.

"He was one of the bad guys."

"I love that movie," Wesley Ruth said. "You know, ole Tom Laughlin learned hap-kido from Han Bong-Soo himself. You know, the Father of Hapkido?"

Quinn nodded.

"Don't act like you don't know these folks," Wesley said. "Y'all train in that stuff, don't you?"

"Mainly jujitsu."

"That's all a lot of joint locks and throws and all that. You mind showing me some-time?"

"Wesley, I need some more folks at my mother's house."

"George was there this morning."

"And Leonard sat his fat ass on the couch watching soap operas with them last night. That doesn't give me much comfort."

Wesley nodded. "We're a little short-handed."

"Heard you got people coming in."

"MBI is sendin' down half a dozen men

today," Wesley said, craning his neck, searching for Mary and his damn coffee. "We're gonna arrest Gowrie this afternoon."

"Even without Lena and that boy as witnesses?"

"Lillie heard enough to pull him in."

"I want to go."

"No way." Wesley shook his head. "These are state men, and it's all got to go by the rules or some liberal lawyer will tear us a new asshole. That boy Gowrie has lost his damn shit, and if he's not careful, I'm gonna punch his ticket."

"How many men?" Quinn asked.

"Six," Wesley said. "Plus George and Leonard. Maybe I can get Lillie to watch your mother and that boy."

"My nephew," Quinn said. "And I got it."

Mary brought Wesley's coffee, and he blew across the lip of the cup and took a sip, wiping his mouth. "That girl and the kid won't get far. No offense, but I don't think that ole truck of yours will make it. His name is Peter Francis, by the way. What'd you call him? Ditto?"

"Gowrie won't go easy."

"They never do."

"How many gun battles you been in, Wesley?"

"Law enforcement isn't like being in the

Army, Quinn," Wesley said. "Y'all get to mow down towelheads with M4s. We got to have probable cause. You gonna eat that ham biscuit?"

"You eat it."

Quinn got up and peeled off the money for the ticket. Wesley stuffed some biscuit in his mouth and took a sip of coffee before he spoke. "Where you going?"

"I'm sitting with my family till you bring him in."

"How hard can it be? You and Boom could've taken them all out yesterday."

"How do you know that?"

"Thing about Jericho is everyone knows what's goin' on. The tough part is provin' it."

"Call me if you find that girl," Quinn said. "And my truck."

"What are you driving now?"

"A pretty sweet black Camaro."

Wesley nodded, eating more. His mouth too full to speak.

Ditto came back to the motel, counting out the sixty dollars he had left from selling Quinn's hunting rifles to those blacks at the feed store. He'd thought about ditching the truck in a creek or river but didn't have the heart and instead found an old barn, nearly toppling over from rot, where he slid her inside and left the keys in the ignition. It was nearly a three-mile walk back to the motel, them heading north instead of south like they had planned. They were holed up in a little town up in Yalobusha County called Water Valley.

Lena had drawn the curtains and passed out in bed with the baby. The baby still not having a name days after birth couldn't be a good thing, but Ditto didn't study on it too long. He was too busy thinking about how to make those sixty dollars last beyond sunset tomorrow.

He could sell the truck, but it would have to be to someone who didn't care too much about registration and all that mess. He needed someone he could trust who wouldn't be a good citizen and alert the law.

Ditto sat down at a little table in the dark, the heater blowing out air that smelled like mildew and cigarette smoke, and ate the last bit of the banana pudding and chicken they'd bought at the town's Piggly Wiggly.

As long as he could get free from Gowrie, it was a good day for him.

He could find a job, didn't matter what it was. Only reason he got mixed up with Gowrie's boys was on account of that stretch at Parchman for burglary of a Goodyear store outside Tupelo. He'd been worried about finding a new set of mud tires for his truck and come out two months later with the Lee County judge sending him down to worry about getting cornholed by all them blacks. Not that he had a real hard time with niggers, he'd been around them his whole life. But a man who hadn't spent time in a state facility had no way of knowing how you had to make your decision on where you stood, and if you just waited there in the middle of the road, you'd find yourself bleeding out your backside or dead. The Brotherhood was a family. You come in with them and you were inside an electrified fence of protection. Any man who judged him for that was an ignorant man at that.

He never wanted to be back there. But when you're headed to the state line with your vehicle running on fumes, sometimes a little prayer wasn't a bad thing.

He slid into bed, counting out the sixty dollars one more time for good measure and then turning to Lena and that sleeping baby, thinking her name was Joy because that was the word that had popped into his mind.

His kissed the girl on the forehead, and then the sleeping child with the sweetest breath he'd ever smelled, and wondered if this wasn't the cleaning of things in his whole life.

You couldn't be Ditto on everything.

Maybe now he'd come back with his own goddamn answer.

The men from Jackson arrived at the Tibbehah Sheriff's Office at four p.m. in their brand-new state cars with handguns and rifles that shone fresh with oil and seemed to be lifted straight from the box. They dressed in civilian clothes, suits for investigators and jeans for those in narcotics, all of them wearing heavy hunting jackets bulging from their Kevlar vests. Wesley Ruth brought them all inside, where they talked in the interrogation room, a spot usually reserved for the coffeepot and open boxes of doughnuts, old file cabinets lining a wall, a stack of unsold calendars to raise money for the volunteer fire department.

"How many?" a gray-headed trooper asked.

"No more than twenty," Wesley said. "I think it's less."

"All of 'em armed?" asked a younger narc guy, sporting a mustache and chewing gum.

"They got some shotguns and rifles," Ruth said. "I believe they may have a couple assault weapons. There's two entrances to where they live, some trailers down by Hell Creek that I'll show you on the map. I'd say some of us take the gravel road in and the second half of us walk the fire road out back. If we get trouble, we got 'em pinched in."

Ruth laid out a topographic map, and the men studied it before they agreed on a plan of assault, piled in their vehicles, and made their way up to the northeast part of the county, winding their way up through the thick young pines on the land Gowrie squatted. Some of the narc guys had brought along four-wheelers, and they drove them down from ramps on the country road, smiling under their baseball caps, with rifles slung off their backs.

Shit-kicking time.

The bureau men followed four Tibbehah County patrol cars, everyone in their department, including Lillie, Leonard, and George, and headed into the land, bumping along the twisting gravel road high on a hill and then dipping east along the slopes of the hard-cut hills into what had been a hunting camp maybe twenty years back, the land still marked with the old owner's name, T. C. McCain.

Lillie drove the department's Jeep, Wesley

Ruth sat beside her holding a Winchester pump between his legs and chewing gum. He hadn't worn a vest, and Lillie had told him he was acting like a hot dog, and he'd said the goddamn thing wouldn't let him breathe.

· Lillie, with her hair up in a ponytail and threaded through the ball cap, bulging with a protective vest, just shrugged and said, "It's your show, boss."

"When'd you start calling me boss?"

"When you started acting like one."

A cold rain pinged the windshield as they wound their way down the hill and stopped down at the trailers and a large burned-out barn. Lillie backed into a cleared piece of land a good distance from the first trailer, where the land began to slope, decent room to get out fast the way they'd come, wheels turned uphill.

She gripped a 12-gauge, pockets bulging with more shells, a Glock on her hip holding seventeen rounds.

"No wonder you intimidate most men," Wesley said, smiling.

"Only the pussies," she said, grinning.

They met up at the foot of the ravine and spread out as the rain really started to hit the cold dry ground. They felt the rain turn to sleet, making the silence seem electric and charged, every one of them watching doors and windows for movement from a faded curtain or down by the charred opening of what was left of the barn, maybe someone popping out from those blackened freezers, lying out like coffins.

They heard the scampering first, and saw the flit of movement from up the hill.

Everyone trained their weapons on the fast brown blur, cocking hammers and sighting down the barrels of rifles. Lillie took in a deep breath as the movement broke from the dead leaves of branches.

A couple skinny pit bulls started to bark, running to them. Wesley kicked the shit out of one, sending it flying a few feet, both dogs scampering away.

"That'll give you a start," Lillie said to an old trooper who brought down his gun, slow and easy.

"I would've shot 'em."

Ruth nodded to Leonard and George, sending them to the first trailer, the state men spreading out, knocking on doors first and then kicking them in, finding trash and upturned couches, plastic bags of trash and clothes, and children's toys. By the fourth trailer, the old trooper was on the radio, and the four-wheelers buzzed on down Hell Creek and crossed along a sandy shoal, hitting their engines into a high whine up a hill.

They found only two vehicles left. One was up on blocks. The other was missing an engine. Both of them had FOR SALE signs in the cracked windshields.

Lillie had pulled the hood of her jacket up over her baseball cap, hands in pockets. Within fifteen minutes Wesley had holstered his .45, calling a huddle with the state men, pointing up the hill to a few more trailers, the men shrugging and trudging up through the small gum trees and pines.

"What do you say, boss?" Lillie asked as she approached him, George and Leonard at her heels. "You want us to stick around and see what shakes out?"

"They're long gone," Wesley said, spitting on the ground. "And they ain't comin' back."

"What a shame," Lillie said, clicking on her safety.

31

"You don't have to stand outside and smoke," Jean Colson said, opening the screened kitchen door onto the back porch, where Quinn stood with a cigar. "You can smoke in the kitchen."

The sun had gone down hours ago, and it had grown even colder than the night before. The porch chairs, left unused for months, were covered with molding leaves. He'd scraped off the leaves with his hands and wiped the muck on the legs of his jeans.

"Just wanted to stretch my legs."

"Leonard is sitting right outside," she said, motioning him in. "Come on and have some pie. Say good night to Jason. He waited up for you."

"Just doing some thinking."

"With your dad's hunting rifle?"

"Just checking it out."

His mother closed the door behind her and joined him on the deck, covered at each end by pecan trees, the ground sloping up to their neighbor's backyard and a chain-link fence, where a dog was barking. She'd left a scarecrow hanging from a stake in the garden, and it jittered and spun in the cold wind.

"So they're gone?" Jean asked.

"Wesley thinks they're gone for good," Quinn said. "I don't see that happenin'."

"You must've made them plenty mad."

"Tried my best," Quinn said, putting down the cigar in an empty flowerpot and sitting down across from his mother. She nodded. Quinn said: "No moon tonight."

"You packed?"

"I don't know," Quinn said. "Not now."

"How's that gonna sit at Fort Benning?"

"My CO knows me."

"They're gone," his mother said. "They're not coming back, and nothin's gonna happen to your old momma."

"I can take a few more days," he said. "They've got me slotted for training, and it's not the same as waiting for rapid deployment. Things are different now."

"Still, won't sit well."

"I can't leave this mess."

"It was your Uncle Hamp's mess."

"How do you figure?"

"My brother was a good man, and a good

uncle to you," she said. "He took over after your dad's failings and did about everything he could right. I love him for that. But he was about as crooked as a dog's hind leg."

Quinn sat up, spilling the cigar ash on the worn rancher's jacket.

"He'd been taking payoffs since he was elected."

"I don't believe it."

She didn't say anything, the wind still blowing around them, amplifying the cold in the thin soles of his cowboy boots.

"You can find what you want when you come back home," she said. "But don't throw away your career on account of this mess. You and Boom ran those men out of town."

"What about Jason?"

"That's what I wanted to tell you," she said, waiting a beat, smiling. "Caddy's coming over."

"When?"

"Tonight," she said, nodding.

"She's taking him?"

"He's her son."

"And you're okay with this?" Quinn asked, picking up the cigar, leaving the rifle on the porch and standing at the railing, looking out at the tilled-up earth where tomatoes and peppers and sunflowers would rise up in the hot summer. "She's the mess."

"Not anymore."

Quinn took a deep breath, cigar in hand, looking across the little garden, and shook his head. "I saw her."

"When?"

"Two nights ago," he said. "She was in Memphis, and she was not fine."

His mom waited, but that's all he'd offer.

"Don't let her take that kid, Mom," he said. "She's far, far gone."

"Don't say things like that," she said. "She's heard about the Bullard girl and all that's happened."

"Who told her?"

"I don't know."

"Anna Lee?"

"I don't think so," his mom said. "They haven't been friends for a long while."

"She ever tell you about Jason's father?"

His mother shook her head and stayed silent. Quinn left the railing and walked back to the chair, standing there, smoking. Jean reached into her housecoat and pulled out a pack of cigarettes, joining him, sharing a weak smile.

They sat there in the cold, the cold feeling good, not saying a word until Jean got up, patted his knee, and went on inside to put Jason to bed.

Sometime later a car pulled into their driveway, headlights washing through the backyard and up into the bare branches of a pecan tree, and then a car door slammed.

Quinn could hear a rush of feet inside the house and Jason's little voice saying, "Mama."

"Hello, big brother," Caddy said.

Quinn looked up from the deck chair and nodded to her. She had cracked open a Budweiser, and had traded out the Dallas Cowboys cheerleader outfit for a sweater and jeans, a leather jacket with fringe like Annie Oakley once wore.

"Heard you been shootin' up town," Caddy said, laughing a little, sliding over the railing and taking a swig of beer. "I did warn you."

"Why'd you come back?"

"To get Jason."

"I'd prefer you left him."

"You don't even know him," she said. "Call me protective, but I'd rather not see him shot."

"He won't get shot."

"You can guarantee that?"

"Yes, I can."

"Jesus," she said. "I'm starting to see how Mom felt about Uncle Hamp. Just because

382

you're blood relation doesn't mean you have to like the person."

"How's the job?" he asked.

"A job."

"You get insurance?"

"Fuck you, Quinn," Caddy said. "We have some girls who worked over in Columbus, and they said the Rangers practically lived at those bars. Don't cast stones."

"How much to head back to Memphis?"

"I'm not a whore," she said.

"How much?"

"You don't have enough for me to leave my boy," she said, finishing the beer and throwing it against a pecan tree, breaking the glass, and turning inside the kitchen.

Quinn smoked some more and finally put out the cigar.

A car started and left.

Quinn walked around the house, spotting his mother sitting in front of the television with a wineglass, her face drained of any expression.

He clicked off the lights and everything was silent, only the gentle hum of the refrigerator.

He made coffee and sat on the porch for most of the night, smoking down two more sticks and walking out to Ithaca Road and shooting the shit with Leonard till the sun came up. As he headed up the drive from the patrol car, he absently picked up a toy truck and placed it under his arm, thinking how toys like that can really take a beating in the elements.

32

Quinn heard stirring in the kitchen and wandered in, kissing his mother's cheek as she fried bacon, and poured himself a cup of coffee, his fourth. He leaned against the counter, the house feeling even more empty in the daylight, and he knew she felt it more than he could. Quinn searched for something to say. He drank the coffee while she cracked a couple of eggs and served him at the table. "You put new wallpaper in here?" he asked.

"You like it?"

"It's pink poodles."

"It's the same wallpaper Elvis used in Graceland for Gladys."

"You headed up to Memphis for his birthday?" Quinn asked, never understanding her devotion to the King but knowing it made her happy, brought her some peace.

"Of course," she said. "Why wouldn't I? You packed?"

He ate and nodded. "I don't like it."

"I'll be fine," she said. "The only thing good about being the sheriff's sister is that I get no shortage of support. Your uncle gave Wesley a job when Wesley couldn't get a job picking up trash."

Quinn smiled. "I'm sorry about Jason."

"He'll be back."

"Can't be good for him."

"She's trying," she said. "Don't be so tough."

Quinn took his coffee mug and looked out the front window, spotting Leonard bracing himself on the door of the patrol car talking to Wesley Ruth, who'd pulled in ahead of him. Wesley looked like a giant next to Leonard, thick chest and fat forearms, a big grin on his face. Aside from his bulging stomach, Wesley still held himself like a pro athlete.

Quinn let the curtain go and told his mother he'd be back a little later.

"Where you headed?"

"I wanted to lock up the farmhouse and close the gate," he said. "Check on Hondo again."

She nodded, both of them knowing that dog was dead, but it was at least something final he could do for his uncle. Maybe he'd see some buzzards circling around the property and he could bury the dog.

"If I don't find him," he said, "don't go out there alone."

"I promise."

"And I'm going to get you an attorney to fight Stagg," Quinn said. "We'll keep that up. Right?"

Johnny Stagg opened up the cattle gate to Judge Blanton's place and drove slow along the gravel drive, a couple pit bulls trailing his Cadillac, barking at him, snipping at the tires, as he approached that old white house, a fire going in the chimney. Those dogs didn't leave him alone until he stopped and got out, shooing them away, not seeing hair of the judge and wondering. He'd been calling all morning and hadn't found him at home or the office.

He knocked on the door and still heard nothing, but saw it was unlocked and let himself in. A propane space heater burned on a wall under a hunt painting and a barrister bookcase filled with rare volumes. Johnny Stagg always respected the judge for being such a learned man. The fireplace smelled of burning cedar.

The silence was so strong, the popping logs nearly made him jump.

He called out to him.

The judge answered from a far back corner of the house.

The judge was in his study, mounds and mounds of books and files and unopened bills and letters around him. All four walls of the room held sagging bookshelves of law and history, mementoes of the past. Blanton sat looking at a computer screen but stood when Johnny Stagg entered and shook his hand, offering a cocktail.

"A little early, Judge."

"Is it?"

"It ain't even nine o'clock."

Judge Blanton rubbed his unshaven face and clicked on a banker's lamp. The greenish light came up on his bloodshot eyes and white buzz cut, which was grown out to the point of lying straight. A tall crystal glass with melted ice gone brown sat at the edge of his desk. Stagg spotted a black-and-white photo of a much younger Blanton surrounded by some Marine buddies. He read the inscription. "You were in Korea? Sure looks cold."

"Let me make some coffee," Blanton said, standing.

"I need help, Judge."

The judge sat back down and nodded.

"I want these Memphis people gone."

The judge nodded some more.

"They might try and kill me," Stagg said, feeling his cheek twitch. "They blame me for Gowrie, and I feel like I got a target drawn on my back."

"What'd they say?"

"When I called back, Campo wouldn't answer," Stagg said. "I've called him about a hunnard times. Some man answered about an hour ago and said to never call this number again."

"What's that mean?"

"Means they're gonna wipe the floor with my ass," Stagg said. "I can't come up with that kind of money. Even if I could, I never made a nickel off Gowrie. Never a nickel. Shit fire."

Blanton shook his head and reached into a desk drawer for some more whiskey. He poured some into the watery glass, again offering some to Stagg, who declined. Stagg felt himself licking his lips as Blanton drained the glass, his Adam's apple bobbing up and down. Stagg could smell the aged whiskey.

"I'll take that coffee," Stagg said.

"Johnny, you mind me asking how you came into contact with such people?" Blanton asked. "You've sunk us."

"You knew."

"Hell I did. Can I ask what you were

promised?"

"Money. Favors. Good-ole-boy promises."

"Ever try another bank?" Blanton asked. "Nobody would've held you responsible for this whole deal not working. You never promised us a sure thing."

"Sweet Jesus," Stagg said, rubbing his hands over his face and neck despite the cold sweating through his undershirt. "You know better than anyone how this state works. Campo promised things you can't pay for. Certificates and contracts and men in Jackson who make things happen. You ever hear that the world is round?"

"Johnny, I could've told you that brass key to the men's club comes with a price." Blanton stood, heading toward the door. "Who are these men?"

"You know these men better than me, Judge. You got yourself a gold key a long time back."

"I'll put on that coffee. Tell me what you know."

"This wasn't my plan. It ain't my fault."

Blanton asked: "What about Hamp Beckett? What was he promised?"

"He didn't give a shit as long as the money come in regular," Stagg said, shaking his head. "These people invited him down to Biloxi, gave him the VIP till they won their money back. They's the ones who broke him. They broke his mind, Judge."

"You tell this to anyone?"

"Hell no," Stagg said. "But he left a note."

Blanton shook his head, eyes bloodshot and dark-rimmed. Johnny Stagg felt his face glow red-hot, like he'd just taken a dump on the man's high-dollar Oriental rugs.

Quinn met Wesley in the front drive, nodding over to Gowrie's 1969 black Camaro. "How do you like my wheels?"

"When are you headed back?"

"Today."

"You plan on driving that machine back to Columbus?"

"Is that a problem?" Quinn asked.

"Probably," he said. "It's a piece of evidence. We thought it had been stolen from the gas station, but Lillie said you took it."

"I guess we'd better drive it back to the sheriff's office, then."

"Things might happen to a vehicle in transit."

"Sure could."

Wesley grinned a little.

"Hell yeah," Quinn said, jumping into the front seat, cranking that big engine and knocking it into reverse, Dynaflow pipes puttering like a speedboat as they pulled alongside Deputy Leonard McMinn and waved.

McMinn tilted his head like a dog hearing a high-pitched sound and raised his hand to wave back.

Wesley dug some dip from the front of his uniform pocket and thumped it with his thumb. "Hit it," he said.

Quinn redlined the motor, taking it on up before knocking it into first gear, the Camaro beautifully hanging there in space, burning the shit out of Gowrie's back tires and sending up black smoke into Leonard's face.

They laughed all the way out to Main Street and then hit the long, long road out of town, taking the Camaro on up to way past a hundred, knowing that no one could touch them, Quinn feeling like he had in high school, only this time with the law riding shotgun.

"This is more fun than that fire truck."

"Bet your ass," Quinn said.

He found a country music station, and they blared some good outlaw stuff from back in the day, zipping down all those hidden country roads, passing forgotten cemeteries and crumbling gas stations, nothing but gravel and dirt. Quinn switched with Wesley, and Wesley took the car bumping up and over the road into an overgrown field, crashing through a rotting fence and spinning out in the mud and dust, nearly getting stuck in a ravine, but then redlining her again and mashing that pedal till they were back onto the country road leading to the farm.

Both of them laughed so hard they almost lost their breath.

The radio played Haggard, "I Think I'll Just Stay Here and Drink," and Quinn couldn't help but laugh at the future sheriff of the county tearing up the back roads. They hit a turn, and Wesley shifted up, taking on the grade of the hills ringing the valley of the farm, the Camaro spinning gravel and dust along the narrow road.

"Who in the hell left us in charge?" Wesley said.

"Some unfortunate folks," Quinn said.

"God help us all," Wesley said, rolling down the window and spitting, running fast along the line of barbed wire, the fence line nothing but a blur. The road would crest the hill, and they'd hit another road that would lead back to his uncle's place, maybe a mile or so away. The land out here was rented by a hunt club and owned by a logging company, as was much of the big stretches of old timber. Quinn recalled all that old-growth timber on the old Mc-Kibben place being logged out, as Wesley turned north and downshifted, running along the ridge of the hill. He wondered if a guy like Johnny Stagg possessed a soul.

"You look out for my momma," Quinn said.

"You bet."

"And do better than Leonard."

"I promise."

"Gowrie will be back," Quinn said.

"Why do you say that?"

"He won't let this rest."

"You worry too much, Quinn."

Wesley slowed at the next curve, that final bend up in the hills that would head east and back down into the valley to the farm. He downshifted and braked to where a couple trucks pinched the road.

Quinn couldn't see anyone standing close and figured the trucks belonged to a couple of hunters who'd been too lazy to find a place to park. Wesley stopped hard, those back pipes chugging away in idle. "What the hell," Quinn said, opening the passenger door.

Quinn noticed Wesley had his hand on his service revolver.

"Hold up," Wesley said, slipping on his sheriff's office cap.

Quinn didn't listen, coming from around the back of the Camaro and finding Gowrie and the skinny boy with the broken wrist threading through the two trucks. A third fella, fat and slow, with a bloodied hand and dead eyes, wearing a rotten smile, held a 12-gauge.

Quinn was unarmed, feeling like his pants were down.

He looked to Wesley. Wesley eyed him for a moment.

"Sorry, Quinn," he said, spitting on the ground and giving Quinn his back. "I promised to keep the peace."

"You son of a bitch" was all Quinn got out before Wesley joined the men, and Gowrie and the boys started shooting.

The fat boy unloaded with the 12-gauge, hitting Quinn hard with buckshot in the leg and ass, and Gowrie fired off a pistol, a bullet grazing his side. He fell ragged and hard on the gravel.

"Mornin', soldier," Gowrie said and laughed.

Quinn crawled behind the Camaro, the engine still running. He heard the men talking, Wesley saying something about keeping the deal, and Gowrie said, "You bet."

"Go ahead and make it look real," Wesley said. "Shoot for the calf or my ass. I brought this little .22."

Quinn sat on his butt, leaning against the Camaro.

He looked around the edge of the muscle car and saw Wesley's back, hand reaching out with a small .22 pistol to hand to the fat man.

Gowrie stood there with his jeans tucked into his boots, loosely holding a .45 auto and smiling. "You bet, boss."

Gowrie lifted the gun and shot Wesley Ruth right in the head and heart with the .45, dropping the big ex–football player to the road.

"Where you at, soldier?" Gowrie said.

Quinn heard the men's feet walking across the gravel, coming around the Camaro, Quinn wondering where Wesley had dropped his gun. He thought about approaching from the other side of the car, thinking maybe he could lift a gun from Wesley's belt and sneak up on the men from behind. But even if he made it, all of them were armed, and he wouldn't have time.

He searched out a tree line, maybe ten meters away, where all kinds of junk had been dropped off by lazy country folks. Old refrigerators and stoves, cans and bottles and toys, and deer skeletons left to rot, meat smelling sickly sweet.

They would hit him, but he could make it to some concealment, maybe lose them back in the woods.

Quinn ran for the forest and the dumping ground, feeling bullets pass his ear as shots zipped around him.

He kept moving. You always kept moving.

Another shot ripped through his back, his shoulder feeling as if it had cracked clean, and he fell down hard on his face, dragging himself through the heaped piles of rotten newspapers and deer guts, beer bottles and car parts. He backed himself behind an old stove, looking down the ridge through a head-high growth of newly planted pines.

He could maybe crawl his way through, make it back down to the county road by his uncle's house and wait them out until he could find some help.

Gowrie whistled, and told his boys he'd seen Quinn run into all that shit yonder.

Quinn felt light-headed as he moved away from the stove, his leg covered in blood, thinking a femoral artery could have been hit, and in that case he was fucked. He ripped the arm off his shirt and twisted it tight around his thigh. His back was covered in blood, but he couldn't do a damn thing about that. He couldn't raise his left arm, but he could use his fingers.

In the field, they'd cut loose his uniform and get some QuikClot into that son of a bitch, that powdery shit saving his life at the Haditha Dam and again along a rocky ridge in the Arma Mountains.

This time, he didn't have body armor or a weapon. You didn't get a Purple Heart for dying in a junkyard.

He heard the fat man breathing before he heard his heavy walk. The skinny fella with the black eyes, still wearing a makeshift cast on his arm, walked in front of Quinn first, kicking at his bloody leg. The fat man followed, out of breath and sweating, mopping his face with his shirttail, showing his blubbery white belly.

"How's it feel?" the fat man asked, unwrapping a stump that had been a thumb.

The fat man kicked at him. Both boys raised their guns and smiled.

33

The fat man's head exploded into a fine mist, and he fell on top of Quinn, the cracking explosion of a big revolver sounding only after. The other man raised his weapon, his shirtfront opening up with a huge hole, blood spreading across his chest as he fell dead, another crack before he hit the ground. Quinn kicked and pushed, and the pain and effort of getting that fat son of a bitch off him was something else, but he gritted his teeth and crawled, his damn right leg not working worth shit, the tourniquet coming loose. He retied it as he heard the gunning motor of the Camaro and saw the spray of gravel, the muscle car bounding southward on the hill, nearly losing traction in that curve but righting itself and disappearing.

Quinn tried to stand but couldn't.

He finally got to one knee, looked up the rutted path from the county junkyard, and waited to see who'd saved his ass. At first he heard padding feet, the sun looking high and pale over the ridge and path. He thought he saw a man in a worn rancher's coat, a cigarette hanging loose from his weathered face, the hill tunneled with bright green leaves with the smell of tobacco in the wind. Sheriff Beckett motioned for Quinn to get a move on, follow him on out.

Quinn's vision kind of kicked in and out, but it was clear as hell when he saw that cattle dog with a gray-and-black quilt coat trotting the path for him, smelling his blood and then barking.

He heard a big baritone voice coming from somewhere up the hill. A large shadow holding a silver Colt .44 in his left hand.

"Hey, Quinn," Boom said. "I been waiting for you. Found Hondo."

"You stay here," Ditto said, behind the wheel of a red GMC Jimmy he'd stolen from a motel in Yalobusha County that morning. Lena nodded while cradling her baby in one arm. Her other hand held that little .22 peashooter she'd brought from Alabama, her saying she should have used it on Charley Booth when she'd had the chance.

Ditto walked to a side door of the movie-house church, recalling a similar place in his hometown of Calhoun City where a crazy preacher thought he possessed a true healing gift. A rich man with the cancer had joined up with them, and for weeks the preacher had laid on hands, asking them all to join in the touch to drive the devils from his soul to cleanse him. Even when the man died, the preacher didn't give up, refusing to let folks take the body from the church, letting the man lay there for nearly a week, telling everyone that he could raise that son of a bitch from the dead.

The preacher finally let them plant the man, still saying he could have done it if the body hadn't been embalmed.

Brother Davis was of the same mold but had always been good to Ditto. Davis knew that Gowrie was crazy as a shithouse rat and would take some pity on their situation.

All he wanted was five hundred dollars, only half of what was come due to him.

Ditto's damn heart jackhammered in his chest as he walked down the vacant aisle, his heart way up in his throat. If one of Gowrie's boys spotted him here, they'd hang his ass high.

He found Brother Davis asleep in the first row, feet kicked up on the stage, snoring. A book by Pat Robertson about saving your family during the End Times was splayed across his lap.

He awoke with his eyes wide, probably expecting the Beast.

"Brother," Ditto said, whispering. "I'm in a mess and need some money. Gowrie wants me dead, and I don't want no trouble."

"Who are you?"

"It's me," Ditto said. "You know me."

Brother Davis nodded, screwing up his face and studying Ditto's profile. "Gowrie's gone."

"What about the money?"

"Don't belong to him," the old man said. "People from Memphis comin' for it."

"I just need five hundred."

"I can't," he said. "Them boys in Memphis gonna take what's theirs and shut us down."

"What will you do?"

"Continue with my ministry."

"You really a minister?"

"Yes, sir. Hell yes, I am."

Ditto shook his head. "I got eight dollars left and a girlfriend with a baby."

Brother Davis: "That feisty girl? I sure like a girl with spirit."

Ditto nodded. Brother Davis licked his

cracked lips.

"Y'all intimate? Did she get nekkid yet?"

"Can I just borrow a little?" Ditto said.

Brother Davis stood and closed his book, finding the stairs to his pulpit and leaning into the podium. A big cross fashioned from stripped and shellacked cedar beams hung from chains. "Let me see the girl."

"Why?"

"She needs to be taught a lesson."

"Good-bye, Brother," Ditto said. "Good luck."

"Just give me five minutes," Brother Davis said, his dirty eyeglasses and golden smile catching in the weak movie-house light. Ditto thought how strange it was that the cross above him had been fashioned from fallen logs and chains from a hardware store. Didn't look too fitting.

"Oh, shit," the preacher said.

Ditto turned.

Up the aisle, a door with a diamond window was kicked open, and walking down the aisle was Gowrie himself, Ditto nearly shitting his drawers, but Gowrie walked right past him and approached the preacher standing in the pulpit. He raised a gun before the homemade cross.

Gowrie wore a ski hat, his eyes wide and electric on that ole meth.

"They got state people down here," Brother Davis said. "They was like fire ants all over your place last night."

"Where's the money?"

"It ain't ours."

"You give it to Stagg?"

Brother Davis shook his head sadly. "Belongs to them boys in Memphis."

"And you're gonna let 'em have it?"

"Don't have no choice."

"Bullshit."

Gowrie shot him in the shoulder and leg, the old man falling to the ground. Gowrie hopped up on the stage like a damn cat and started to kick the old man, asking him again where he'd put the goddamn money. He walked to the edge of the stage and unhitched the cross from the chains, it falling down near the preacher's head.

"Them folks will kill me."

"I'll kill you."

"It's done."

"You lyin' shithole preacher, where'd you put the money? You lyin' shithole preacher."

The old man pointed with a bloody hand behind the curtain and said something about the cash being in a box of hymnals by the door. Gowrie squatted down and checked the box, counting handfuls of cash in his thick little hands.

"This all you got?"

"We never had no more."

"You damn liar."

Gowrie stood over the old man, kicking him in the head again and dragging his bloody ass to the cross.

Gowrie wrapped the old man in the chains and hoisted him into the rafters of the old movie house. Ditto breathed his first breath, thinking maybe the son of a bitch had forgotten about his presence.

"Come on, you little fat shit, and help me get what's mine," Gowrie said, tying the chain to the wall, leaving the gold-toothed preacher hanging and dropping blood to the wood stage and searching for just the right prayer to set himself loose.

Ditto scrambled to his feet and ran to follow, wiping his sweating hands on his pant leg, mouth trembling, and pissing a bit on himself.

"Where we headed?"

"Where Johnny Stagg got my goddamn money."

Lena saw Gowrie park behind the movie house and come right through the front door. She slid down in the seat of the car, closing her eyes and shushing her baby, who'd taken that very moment to start wailing, now calling the baby Joy, something that Ditto had come up with, maybe the first sensible name she'd come across in some time.

Ditto inside with the preacher, Gowrie coming in the rear.

Not an ideal situation.

But the boy had left the motor running, and she could just slide on over and get as far gone from Jericho as a half tank could get her. Instead, she just waited there, closing her eyes and praying a bit, hoping the Lord would find her thoughts a lot stronger than Brother Davis's. She waited to hear gunshots and prayed that Ditto would make it through. That little fat boy had more guts than any man she'd met in her life.

A good ten minutes passed. She heard gunshots.

She crawled behind the wheel, holding the baby in the passenger seat with her right hand, using a pillow from the motel to corral her on the seat. She knocked the car into gear and moved up in front of the movie house, seeing the door was wide open.

Her hands shook. Even Gowrie wouldn't shoot a girl with a baby.

She'd point that ole peashooter at him and give him a talkin'-to. She would leave with her little fat boy, money or not.

She didn't want their goddamn money and would tell him so.

She reached for the crying baby and got out of the car, holding Joy and that .22 so tight. She felt like she was walking all sluggish in water, her blood running so fast, her mind a hot tangle of thoughts. She heard a man crying but saw no one until she looked up from the pulpit.

There she saw golden-mouthed Brother Davis hanging from the cross, the cross swinging like a pendulum from a mess of chains.

"Help," he said. He was bleeding bad, gray-faced and dying.

"Where's Ditto?"

"Please," Brother Davis said, screaming. "He took all I got but said it wasn't enough."

"Where are they?"

"Help me."

"Speak, you old wretched man."

"They gone to the bank."

34

Quinn stood up from the hospital bed wearing one of those paper nightgowns that left his naked ass hanging out as he made his way to a water pitcher. He was weak and light-headed, not feeling much in his body at all, his right leg stinging like it was asleep and fingers fat and clumsy in a sling. He'd watched Luke Stevens dig the buckshot out of his leg and ass and then work on that bullet in his shoulder, saying the blade had been cracked and Quinn would need to see a surgeon in Memphis or over in Columbus. Luke wanted to knock him out for the whole thing, but Quinn wanted only something local for the pain, to have that shit dug out of his body and be sewn up. Of course Luke tried to explain to him that the process was a little bit more complicated. Quinn's muscles had been torn, bones cracked, and he'd lost a damn good bit of blood.

Quinn drained the water glass and eased his way to the bed.

That was about the time Johnny Stagg walked into the room.

"Son of a bitch," Quinn said, closing the back side of the gown. "You got to be kidding me."

"Judge called Benning," Stagg said. "He wanted me to relay that."

"What'd he tell them?"

"Said you'd been ambushed by some poachers."

Stagg wore a checked button-down shirt with a V-necked tennis sweater tucked into a pair of pressed gray pants. He looked like the gardener who'd stolen the millionaire's clothes.

"Y'all make for a nice pair." Quinn laughed. "You know what happened to my damn pants?"

"I imagine they cut 'em off you," Johnny Stagg said, nodding down to the wound on the back of Quinn's leg. "That don't look so good."

"Yeah, it stings a little when you get shot in the back," Quinn said. "You gonna leave or you want to be tossed out of the window?"

"I wasn't a part of this," Stagg said, looking down to his tasseled loafers or maybe the worn linoleum floor. "I wanted to look you in the eye and tell you."

Quinn held up his hand and shook his head. "What do you want, Johnny?"

"Gowrie and me weren't partners," Stagg said. "All I wanted to do was jump-start the economy of this old town. There was gonna be a regional hospital taking over for this old rotting place. A Walmart, too. You got my word."

"True gold."

"If we'd known what was going on . . . I wouldn't have made a deal for nothin' in the world."

"One of my best friends was just gunned down in front of my face," Quinn said. "Gowrie shot him in the head and heart right after he'd turned on me. I guess you wouldn't know a thing about that."

"What Wesley done makes me sick to my core, but he doesn't stand alone," Stagg said, looking solemn behind that craggy mask. He reached into his pocket and unfolded a letter, placing it in Quinn's hands. "This belongs to you and your momma."

Quinn knew it instantly as his uncle's handwriting.

"I was gonna burn it," Stagg said.

Quinn read the short note written to his

mother, flecked with blood:

I walk a lonely road, Jean. It's never been a straight path and you loved me despite it. I killed a young woman named Jill Bullard. She was a witness to a fire in a drug house. She kept coming back for money after. I, and I alone, shushed it up. Don't look for answers because that's all there is to it. "Come to me, all you who are weary and burdened, and I will give you rest." — Matthew 11:28. Your loving brother, Hamp

"You see now?" Stagg said. "You can read the truth right there. Your uncle killed to cover up for Gowrie. He let all this shit grow wild. He couldn't live with it and did the honorable thing."

"Why don't you bring that note to Jill Bullard's family in Bruce?" Quinn asked. "You explain it, Johnny."

"You can make it right."

"How do you figure?"

"Kill the man who tarnished your uncle," Stagg said, looking him hard in the eye. "Gowrie just killed Brother Davis and looted his church. He's high as a kite and wants to burn Jericho down."

"You tarnished my uncle. You just want me to save your ass and get that money back. How much are you on the hook for, Johnny?"

411

"Gowrie got more than a hunnard thousand dollars in donations. Crucified Brother Davis on some cedar logs."

"Who are these people in Memphis?"

"I need that money," Stagg said. "I'll give you a cut. You can keep all your land. I'll buy that slice of 45 for whatever you think is fair."

"Let me think on it."

"Gowrie's tearin' shit up. We got five deputies left. What can they do?"

"Wait for the help that's coming."

"What do you want, Quinn? I got to get that money or they'll kill me."

"I thought about it."

"And?"

Quinn offered his hand with a smile. "Good luck, Johnny Stagg."

Ditto never signed up for this bullshit. But when a fella like Gowrie puts a gun to your head, you tend to listen up.

"Grab that bag," Gowrie said, stopping the Camaro with a skid on the town Square.

"The one with the Little Mermaid on it?"

"You see another?"

"The big suitcase is filled with the preacher's money."

Ditto reached into the backseat of the car and grabbed the child's duffel bag. The bag wouldn't hold a full-grown man's shoe. "I can't get nothin' in this."

"Go get a trash bag."

"Where?"

"Come on," Gowrie said, the big motor idling. He walked straight on into the Citizens Bank Building, bigger than shit. He strolled right up to the windows to the only teller working and grabbed her by the back of the neck. "Give it up."

He wheeled the gun around to a couple men and a big woman sitting at desks with computers and said, "Y'all come on over and join us. Anyone does something that doesn't sit well and I'll blow this woman's goddamn head off. Hands behind your heads. Hell, you got it. You got it."

The office people walked over slow and easy, Gowrie pointing to the floor, where they got down on their knees and laced their hands over their heads. The office looked like it hadn't changed a thing in about thirty years, with old-timey wood paneling and green vinyl furniture. A picture of a smiling black woman promised FREE CHECKING!

Ditto just stood there — waiting any second for someone to bust in the door and start shooting — and glanced up to a corner and saw a security camera. He looked the other way and saw another. He looked right ahead of himself and saw another taking his damn picture.

Son of a bitch.

Maybe he could give some kind of sign, something that the police could see to know that he wasn't an active participant in the matter. But as long as Gowrie walked right by that GMC Jimmy they stole and left Lena and her baby alone, he was fine with whatever came of this.

"Don't give me a dye pack, neither," Gowrie said, shoving a gun into the teller's face. "Something explodes on me and I'll come back to this town again and take a shit in y'all's commode."

The girl, young and doughy, wearing a good bit of makeup and gold jewelry, nodded and said, "Yes, sir."

Yes, sir, to Gowrie.

"Give me that bag, dipshit."

Ditto handed him the Little Mermaid bag, and the teller looked right past Gowrie to Ditto and gave him a confused look. Gowrie saw the exchange and said, "Fill her up."

"How much?" she asked.

"Everything," he said.

"It won't fit."

"Then get yourself another bag."

"Yes, sir."

"Mr. Stagg on the board here?" Gowrie

414

asked while she worked. The girl didn't know what to say and just shook her head.

The big woman in the flowered dress, the woman who seemed to be in charge, didn't bother to look up, her hands still laced over her head, but kind of mumbled, "Mr. Johnny Stagg serves on this board."

"Tell him I got what's mine," he said. "The rest he can shove up his ass."

The door bust open and five of Gowrie's boys came in with some pillow sacks and smiles on their faces. They looked like this was all in good play, like those Army maneuvers in the woods, and if they got shot it wouldn't be bullets but paint.

None of 'em had turned twenty yet, including that son of a bitch Charley Booth. All of 'em, dirty and bald-headed, in heavy coats and gloves. None of 'em had shaved in days, and they stunk. How in the hell had Ditto ended up here?

Prison would be a hell of a vacation. He'd shack up with the biggest nigger in the place to get free of this shit.

Gowrie reached over the ledge of the teller's booth, making the little girl with all that makeup jump. She put her hands up in the air, leaving hundred-dollar bills scattering to the floor. "I'm so sorry. I'm so sorry."

Gowrie just laughed, fishing a Blow Pop

from a candy jar and tearing off the wrapper. "Throw in all these, too. You don't need to paint yourself up like a whore . . . And smile sometime. Son of a bitch, this old town is sad."

Quinn had to lay facedown on the bed to relieve the pressure on his backside. He had a pillow up under his face so he could watch the door, converse with the nice black nurse who'd come in to check on him every fifteen minutes. She wanted him to take some more pills, put him on a pain drip, but he said no thanks and asked again about his clothes.

She said they'd been thrown away.

"Even my boots?"

"Even the boots."

He tried to close his eyes. He heard a knock on the door.

Anna Lee Stevens walked in and stood over him, then sat at the edge of the bed and looked down at the bandages on his legs and back. She touched his arm and smiled. She'd been crying.

"Luke got called," she said. "We thought you'd died."

"Wouldn't have hurt as bad."

"What happened?"

"Boom brought Hondo back."

"Who's Hondo?"

"My uncle's dog," Quinn said, smiling.

"You're laughing?"

"Why the hell not? Beats crying."

"And Wesley? He's dead?"

Quinn was silent.

She moved her fingers back and forth across his forearm and just stared at him, grabbing his watch and starting to cry a bit. Quinn watched those sleepy eyes and her soft red mouth as she leaned over and kissed him on the forehead.

"What's that for?"

"Because I felt like it," Anna Lee said. "You need it."

"I didn't kill Wesley."

"I'm so sorry, Quinn," she said. "Those men should all die."

Quinn grabbed her wrist lightly and lifted his head, their faces maybe two inches apart. He could feel her breath on him before she shook her head and stood.

She got halfway to the door, turning back once to smile.

"Anna Lee?" Quinn asked.

Lillie Virgil burst into the room and nearly bumped into her, dressed in full Tibbehah County Sheriff's gear, with ponytail threaded through ball cap and holding a police radio. "You look like shit," she said. "Hey, Anna Lee."

Anna Lee smiled at Quinn before heading out. Quinn wondered what her husband had done with the bullets he'd dug out of him.

"So you got shot in the ass?"

"Just some buckshot," Quinn said. "And a bullet in the shoulder."

"I thought bullets bounced off Rangers."

"You're in a good mood."

"Why the hell not?" Lillie said, standing over him and then turning her back to answer a call on the radio, a lot of squawking and static, but it was clear some shit was going on at the Citizens Bank Building. "Gets better and better."

"Wesley sold me out."

"Boom told me."

"You expected that?"

"I wasn't surprised," she said. "I never wanted him a part of what we'd been up to."

"He was my friend."

"We can sing 'I'll Fly Away' sometime later," she said. "I got ten troopers blocking the roads out of the county. We got Gowrie bottled up, and now he's come right back for more. I think he's lost his goddamn mind. Ain't no way this will end pretty. He either surrenders or gets killed."

"How many with him?"

"He's got seven of his boys and I got five,

counting me," she said. "He killed that preacher."

"Johnny Stagg offered me a reward to get back his collection plate," Quinn said.

"And you told him to go fuck himself."

"You should probably wait for some more folks," Quinn said. "Who's in charge anyway?"

"I guess that's me," Lillie said. "We got deputies headed this way from Webster and Choctaw."

"Folks will say a woman shouldn't take action," Quinn said, playing with her. "That Tibbehah always needs outside help."

Lillie studied Quinn's face as he moved slowly off the end of the bed, slipping down light and easy on wobbly legs. They held steady but hurt like hell, the medication wearing off.

"I can see your ass," Lillie said.

"Troopers got him bottled in," Quinn said. "He's in the bank right now. No other way out?"

"Pretty much."

"And he's killed three men we know about."

"And Jill Bullard."

Quinn shook his head, handing her the suicide note Johnny Stagg had given to him. Her face dropped a bit, eyes lifting up and meeting Quinn's. She shook her head like she didn't believe a word of it even though they both damn well knew it was written in Hamp Beckett's own hand. Shit, it was flecked with his blood.

"I don't believe it."

"You should," he said. "We can debate it later."

"We could just wait around."

"Yeah," Quinn said, grinning. "Sure thing."

"Let everyone think that this whole county is corrupt and weak."

"Would you please have someone get me a pair of jeans, a gun, and boots," Quinn said, winking at her. "I'd like a shirt and jacket, if that wouldn't be too much trouble."

Lillie wadded up the suicide note and tossed it in the trash. "Be right back."

"And Lillie?"

She hung at the doorway, hand on the doorframe. She had to lift her chin to see him from under the dropped bill of the ball cap.

"We'll need some more local folks to make a stand."

35

The old men seemed frozen in the same spot at the VFW where Quinn had joined them one week ago after the funeral, where they'd first asked him to pull up a chair, share in some whiskey, and explained how his uncle stuck a .44 in his mouth and pulled the trigger. They all looked up from their ceremonial cups of coffee, seated at a corner table below a group photo from 1993 of the same men plus his uncle. Mr. Jim pointed to a chair — his uncle's chair — and asked Quinn to join them, saying he was headed down to the barbershop and he always cut the hair of active service members for free. "High and tight," he said. "I can give that Ranger cut as good as anyone."

"We need help," Quinn said, explaining the situation.

Varner walked behind the VFW bar, reaching for an M40 sniper rifle that hung in a red velvet perch. He checked the sight and racked open the chamber. "I keep ammo at the store. I can take a fair shot from the water tower."

Quinn nodded.

"You loan me a gun?" Mr. Jim asked Lillie. "All I got is a peashooter I keep by my cash register."

"Yes, sir," Lillie said. "Two more of my deputies just quit. I'm down to Quinn, Boom, and two others. Four boys just got in from Choctaw. Two from Eupora. Troopers got the highways out of town."

"What about you?" Quinn asked Judge Blanton.

Blanton hadn't moved since Quinn and Lillie had walked in, sitting still with a hand around the heat of the coffee mug. He looked hungover, with half a cigar going in the saucer. "You sure about that?"

Quinn nodded.

"I got a shotgun and an old M1 in my trunk," Blanton said. "Just got it out last week to show the boys. Works as good as ever."

"Gowrie's bottled up in the Square," Quinn said. "We need to hold him there, make sure they don't move."

"Wesley really threw in with that sack of shit?' Varner asked. Quinn nodded.

"Who's driving with me?" Varner asked.

"My finger's startin' to itch."

Gowrie strolled down the rows of the Dixie Gas convenience mart, throwing chips, beef jerky, and liter bottles of Mountain Dew to his boys. They'd made it all the way out of town only to spot that roadblock with two state patrolmen, Gowrie not saying shit, only working that black Camaro into a wide U-turn and trying for another route. After the third roadblock, he drove back to the gas station, filled up the beast, and told the two cars following him to do the same. "It's gonna be a battle," he said. "Git some supplies."

Daddy Gowrie drove the second car with Charley Booth riding shotgun, his cherry red El Camino with bucket seats complete with a nekkid-woman air freshener. He wasn't so sure about his son's plan and told Ditto, while everyone looted the store, the store clerk down on his face, counting squares.

"I think my boy's brain has corroded."

Ditto nodded.

"Why the hell you come back?"

"For money."

"Money and pussy has killed many fine men."

"You want to run?" Ditto asked.

"He'd kill me. He'd kill you, too."

"I just as soon try," Ditto said.

Daddy Gowrie topped off the tank and hung up the nozzle. "No. I said I'd back him. He's my boy."

"You shoot me if I run?" Ditto asked.

"Probably."

Ditto looked to Main Street, running south into Jericho's downtown. His eye caught something high up, just in line with the winter sun. Someone was crawling up that old rusted water tower with a rifle on his back.

"What you looking at?" Daddy Gowrie asked.

"Nothin'," Ditto said, smiling. "Let's go."

"Hold on," Daddy Gowrie said. "Wait one minute."

Ditto turned and saw that Jimmy parked across the road, Lena marching toward the gas station with the baby in her arms. His mouth stayed open, not sure what the hell to say.

Charley Booth ran out to meet them and pulled them on inside.

"You ever seen two roosters git into it?" Daddy asked with a rotten smile.

Lillie gathered the men on South Main, right by what had been the train depot, deputizing Blanton, Ed Varner, Mr. Jim, Boom, and Quinn right on the spot. Varner asked if this was all legal, and Judge Blanton said that Lillie was acting sheriff and she could deputize who she saw fit. That seemed to satisfy Varner, and he set off down the road for the water tower, telling Quinn he'd take the shot on Gowrie if he'd poke his head out just a little.

"What about George and Leonard?" Quinn asked.

"Who do you think quit on me?"

"In with Wesley?"

"Just cowards."

Lillie held a 12-gauge and chewed gum, moving in the direction of the town Square, where they'd walk north toward where Gowrie's men had met at the old Dixie Gas station. Judge Blanton held a beautiful old Browning Sweet 16 in his liver-spotted hands. Mr. Jim hobbled next to him in his Third Army hat, cradling a 12-gauge pump.

Boom held a deer rifle, the .44 Anaconda tucked into his belt.

Quinn carried Blanton's old M1, the clip loaded and a spare in his jacket pocket. The old man said it had been his and he fired it once a year, still in fine working order.

They all crested the hill of the railroad tracks and moved on into town, passing a barricade set up by a couple policemen down from Eupora. Lillie nodded, the group of five walking together, Quinn scanning the town for any movement from the doorways or the roofs of the storefronts.

He picked out Ed Varner, that old crazy bastard, on the rusted water tower where he'd already found a perch for the sniper rifle, aiming it down toward the north end of the Square and the old gas station.

"I didn't ask him to do that," Lillie said, walking beside Quinn.

"You didn't have to."

"Can he make that shot?"

"In his sleep."

Blanton hobbled alongside Boom, Boom's left arm hanging loose with the rifle in hand. Mr. Jim kept that shotgun pointed upward, walking nice and easy, as if they were at a Saturday quail hunt, moving on past the Coulter's Flower Shop, past what had once been the hardware store, pharmacy, and general store. Nothing but shells now. Plywood covered the busted-out windows of the Odd Fellows Hall and the check-cashing business on the bottom floor.

The town gazebo sat empty. The whole town emptied out after the bank robbery, the old brick buildings standing crooked and worn in the weak winter light, a cold wind slicing through alleys and roads. You could hear sirens and the sound of a helicopter, Lillie saying it flew down from Lee County. More support heading into Tibbehah County every minute.

"They're not going anywhere," Quinn said.

"I want you to blast Gowrie's ass."

"How you doin', Boom?" Quinn asked, passing the veterans' monuments, with old artillery parked at the base, an American flag and a POW flag flying overhead.

"I think I like being a deputy."

"Better than jail?" Lillie asked.

"Better than jail," Boom said.

The monuments had so many names etched in granite from World Wars I and II, Korea, Vietnam, the Gulf War, and what they were calling the Global War on Terror. Six names added in the last ten years. Quinn knew them all.

The four-sided town clock sat in front of the old five-and-dime, still working, reading nearly three o'clock.

The helicopter beat overhead. The police sirens came from all directions.

Someone had cut the power to the service station, and Gowrie's boys met up in the candy aisle, Gowrie talking about how the government had wanted to implant micro-chips in every citizen but had to settle for digital watches. "That's why you won't catch me wearing jack shit."

"Just askin' the time," Ditto said.

As soon as he'd seen Lena, Gowrie had smiled like he'd just won the Tennessee Lottery, reaching for her and the baby and telling them they were having a hell of a party at Dixie Gas today. He offered her some chicken wings and beer. "You just what we needed."

Ditto took her to the back of the store by the beer coolers, wanting to ask her what in the hell she had just done. He had the matter well in hand and she just strolls on into this situation. But he didn't speak while Gowrie could listen, waiting till Gowrie got off his ass and walked to the edge of the big window facing the pumps.

Gowrie spotted ten patrol cars barricading the path from the station, about three hundred feet from the door.

"Some fun," Gowrie said. "Y'all ready?"

The phone to the store kept on ringing till Gowrie shot it and started to prowl around and smile, saying all the training at the compound was coming to a head. He said once they got in their vehicles, using the girl and baby as a shield, they could bust right through the barrier and shoot down a couple cops, too.

Gowrie hated cops.

Ditto recalled one plan he had involved them in, blowing up a police station in Memphis. Gowrie got real excited about it one day after church, and then the idea seemed to slip his mind.

"You love her?"

Ditto looked up to see Charley Booth, working on a Hershey bar in one hand and a sack of peanuts in the other. Lena said, "Ptttt," and turned her head.

"That's no concern of yours," Ditto said.

"That's my baby she's holdin'."

"This what you wanted for your baby, you dumb shit?"

Charley Booth leaned down and whispered, "Not really what I was aiming for."

"Y'all shut the hell up," Gowrie called from the front of the store. "I think they want to talk, lay out those terms and bullshit. Well, they can suck my ass. I'll kill everyone in here if they keep crowding me."

Daddy Gowrie had found a spot up by the cash register, where he thumbed through porno mags and drank a beer, every so often giving a low whistle and saying, "Hot dang."

Ditto looked to Lena and mouthed the word "Why?"

■ ■ ■ ■

Boom rested the deer rifle in the open window of a sheriff's office patrol car and smiled.

"You got him?" Lillie asked.

"I do."

"I figure you take out Gowrie and we shoot the windows in with some tear gas," Lillie said. "How's that sound?"

"That'll work," Quinn said.

"Hold on," Boom said, peering through the scope. "Y'all know they got a girl in there with a baby?"

"Shit," Lillie said. "Your friend?"

Quinn took the field glasses Lillie passed to him and watched the girl arguing with that boy Ditto and some skinny little white boy with jug ears.

"Yep."

"Shit," Lillie said.

"This complicates things," Quinn said.

"I can take out Gowrie," Boom said. "What do you say, Lillie? Shit."

"What?" she asked.

"Son of a bitch moved."

Quinn handed her the field glasses and nodded.

"What do you say, Ranger?"

"I can clear that room in under twenty seconds."

"What about your girl and baby?"

"I can work around them unless they make a break."

"Let's go," Gowrie said.

He had his sweating forearm around her neck, Lena trying to breathe and hold Joy at the same time. The baby was screaming and Gowrie was yelling, making her move faster than her legs could work. She wanted him just to ease up a little, let her catch a breath before they broke out, because if she couldn't breathe she'd drop the child.

He kicked open the gas-station door and walked her out onto the pavement, pointing the gun to her head and then back at the long row of policemen and cruisers. Lena had just a single moment of clarity then, looking at all those red and blue lights, all those guns aimed at Gowrie, and kind of took comfort that this wasn't something being done at Hell Creek but in plain view of so many people.

If she or her baby died, someone would at least know about it.

He tightened the grip around her neck, his mouth hot and wet in her ear. "Get in the fucking car."

He let off her neck and opened the passenger seat to the old muscle car. She tried to get inside, hold that baby close, but not fast enough for Gowrie, who kicked her in the ass and sent her toppling over, nearly crushing her child. She screamed at him and then just started screaming at all of it — at Charley for all he'd done and then Ditto for bringing them back here and then herself for the goddamn mess she'd caused. She'd thought she could grab Ditto, make Charley Booth see that some men were a hell of a lot smarter and stronger.

But Gowrie just ate her up.

She was in the car now, the .22 tucked into the blanket with Joy.

The keys were in the ignition as Gowrie tried to crawl over her.

She started the car with a free hand, baby in her right arm, and slipped her foot onto the pedal, knocking the car into first gear. The car lurched forward in a rush before she hit the brake, and Gowrie smacked his head against the windshield, spiderwebbing the glass, as Lena took a shaky aim at his chest with that ole peashooter and fired three times.

Her baby screamed. Gowrie fell out of the open door and rolled onto the grease-stained asphalt and ran for his boys.

She took her foot from the accelerator, slowing at a pile of creosote crossties, trying to stop that war-cry scream. Her baby screaming and crying.

Two cops looked into the window and tapped on the glass. The engine revved, but she wasn't going nowhere. She tried to calm Joy, that .22 still frozen in her fingers.

She looked at herself in the rearview mirror, the red eyes, and tears causing some confusion. She climbed out, tossed the gun in the dirt, and saw Gowrie surrounded by his shitty daddy, Charley Booth, and two more boys.

Ditto wasn't anywhere to be seen.

Quinn Colson, two old men, and that big black man with one arm walked onto the grounds of the station. That woman deputy stood with them, aiming a rifle at Gowrie and his boys. Gowrie, bleeding in ragged spurts onto his T-shirt, seemed to think this whole mess was funny.

His gun was out.

All of 'em had guns out.

What followed lasted only thirty seconds but would often take hours to debate.

No one ever said who fired first, but it was thought the first shot came from the town water tower, no one being able to say — officially — who was up that high.

Gowrie was knocked back, covered in so much blood it was hard to tell where he'd been hit, and his daddy whipped his pistol up before being shot twice through the throat. He fell to the ground, crawling for his El Camino and making it only to the door handle before he died.

Charley Booth made a run for it, turning once to fire his revolver at the cops and getting two rounds of 16-gauge shot through him, opening up his chest like two solid fists. He bled out within a minute.

The other two boys, names later released before they headed to Parchman, dropped their guns and put up their hands. A large black man with one arm knocked them to the ground, holding them underfoot.

Lillie Virgil was down, shot in the calf. Judge Blanton was flat on his back on the cracked asphalt, blood around his head like a halo.

Gowrie crawled back into the gas station and slammed the glass door shut behind him, breathing like a caught fish. The clerk had made a run for it, leaving the back door wide open, the wide expanse of a muddy field showing in a clear frame.

Gowrie saw the shadow of a man enter and then disappear like a wraith.

■ ■ ■ ■

"Hey, soldier," Gowrie said, yelling, spitting blood. "Come on down and we can hammer this shit out. I didn't kill your uncle. You hear me? I didn't kill him."

Quinn wanted to ask him about Wesley Ruth and Johnny Stagg and those men from Memphis but instead just hobbled around the aisles of the darkened convenience store, holding a fully loaded M1, hearing Gowrie breathing and cussing. His mouth giving him up as Quinn passed by a NASCAR display for Pepsi and bags of potato chips and pork rinds.

Quinn wanted to kill him.

He'd figured on killing him.

Quinn eyed Gowrie in the wide picture of the shoplifting mirror. Gowrie was on his ass with a pistol, holding his bloody stomach and spitting blood. The floor was slick with all that blood where he'd been crawling on his belly.

"How you doin'?" Quinn asked, limping slow.

"Peachy, soldier."

"You know, you remind me of a fella I once met in the Kandahar Province," Quinn said. "You ever hear of that place?"

435

"I ain't stupid."

"He ambushed me just as I was about to get on a helicopter," Quinn said. "Tried to slit my throat."

Gowrie didn't say anything.

Quinn wavered from the pain and gritted his teeth as he crept down the aisle, realizing he was dragging his back leg. "Even after I shot him and cuffed his hands, he kept asking me to kill him. Why do you figure?"

Gowrie was silent, and then said: "You gonna shoot or teach me a goddamn parable?"

Quinn could turn on the next aisle and aim straight down the row with that old M1. Gowrie was already immobilized and sitting pretty. He could take the shot so damn easily.

Quinn stepped back, feeling as if a knife had sliced his hamstring and ass while he retraced his steps back down the aisle. The shot would've been so easy and quick.

"Do something," Gowrie yelled.

Quinn looked up at the round mirror at Gowrie, eyes closing and opening, spitting blood, and trying to keep from passing out. Quinn shook his head and limped forward.

With his good arm, Quinn pushed over the candy-and-gum display, the old metal cage crashing on top of Gowrie. Gowrie kicked and flailed to get loose and rush Quinn.

Quinn staggered over to him, swinging the butt of that ancient rifle at Gowrie's head, the shitbag's pistol clattering to the floor. He punched Gowrie in his throat and bloodied chest. Quinn clenched his jaw in a mess of pain that almost brought him to his knees. He dropped on top of Gowrie, grinding his knee into the spot he'd stuck with an arrow not long ago. "You want it bad, don't you?"

"What the fuck? Goddamn."

"You want to be somebody."

Gowrie's mouth rushed with air, eyes watering. The smell of him was something tremendously sharp and rotting as Quinn held him down flat to the floor. Lawmen filled the room, Lillie limping behind them.

"You'll be sorry you didn't pull the trigger," Gowrie said, whispering with a bloody smile. "You think those boys are the best I got? I'm coming back to kill you."

"Counting on it."

Lillie helped Quinn to his feet as two deputies wrestled Gowrie from the floor. When he was gone, only a slick trail of blood left, she turned to him. "The judge is dead."

Quinn nodded. He picked up the old

man's gun and walked out into the daylight, the Dixie Gas sign reminding him of a flag.

36

Lena took a job at a barbecue house between Tupelo and Birmingham, a little
choke-and-puke perched on the side of a
sloping green hill, everything coming on
green in the early spring, where they paid
her a decent wage and she could afford to
keep a trailer, saving up for a little car,
maybe heading on sometime. But the people
who owned the restaurant were good
people, let her cut out early to get Joy from
the Little Angels day care. Lena spent most
nights in front of a small television, where
she'd rock and feed Joy, place her feet up
on a busted coffee table and just rest. She
hadn't thought about Ditto for some time,
it being nearly four months since Charley
Booth had been killed in Jericho. But in the
second week of March, a day when it was
raining a shit storm outside, and truckers
came in soaking wet and shaking like dogs,

he touched the back of her sleeve and just smiled.

She'd missed that pig-faced boy.

She got a break thirty minutes later, her clothes smelling of hickory wood, and hands dry and cracked from washing dishes. The storm had moved on, and she found him sitting on the hood of a brand-new Dodge truck beaded with rain and wearing a pair of rattlesnake boots and holding a black cowboy hat in his hand. She'd never figured Ditto for the cowboy type, but it was an image. The pig-faced boy came to impress her, and he kissed her on the cheek, his own cheek flushing a bright red.

"I got money," he said. "I took a job up in Memphis."

She nodded.

"You weren't easy to find."

"I didn't know you were looking."

"I wasn't sure who was looking for me."

"You didn't do nothin'."

"I'm not innocent, neither," Ditto said, fingering the brim of the cowboy hat in his hand. "How's Joy?"

"Good," she said, squinting into the sunlight behind his back. "Why'd you come here, Ditto?"

He slid off the hood of the truck and took her hand. "I'd like to look out for y'all.

Come on with me?"

The air was choked with all that hickory smoke, burning off hazy and slow in the golden light. The green hills rose and broke with wet green trees and grasses growing knee-high. Eighteen-wheelers zoomed past them, scattering the smoke and peaceful views.

She smiled at the boy. "I appreciate what you did."

He nodded. "But you won't come?"

"How'd you get all that money?"

"It's kind of hard to explain," he said. "But some ole buddies of mine sure have set me up."

She touched his face and kissed his thin lips. The boy had poured nearly a quart of aftershave over himself. "What happened to Gowrie?"

"Parchman Farm."

"He get the chair?"

"He killed a lawman," Ditto said. " 'Spec so."

The boy looked sad and clumsy, fumbling in the pocket of a new snap-button shirt for some cigarettes and lighting them with shaking fingers. But he smiled anyway, trying to look loose and cool on the hood of that brand-new Dodge.

"You won't come?" he asked.

Lena shook her head. She smiled at him.

"I was glad to know you."

"You ever hear what happened to that soldier that got Gowrie?" Ditto asked. "I wanted to apologize for thieving his ole truck and stealing them guns."

"He get 'em back?" she asked.

"Don't know."

"That old Ford wasn't worth much."

Ditto finished the cigarette and stomped it out in the gravel, walking around the side of the new Dodge and pulling out a big pink gorilla. The ape was so large it was bulky to carry, at nearly half the boy's size. "You are still calling her Joy?" he asked, shielding his eyes from the sun coming out behind the clouds.

"I sure am," Lena said, checking her watch, scooting off the truck. "I got to go. I'll let her know you brung this."

For all Quinn's complaints about becoming a Ranger instructor, riding the damn desk was a hundred times worse. As a platoon sergeant, there were always forms and paperwork and details to keep track of. But sitting in front of a computer all day, working on other folks' shit, was a little slice of hell. He'd crack his office window at Benning with a brick and could smell the Chattahoochee River from where he sat, wanting so much to get on his boots and hike far into the Cole Range till he dropped from exhaustion. But he still walked with a limp, and the doctors there in Columbus said he might always keep it.

The sling was off, and he was able to head to the range and shoot. He taught weapons classes to the kids coming in, and they'd ask him about that limp, hearing that Quinn had been at Haditha and made several trips into Afghanistan.

He'd tell them he fell off a bicycle and leave it at that.

The only good thing about riding the desk was that most your weekends were free. And he'd found Columbus, Georgia, to be a pleasant old town. They had a big wide boulevard along the Chattahoochee, with brick storefronts that reminded him of movies from the thirties and forties.

He often met other older Rangers at bars there, leaving the topless joints and roughneck spots on Victory Drive for the younger men. They'd drink beer and raise a little hell.

Sometime in early March, Quinn got a phone call at his apartment on base, and he drove through the gates at Fort Benning into the downtown. He dressed in civilian clothes, starched khakis and a pressed blue button-down. His hair had been barbered the day before, and he had even pulled out a pair of brown cowboy boots his mother had sent him for Christmas, the card coming from her and Jason.

Jason back with her now.

Quinn walked into Ruth Ann's, a favorite diner of the men at Benning. Ruth Ann's had been there for decades on Veterans Parkway, about the only place in town that could serve a breakfast as good as Jean Colson's.

Lillie Virgil got up from the booth and hugged Quinn tight. She'd worn her curly hair down, with snug blue jeans and a loose white tunic with all kind of designs.

"No gun belt today?" Quinn asked, taking a seat across from her.

She shook her head. "That drive's nothing. When are you coming home?"

"Summer," he said. "I promised to see Jason on his birthday. I bought him a Ranger T-shirt from the PX and some toys. Would you bring them back for him?"

"Lots been going on since you left," she said, smiling. The bright afternoon brought out Lillie's natural glow, little makeup and plenty of freckles. She had little gold hairs on her arm and wore silver bands on her wrist.

"You ever get tired of wearing that uniform?" he asked.

"Do you?"

"I'm not wearing one."

"Haircut gives you away."

Quinn smiled. "Can you stay the night?"

Lillie looked at him. She smiled a bit and shook her head. "You know I've been running for sheriff?" she asked.

A waitress came over, and they ordered a couple of burgers and Cokes, extra fries and some onion rings. When the old woman walked away, Quinn said he'd been keeping up with all the Jericho news from his mother. "She likes to talk."

"You know there's never been a woman sheriff in Mississippi?"

"No kidding?"

"Don't shit me, Quinn," she said. "You can imagine the rumors going around the Square."

"That won't matter."

"How do you figure?" Lillie said.

"Because that county would be lucky to have someone with your experience," Quinn said, looking up only a moment to thank the old woman for the Cokes over ice. "You helped bust up forty years of corruption about to be carried on by Wesley."

"I'm going to lose," she said. "It's already done."

"Against who? Leonard?"

"Johnny Stagg."

Quinn took a sip of Coke and leaned back into the diner's booth, stretching out his arm on the backrest. On the wall next to him hung a picture of a boxer from sometime in the Depression named Lamar Murphy, the Red Irish Kid. He had intense eyes and a good stance. Quinn figured on him being a good scrapper.

"He let go of the farm and land," Quinn said. "I kept the parcel. He can't have it."

"You okay with him being sheriff?"

"What kind of experience does he have?"

"It's an elected position," she said. "Most sheriffs in Mississippi never started out in law enforcement."

"You've got a college degree," Quinn said. "You were a cop in Memphis and how many years down in Tibbehah? You know everyone."

"Stagg has money."

"God, I'm sorry, Lillie. I really am. You want to get piss-drunk tonight?"

"Maybe," she said, meeting his eyes. "If you'll consider why I drove five hours to see you."

"I should have called you," he said. "God knows, I wanted to."

"Be quiet for a second," she said, grabbing his hands across the table. "You should run. You can beat Stagg so damn easily."

"I got ten years till retirement."

"You think Tibbehah County can stand ten more years of Johnny Stagg in charge?"

"Not my problem," Quinn said. "The Army is my career."

"I noticed you're still giving to that leg where you got shot."

"I know men who lost part of their legs and still serve," he said. "You know, I've been in since I was eighteen. Most of my time here at Benning. You can't just walk away from that."

"You wouldn't be walking away from anything."

"I can't."

"Just consider it."

The hamburgers came, and they ate for a long time without talking, only Lillie asking for the ketchup and a couple napkins from Quinn's side of the table. "Can you stay the night?" he asked again.

"Why?" she asked.

"I like seeing you."

"Anna Lee is pregnant."

"What does that have to do with us?"

"Plenty."

That kind of soured things for a bit before Quinn walked Lillie to her Jeep, Lillie saying it would probably be best if she turned back around and headed home. "I got two church services to make tomorrow. Plenty of hands to shake."

"You can beat Stagg," he said. "People respect you. No one respects him."

"It's done."

"I can't quit, Lillie," Quinn said, hugging her again and stepping away. "It's not possible."

"How's that desk?"

"It makes my ass hurt, sitting all day."

"You think all the troubles we got end with one shitbag who set up camp? Gowrie is one of many."

Quinn reached for her Jeep door and opened it. He could smell her clean shampoo smell as she moved in close.

"Think about," she said.

Without warning, Lillie leaned over and kissed him hard on the mouth, got into the Jeep and slammed the door. She backed out, Quinn paralyzed where he stood, smiling. She rolled down the window. "I won't stop trying with you."

Quinn smiled and waved, watching her pull out onto Veterans, turn west and dis-

appear, his mind working over the possibili-
ties.

ACKNOWLEDGMENTS

Special thanks to Colonel George Reynolds, USA (Ret.), for his support, stories, and friendship while serving at Camp Phoenix in AFG, and also to my buddy Jason, former saw gunner and fire team leader, 2nd Platoon/ Alpha Company of 3/75 Ranger Regiment, for telling me a hell of a lot about Quinn.

As always, appreciation to my family: Doris and Charlie, Paige and Jim and the boys, and Angela and Billy. Thanks also to Tim Green for twenty years of support and friendship.

And to the Putnam team of Neil Nyren, Sara Minnich, Michael Barson, Claire McGinnis, and Ivan Held.

Of course, nothing would be possible without my tough and loyal agent, Esther Newberg.

And a decade of thanks to my friend David Thompson, a brilliant and funny true pal who is gone way, way too soon. You are greatly missed.

ABOUT THE AUTHOR

Ace Atkins, a former journalist, has written eight previous novels. He began his writing career in 1998, at age twenty-eight, when the first of four Nick Travers novels was published. In 2001, he earned a Pulitzer Prize nomination for his investigation into a 1950s murder. That murder inspired his 2006 novel *White Shadow*, which was followed by three further history-based crime novels, *Wicked City, Devil's Garden,* and *Infamous.* Atkins lives in Oxford, Mississippi.

The employees of Thorndike Press hope you have enjoyed this Large Print book. All our Thorndike, Wheeler, and Kennebec Large Print titles are designed for easy reading, and all our books are made to last. Other Thorndike Press Large Print books are available at your library, through selected bookstores, or directly from us.

For information about titles, please call:
  (800) 223-1244

or visit our Web site at:
  http://gale.cengage.com/thorndike

To share your comments, please write:
  Publisher
  Thorndike Press
  10 Water St., Suite 310
  Waterville, ME 04901